don't

wake

me

don't
wake
me

don't

wake

me

martin
krüger

THOMAS & MERCER

Text copyright © 2019 by Martin Krüger
Translation copyright © 2020 by Jozef van der Voort
All rights reserved.

Previously published as *Weck mich nie* by Edition M in Luxembourg in 2019. Translated from German by Jozef van der Voort. First published in English by Thomas & Mercer in collaboration with Amazon Crossing in 2020.

Published by Thomas & Mercer, in collaboration with Amazon Crossing, Seattle

www.apub.com

Amazon, the Amazon logo, Thomas & Mercer and Amazon Crossing are trademarks of Amazon.com, Inc., or its affiliates.

ISBN-13: 9781542019620
ISBN-10: 1542019621

Cover design by Plum5 Limited

Printed in the United States of America

First edition

Darkness reigns at the foot of the lighthouse.

– Japanese proverb

PART ONE

AN OLD HOUSE BY THE SEA

PART ONE

Chapter 1

Last time it was different, she thought.

Deserted houses stood along the road beside rugged, moss-covered crags that jutted steeply from the landscape like pale bones. Sailboats under their winter covers drew past her windscreen, followed by a bed and breakfast with a *Vacancies* sign swinging in the wind. A boy and girl were selling vegetables from a stall at the end of a track that led to a farmyard. Jasmin Hansen waved at them as she passed, but they didn't wave back. A breath of cold air from the nearby Norwegian Sea penetrated the narrow gap in the car window.

Her fingers drummed nervously on the wheel. The radio was playing an old song by the Rolling Stones about a traveller seeking shelter from the storm. *Seems apt*, she thought. *Always on the run from a lowering sky – except you brought your own dark clouds with you.* She had hired the Volvo in Oslo and driven up along the coast. Although she'd set off under late-summer sunshine, slate-grey clouds now covered the sun.

'Everything is OK,' she'd said to Jørgen when he called her for the first time, only three hours into her journey. 'Everything is OK.' Her overprotective Jørgen . . . and yet she'd felt like she was lying to him.

Her eyes flickered up to the rear-view mirror. Paul had fallen asleep, his mouth half-open, his chest rising and falling in a gentle, even rhythm. His Nintendo 3DS was still lying beside him, quietly playing a tune. *Paulie*, as Jørgen sometimes called him – though Jasmin didn't particularly like the nickname. Beyond him, in the boot, Bonnie, their three-year-old Labrador, was also asleep.

Jasmin stopped at an old, storm-battered and somewhat rusty petrol station at the entrance to the village and refuelled her Volvo XC60. She could smell the sea and the endless pine and spruce forests. Paul didn't stir as Jasmin gazed at him lovingly and opened a door to let cool, fresh air into the car. Her son sighed quietly in his sleep. He was tall for a five-year-old; she'd had to buy him new clothes just a few weeks ago. He kept growing and growing – he'd be taller than her before long.

We can do this. Together. And when we get back, everything will be OK again, she told herself. That thought was what kept her going.

'The next ferry might be the last one today,' said the old woman behind the counter as Jasmin paid for her petrol and three pre-packaged sandwiches. 'There's a storm brewing, I can feel it in my bones. And you're new here, young lady, aren't you?'

'My son and I are on our way to Minsøy.'

The old woman opened her near-toothless mouth and laughed. 'Then I'll wish you good luck.' Jasmin was already at the door when she heard the woman add, 'The island isn't what you think it is.'

After that, the forest.

Densely clustered pines, silver birches and beech trees reared up against the blue-grey backdrop of the overcast sky. Their leaves had begun to change colour here and there, sprinkling the thick greenery with spots of yellow and orange. At one point, Jasmin thought she saw an elk peering out from among the tree trunks – its mighty antlers covered in moss and lichen it had picked up from the undergrowth, its fur damp with dew.

4

There was a child standing in the road.

Jasmin wrenched the steering wheel to the side. The tyres screeched as the car swerved, skidding along the road. Then it came to a stop, pitching Jasmin forward into her seatbelt.

'Hey!' she yelled out of her hastily wound-down window. 'What the hell are you doing? You should be more careful!'

The child was wearing a yellow raincoat with a pointed hood that concealed its face. Slowly, it walked down the road towards the car.

'Where are your parents, kid?' she asked more gently.

The child looked up at her and Jasmin found herself staring into the impassive face of a young boy, who returned her gaze with his ice-blue eyes before walking past her in silence and stepping into the forest. The yellow of his coat disappeared amid the foliage.

'Mummy?'

Jasmin whirled round in shock. Paul was staring at her wide-eyed, rubbing the sleep from the corners of his eyes. 'What . . . what's happening?'

Jasmin swallowed to dispel the strange, bitter taste in her mouth. 'Nothing, honey.'

'Are we there yet?'

'Not yet. But we don't have far to go, and then we'll be on the ferry.'

'On the sea?'

'Yes. On the sea.'

'How far is not far?'

Jasmin reached back and stroked his corn-blond hair, which was so similar to her own. 'Just to the end of the road.'

5

The ferry emitted a long, drawn-out blast on its foghorn and puffed grey clouds of exhaust into the air, which spread out over the dock like dark wafts of mist. Jasmin took Paul by the hand and together they stood by the railing, looking down at the boiling spray while the cold wind blew fine droplets of water onto their cheeks. Seagulls accompanied them for the first hundred yards before turning back towards the mainland, leaving them to sail out alone into the fog, which enveloped them within a few minutes and smothered every sound beyond the crash of the waves against the ship's hull and the rumble of the engines.

'I'm cold,' said Paul, tugging on the sleeve of Jasmin's coat. She bought him a hot chocolate from the on-board cafe and they sat down to drink it together. Jasmin picked up a newspaper someone had left on their table and, her fingers clenched round her cup, she searched through the pages for the words *Unknown victim, unidentified body discovered*. But of course there was nothing. She exhaled in relief, like every time, but she still couldn't shake off the vague feeling of tension that dogged her wherever she went. *One day you'll find it. One day it'll all catch up with you.* She felt certain of that.

A man in his sixties in a moss-green raincoat that dripped water onto the floor sat down with them and warmed his gnarled fingers against a large mug of coffee. He looked across at them both with a cheerful smile on his weather-beaten face.

'I see somebody's thirsty,' he rumbled. 'My daughter always used to like a hot chocolate too when we took the ferry to the mainland each week.'

'There's nothing better to warm you up in this weather,' Jasmin replied, dabbing her lips with a serviette. She always found it oddly uncomfortable when strangers struck up conversation with her like this, and each time it took her some effort to respond.

'Minsøy is hiding in the mist,' the old man continued after scanning the horizon through the porthole. 'She always does that.

The island is like an old lady – she has her secrets. Secrets she wants to keep, at all costs.'

'Do you know Minsøy well?' Jasmin's thoughts turned to the only large settlement on the island: the village of Skårsteinen, with its two thousand inhabitants, where she and Jørgen had spent the night when they viewed the old sea captain's house for the first time. It had been a mild spring day; she recalled the gentle breeze that had blown in from the sea. They had bought it a few months later. *It was our little refuge*, she thought. *Up until that day.*

'I run the grocery shop on the main street together with my wife, and she'd worry about me if I missed the ferry. The summer is coming to an end and the sea is getting more treacherous by the day. The tides are changing, and when the wind finally shifts to the north, the last residents will take to their heels, leaving only the people who've always been here and those who can't get away.' He gave her a scrutinising look. 'Or those who deliberately choose to arrive now.'

'My husband and I own a house on Minsøy.'

'A *summer* house, you mean.'

Jasmin took a sip of her drink, which had now gone cold. 'Is that a bad thing?'

A solemn smile played over his bearded lips – solemn and yet warm. 'That depends if you're a summer or a winter person. But you've actually already answered your own question. You're looking for something, one way or another, aren't you? Just like most of us are.'

'I'm looking for . . .' From the corner of her eye, Jasmin saw Paul stand up, walk over to the window and press his nose to it. Rain was whipping against it and running in rivulets down the thick glass. 'I guess . . . for myself.'

'I'm sure you'll manage it in the end.' The old man extended his hand – a huge bear's paw that bore the marks of hard physical labour – and Jasmin shook it. 'Karl Sandvik,' he introduced himself. 'Come and see us if you need anything. Our door is always open and my wife loves meeting new people.'

'Thanks,' Jasmin replied. 'Jasmin Hansen. Thank you very much.'

'It's always good to know there are still young people out there who are made of sterner stuff. Which house did you say was yours?'

'Number 7. On the south coast, close to the beach.'

'Ah.' Sandvik stroked his beard. 'The old captain's house. Nice spot, with the forest and the sea views. Well, I'll see you again, I hope.'

'Absolutely.'

Sandvik nodded and looked back at the window, where Paul was still peering out and drawing letters in the condensation on the glass. 'There she is,' he said. 'Minsøy.'

Light-grey rock was emerging from the mist, which soon gave way to darker grey, followed by steep slopes, cliffs, a shingle beach on which the waves were crashing with full force. Jasmin could see the lighthouse and its beacon, the road running along the cliff edge, and the rooftops of Skårsteinen in the distance.

The island was wild, rugged and beautiful, an almost pristine patch of earth. The port drew nearer and the ferry slowed down. For a moment, the blanket of clouds parted and let a few rays of sunshine through.

See? they seemed to be trying to say. *Not everything is dark.*

'We made it.'

Chapter 2

Jasmin Hansen had liked the house at the end of the road from the moment she saw it. True, the roof was a little crooked and the red brickwork on the windward side was overgrown with moss and encrusted with salt, but it was still in one piece, as if it had resolved never to bend before the onslaught of the sea and the storm gales. It felt familiar, a place she could retreat to and clear her head. That was something she desperately needed right now – more than ever before in her life.

'Here we are,' she announced, her heart pounding. 'I think it'll suit us very well, don't you?'

Paul leapt out of the hire car as soon as she opened the door and Jasmin followed him with a smile as he dashed up to the house, closely followed by Bonnie, who held her head up to sniff at the breeze after the long journey.

Bonnie and Clyde, Jasmin thought. *If Jørgen and I had bought a second dog, we couldn't have called it anything else. But that'll probably never happen now.*

The crunch of car tyres on gravel prompted her to look back over her shoulder. An old Volkswagen was coming up the drive, and the man who got out shortly afterwards looked like he'd been poured directly into his blue winter coat.

'Jasmin Hansen,' she introduced herself. 'I'm—'

'Of course, I know who you are,' he answered in a gruff voice. 'Knut Jüting, but I'm sure you know that already too. So you made it over all right?'

'The sea was a little rough.' Jasmin smiled noncommittally.

'They've been saying on the radio that the first big autumn storm will be arriving very soon, young lady, and I can't argue with them. I can sense it. There's an ache in these old bones that I haven't felt for a long time.' He handed her a keyring with three keys attached, one of which was larger than the others. 'Front door, the shed at the back of the house – the door sticks a little so give it a good shove and don't be timid about it – and this one's for the boathouse down on the beach behind the forest.'

'Wonderful,' Jasmin replied. Knut Jüting – who looked after a few of the empty houses on the south coast of Minsøy – shook her hand. She felt calluses and rough skin that spoke of hard graft on the high seas. 'What were they saying about the storm?'

'It's getting closer,' Jüting replied. 'But the roof is sound, Ms Hansen, don't you worry about that. I made sure of it.' He held up a bulky old mobile phone that he must have bought years ago and never traded in for a better model. 'And if you have any problems, give me a call. It isn't very far to the village.'

'Just follow the road, right?'

'Just keep following the road,' he replied, walking back to his Volkswagen. 'That's right.'

Jasmin found Paul and Bonnie in the overgrown garden behind the house. The birch trees were clustered beside the fence and she could barely make out the narrow path under the long grass – the path that led down to the beach.

'Who wants to take a look around inside?' she called. 'And who wants a cup of hot chocolate?'

Bonnie barked and Paul giggled as the dog licked his face. Jasmin walked back around and unlocked the front door. There was a bright piece of mirrored glass mounted in the dark oak to let people inside look out. The door swung open with a squeal.

A musty, dusty odour hung in the air, with something else underneath it that she couldn't identify – maybe mould, or maybe something rotten. Had an animal got in through a broken window and been unable to find its way out again? It was a possibility – the house had been unoccupied for years.

Five years, to be precise.

You're back, she thought. *After all this time, you're back.*

She and Paul stepped through the front door into a hallway designed to keep the cold out of the rest of the ground floor during winter. On the wall to their left was a brick fireplace with an oil painting hanging above it that showed an old ship crossing a choppy sea, its square sails bellied out in the wind.

The floor and the sideboard were covered with a layer of dust in which Bonnie left pawprints as she trotted curiously through the hallway towards the kitchen. 'Here, Bonnie.' The dog returned obediently to Jasmin's side and looked up at her expectantly. Jasmin didn't like the idea of her tearing off through the house and possibly disturbing some animal that had taken up residence inside. The caretaker had dropped in regularly to check up on things, but he evidently hadn't viewed cleaning as one of his duties.

'Maybe we should start by looking for the vacuum cleaner,' said Jasmin. 'But before that . . .' She flicked the light switch. There was a buzzing noise, as if the old and long-unused bulbs were protesting, but then warm light flooded into the hallway. One of the wall lights gave a bright flash before going out with a pop, but the rest of them stayed on.

She walked through to the kitchen, which had a gas cooker and a small round dining table below a window looking out onto the back garden, where white poplars and birch trees were swaying gently in the wind. A gingham cloth still covered the table where they used to eat together, back when everything had been so much easier and more carefree, with the mild summer sun shining in through the casement windows. On the right a wood-panelled hallway linked the kitchen to the living room. Jasmin briefly put her head through the door. The green, floral-patterned sofa Jørgen hadn't wanted to part with was still standing on the walnut floorboards in front of the French windows that opened out onto the veranda, from where a set of steps descended to the garden and the path that led through the woods and down to the beach.

It began to drizzle, the rain pattering gently against the window. Goosebumps crawled over Jasmin's body. In her mind's eye, she saw a harsh white light – a blinding flash – and with it came memories she would prefer to suppress, locked away in a box deep in her subconscious.

Squealing tyres. The figure in the headlights, close, far too close. The driving rain that obscured her view, the drumming of the water on the windscreen.

Water like blood flowing over the ground. Blood mingling with the rain and soaking the soil.

Her own scream reverberating in her ears.

Then the impact.

'Mummy?'

Jasmin gave a start.

Paul was standing in front of her. 'I've found the vacuum cleaner,' he explained, looking at her with wide eyes. 'It's red and enormous.'

'You've . . .' It took her a few seconds to gather herself, to organise her thoughts. *Breathe*, she told herself. 'Thanks, honey.' She glanced over at the window again, at the tops of the birch trees swaying back and forth. 'Do you want to have a look at the back garden with Bonnie? But don't go any further than the trees at the bottom so I can see you, OK?' She opened the door to the veranda, and Paul and Bonnie bounded through it.

Her son's gleeful laughter rang back to her as she watched him go. *You have to be there for him. It's the only thing that matters. Trying to recover your memories here, to remember everything you've forgotten – all that is important, no doubt, but it's not the priority.*

The priority is to get back to your old self.

That's the only way you can be there for Paul in the way he deserves. And once you've managed it . . .

No. She didn't want to think about Jørgen now.

She found the vacuum cleaner where she remembered leaving it, inside a storage cupboard next to the kitchen. A fat spider crawled out of the nozzle as she dragged it towards the hallway, but it still worked just fine. An hour later the ground floor looked presentable, and Jasmin went back and forth several times from the car to the house as she unloaded their bags and suitcases. Bonnie sat at the bottom of the stairs and watched her, while Paul had found a stick in the garden and was duelling with an invisible foe by the front door.

She brought in her bag of documents last of all, before climbing the steep staircase and casting a glance into the bedroom. The curtain was slightly open, as if somebody had been standing there a few seconds ago and looking out of the window.

It'll be all right.

It has to be.

The tap in the bathroom produced a thick, gurgling flow of reddish-brown liquid. The pressure was good, but that was all. She left it running for a few minutes until the rust was flushed out of the pipes, leaving nothing but clear water that stubbornly refused to warm up.

'Would you do me a favour and unpack your bag? Your things are in here.' The room Paul would be sleeping in was south-facing,

13

overlooking the garden, and lay directly opposite her own. 'I'm going to pop down to the cellar to look at the heating.'

And hopefully not at the spiders, she thought.

The plank door to the cellar gave a squeak as she lifted the simple metal hook that kept it locked from the hallway. Jasmin groped for the light switch, but when she found it, the bulb momentarily flooded the room with light before going out again. The cellar stairs fell steeply away before her – and down at the bottom . . .

For a moment, she felt certain she'd seen something looking up at her during that fraction of a second. Something scuttling over the floor on all fours. But not an animal.

'Oh, Jesus,' she whispered. In the kitchen, she found a box of matches and candles – *always a good idea to keep that sort of thing on hand out here*, she heard Jørgen's voice echo through her mind – and a sharp knife.

The staircase creaked as she descended. It sounded like the rattle of a dying man. Houses this close to the water shouldn't have a cellar, one of the neighbours had told her – but nobody cared about that on the island.

In this place, you just have to get by. Nature doesn't care about you. It merely exists.

There were shovels, spades, a pickaxe, all leaning against the wall. A green gun cabinet gave a rusty squeak when Jasmin put her hand on the door. Inside it lay an old hunting gun – a pump-action shotgun. Her heart was pounding. The hot water tank loomed out of the darkness like an oversized magician's top hat – a magician who had been playing some very odd tricks down here.

Beside it, she found the boiler. The large switch controlling the power supply to the gas burner was turned off.

Of course it is. Jørgen always remembered things like that. Or was it the caretaker?

Jasmin flicked it to the 'On' position and the burner rumbled back to life. So much for that. On a shelf covered in cobwebs, she found a handful of fuses for the box in the hall, as well as a torch with no batteries.

She would have to head into the village first thing in the morning to pick up the other supplies. That was no bad thing, since it would bring her among other people. *Exactly what you need.*

Right?

Right?

Jasmin swung her candle around. A draught caused the flame to flicker. She had never liked this dank, mouldy old cellar. In the corner she saw a rowing boat propped upright against the wall, its red hull gleaming in the candlelight like fresh blood. Somewhere in the darkness, she could hear the rustle and crackle of leaves that must have been blown in by the wind.

The door in the far corner was slightly ajar.

That *never* happened.

That door had *always* been kept locked – she'd insisted on it.

Jasmin felt her pulse quicken and a shiver ran up her back, as if the temperature had suddenly dropped by several degrees.

She took a few steps backwards.

Through the gap in the door, she saw an eye peering in. Silver-edged, with a pupil that held a red gleam.

She blinked: it was gone.

Jasmin whirled around and sprinted up the stairs. She slammed the wooden door shut behind her and threaded the metal hook through the catch, before dragging a cabinet from its usual spot against the wall and pushing it in front of the door. The shoes stored inside it clunked around noisily.

Her hands were trembling.

There wasn't anything down there. It was just your imagination mixing things up, after everything you've been through.

15

'I've found it,' said Paul behind her. Jasmin gave a low cry and spun around to face him. 'Upstairs . . . there's a broken window,' he explained with a somewhat guilty expression.

Jasmin blinked. 'What did you find?'

'It's a fox.' Paul pouted. 'Well, actually Bonnie found it, not me.'

The animal was lying inside a wardrobe at the end of the upstairs corridor. The floorboards here were creaky and the outline of the watermark left by a leak in the roof some time ago was still visible on the wallpaper. Jørgen had fixed the roof, Jasmin recalled, and had almost fallen off at one point, but he'd laughed it away. He always faced every difficulty with a smile and a shrug. For a moment, she found herself yearning for him – wishing he was here to take her in his arms.

Then she suppressed the thought.

You need to do this alone.

He doesn't believe you.

Nobody does.

But can you blame them?

The fox couldn't have been dead for very long – perhaps a day or two. The smell emanating from it was unpleasant, but nowhere near as strong as when she'd first entered the house. The stench was gone from the rest of the rooms, the wind having driven the stale air out through the open windows. Jasmin fetched her work gloves from the storage room and carried the corpse outdoors.

The tall grass in the back garden brushed against her legs and whispered quietly in the breeze. 'We have to bury him,' said Paul, who had followed her outside. Bonnie was lying on the veranda watching them; her dark, floppy ears pivoted attentively in their direction so she could keep track of what her humans were up to.

Bury him.

Jasmin glanced at Paul. He'd brought a small shovel with him and was yawning with all the weariness of a five-year-old after a tiring day like today. She stroked the top of his head. 'Let me do it,' she replied. 'Later on.'

'Do you promise?'

'Of course. Scout's honour.'

Paul reached into the pocket of his blue raincoat and showed her a small figure of an animal made of folded paper. It looked like a fox. Ever since her sister had taught him about origami, Paul had been quite a fan of it; his guidebook and the heavy paper that folded so well were the first things Jasmin had packed. 'I made this. For him. I think we should give it to him as a present.'

'Is that from your book? I didn't know . . .'

'No, it's not.' Paul shook his head. 'I made it up myself.'

'It's very beautiful, honey.'

'So he isn't so alone, you know? I don't think he should be alone.'

'No,' she replied quietly, swallowing to clear the lump in her throat. 'He shouldn't.'

Jasmin spent the rest of the afternoon cleaning the house, clearing the cobwebs from the corners, dusting the curtains and the furniture, making the beds and lighting a fire in the stove.

She and Paul had a light dinner while Bonnie ate her favourite dry food from her bowl. Then Paul tested out the television in the living room to see if it still worked.

As it turned out, it did. With her little boy snuggled up beside her, Jasmin was able to relax somewhat for the first time since leaving home. They watched a quiz show, and the quiet hum of the washing machine at the other end of the hall made her drowsy. After an hour, Paul began muttering softly in his sleep, and she carried him gently upstairs and tucked him into bed.

'Sleep well, champ.'

'Will you read me something?' He blinked up at her through his half-closed eyes and Jasmin couldn't help but smile. The box of books she'd brought with her was still out in the corridor. 'You can barely keep your eyes open as it is. Just go to sleep.'

'Night, Mummy.'

'Good night, little bear.'

Jasmin left the corridor light on and went back downstairs, where she peered through the windows and turned the key again in the front door. The bolt gave a convincingly metallic clunk, which reassured her a little.

Was that the staircase she could hear creaking? Was there something coming up from the cellar? Pushing at the door, rattling it against the cabinet? She blinked and rubbed her eyes. Clearly she was overtired.

Jasmin's thoughts turned to what had happened down there. She'd never forgotten it – had never been able to forget. The man who'd presented the property to them had given them a tour, showing them the garden, the path down to the beach, the whole house from the cellar up to the attic – and then, while they were sitting together over a cup of good, freshly brewed coffee, he'd told them the story. 'I can't sell it to you,' he began, 'without mentioning it, as it wouldn't be right otherwise.'

Jasmin had glanced across at Jørgen, who'd responded with a smile, as if to say: here come the ghost stories, but whatever he tells us, the two of us have already fallen deeply in love with this little old house. Yet what the man said next wiped the smiles from both their faces.

'Somebody died here. It was suicide, downstairs, in the back room of the cellar – that was where they found him hanging from one of the beams running along the ceiling, his face all—'

Jasmin had rushed out of the room, her hand pressed to her stomach, which was clenched tight beneath her cardigan. 'We don't have to buy it,' Jørgen had said as they drove off afterwards. Jasmin had looked over her shoulder. The old captain's house had gleamed in the light of the setting sun.

Come back, it seemed to be calling to her.

Now you've stepped over my threshold, I'll never let you go.

Somebody died there, she'd thought. *But that's all. You've never been superstitious or sensitive to vibrations, like your mother. The house is gorgeous and so close to the water – it'd take us a long time to find anything better.*

And so she'd pushed all doubts aside.

All the same, she had never set foot in the back room of the cellar again.

Chapter 3

The night was clear and the stars glittered like ice crystals woven into a soft blanket of blue-black velvet as Jasmin dug a grave for the fox in the back garden. The wind whispered through the dry leaves of the poplars and birches as if it were trying to tell a long-forgotten story. She worked first with her spade, then the shovel, digging a good two feet into the earth. Carefully, she lowered the fox into the hole and placed Paul's origami figure beside it.

So he isn't so alone.

The things Paul comes up with.

In the nearby forest, a branch cracked. *Like a heavy boot treading on it*, she thought. Jasmin's eyes scanned the darkness anxiously, but she couldn't see anything beyond the inky, formless void that the world had vanished into tonight. A bush waved in the wind, its branches like the outstretched arms of a stranger.

Jasmin threw the spade and shovel over her shoulder and went back to the house, leaving small clumps of soil behind her on the steps.

Clear evidence, she thought. *Guilty as charged, Ms Hansen, with the sentence to follow.*

Her shoulders and arms protested painfully, but it had been good, honest work, as her mother always used to say, and it seemed right to her not to simply throw the cadaver into the forest. Quite apart from the fact that Bonnie might have found it again and – God forbid – dragged it into the house, which would have left Paul deeply disappointed in Jasmin.

And that was the last thing she wanted.

Jasmin looked at herself in the mirror of the small, eggshell-coloured bathroom. *You're tired. And you're still a long way from your usual self.*

The accident.

It's in every muscle, every bone in your body, burned deep into your soul.

And nobody believes you.

That was the worst part of it. Jasmin undressed. The pale scar left by her stitches stood out against her skin. It had only been a few months ago but the scar already looked much, much older. The impact had driven part of the dashboard into her side – it had been close, very close.

But you're alive.

You're alive – while that man . . .

She suppressed the thought, pushing it aside like an ugly, heavy box that blocked her path, and got into the shower. The water was hot and the pressure strong, a blessing after her tiring day. She closed her eyes and listened to the quiet patter of the water and the gurgle of the plughole, which mingled with the soft rustling of the wind outside. A shutter clattered noisily against the side of the house as the spray massaged her tense shoulders.

The light had taken on a blood-red colour, as if to reflect how she felt. It was as though her left side was filled with hot coals – a pain that radiated up to her temples and down to her calves. They had told her afterwards she'd kept shouting for her husband and son every time she woke up, panicking, terrified – and that hadn't been the only thing she'd yelled either. 'Out of the way, get out of the way!' she'd cried, as if trying to warn somebody.

The man she saw leaning over her when she woke up, his familiar face emerging from the blurred, foggy darkness of her unconsciousness, was not Jørgen. She was looking not at her husband, but at the Nordic blue eyes of Sven Birkeland; at the cool, appraising gaze of the specialist registrar at the Oslo University Hospital, Ullevål – the man at whose side she normally stood every day in the operating theatre.

Jasmin opened her mouth and felt the dried-out skin on the corners of her lips crack painfully. She was thirsty; her throat was parched, as if she'd just walked through a desert. 'What's going on?'

'Easy, Jasmin. Take it easy.' He touched her hand and looked at her half-affectionately, half-worriedly. His concern alarmed her more than the pain – but not as much as the blank space in her memory. And this dull ache, where did it come from?

'What happened?' Jasmin cleared her throat, sending a new wave of pain coursing through her body. *Somebody must have sawn your head open and jabbed shards of glass behind your forehead – there's no other way to explain this agony.* 'It – it hurts so much.'

Sven glanced to one side and Jasmin noticed the drip attached to her arm. The rest of her body was hidden under a white blanket. She could smell the astringent odour of disinfectant. It felt as familiar to her as Jørgen's touch.

You're in Ullevål. But you're not at work. You . . .

'Jasmin, you've had an accident. We're looking after you. Everything is OK, you'll be back on your feet soon enough.'

Jasmin grasped at his fingers. 'Tell me the truth!'

'It was a car accident. You hit an animal.'

'What? An animal?' *This doesn't make sense*, an inner voice told her. *Something doesn't add up here . . .*

'That's right, sweetheart. A deer, and a pretty big one at that. You're hurt, but it's nothing we can't fix. You know what we always tell our patients . . .' He smiled, and the gesture consoled her somewhat.

'We do this all the time,' she said, finishing his sentence.

'Look at it this way: now you get to experience all the advantages of this hospital from a different point of view. Isn't that great?'

Jasmin awkwardly lifted her hand and pointed at the drip and the morphine pump below it. 'Give me more. Everything hurts.'

'Sure thing.'

'What about Paul? And Jørgen?'

'They're fine.' Sven hesitated, though it was such a brief, barely perceptible pause that Jasmin didn't quite register it in her hazy state of mind. 'They've been waiting outside the whole time. But I think you should try and get some more sleep now, don't you?'

Jasmin closed her eyes. Even this short conversation had cost her an unbelievable effort. She felt an irresistible urge to drift off to sleep, the pain that radiated from her side gradually dwindling into a dull, insignificant background buzz with each passing second.

'That sounds good. Tell Jørgen I'll . . . I'll be back on my feet soon.'

'That's right, Jasmin. You definitely will be.'

Chapter 4

A rain-slicked road. Headlights illuminating the white lines as they rushed past. The wipers sliding back and forth over the windscreen as if in never-ending mutual pursuit – two foes unable to ever quite catch up with each other. And all the while, the rain hammering down relentlessly over everything, obscuring her view.

Jasmin peered through the windscreen. She'd taken her foot off the accelerator and was driving just below the speed limit. The last road sign now lay behind them, and the trees that lined both sides of this narrow country road were drawing ever nearer – huge, ancient giants with thick trunks.

A long way from civilisation, she thought. *And from any mobile phone coverage.*

Eyes glittered in the headlights along the sides of the road. There were a lot of animals about tonight. At one point Jasmin saw a wolf calmly turn its sleek head in her direction, the rain dripping from its grey fur.

Then she saw the headlights in the rear-view mirror.

Two huge, brilliant white flares, like a pair of eyes. 'That moron is still on full beam,' she said to herself. 'Hasn't he realised? No, of course he hasn't, as he wouldn't be doing it otherwise.'

The headlights came nearer and nearer – a big four-by-four whose driver was evidently in a hurry. 'Overtake me, you lunatic!'

Jasmin slowed down even further and steered her small car closer to the verge in order to make space on the narrow road. 'Overtake, there's nobody coming! And then get out of my hair.'

But the Jeep made no attempt to overtake. Instead, it drove up close to her bumper, forcing Jasmin to pull the anti-dazzle lever on her rear-view mirror. She glanced over at the passenger seat where she'd left her handbag. *Do you have your phone with you? Or did you leave it at home? What exactly is going on here? Why are you so flustered?*

The Jeep drew even closer. Jasmin tried to see who the driver was, but she could only make out a silhouette and it was impossible to say if it belonged to a man or a woman. One thing was clear though: this person wasn't going to give up.

Sweat beaded on her forehead; droplets trickled down between her shoulder blades.

'What do you want from me?'

Her stomach lurched as she realised her car couldn't possibly withstand the weight of the Jeep, and it would only take one little bump for her to veer off the road, judder over the rumble strip and career down the verge.

Jasmin knew what the outcome of that kind of accident could be. She'd seen the victims – had stood in theatre on countless occasions and monitored their vital signs and dosages in her job as an anaesthetist.

Suddenly, the Jeep swerved into the other lane, accelerated sharply and overtook her. Jasmin glanced across at it, but all she could make out was a pair of hands gripping a large steering wheel. Moments later, she could see only the Jeep's tail lights ahead of her, which quickly vanished into the darkness. Jasmin exhaled in relief.

Good riddance, she thought, and tasted blood in her mouth – she'd bitten her lip out of sheer anxiety. *Now get yourself home. Nice and steady. Whoever that was, he was probably just playing a stupid joke on you. Maybe he was drunk.*

Someone else will take care of him.

He's not your problem now.

Yet whatever she told herself, her pulse kept racing, as if she instinctively knew the threat hadn't subsided. Suddenly, another set of lights flashed into view ahead of her, in the opposite lane, at the far end of the road.

She heard a clattering noise in front of her, much closer than the Jeep, and she woke up with a start. Water was flowing over her head, her face, her body. Bewildered, she found herself standing in the shower and realised her bottle of shampoo had fallen noisily to the floor, bringing her back to the here and now. She'd been dreaming. The now-tepid water must have made her drowsy, but the fact she'd nearly nodded off in the shower from sheer exhaustion seemed utterly irrelevant. *You remembered something. The moments before your accident. There was a car – a Jeep – and then . . .*

Then you woke up. Jasmin picked up the shampoo. *Stupid bottle. But still, it's progress.*

You're on the right track. It was a good idea to come here. The new surroundings are stimulating your thoughts and you're going to remember, like you hoped. It's all going to come back to you.

Including the truth.

Yes, maybe even the truth.

You need to find the triangle. The upside-down triangle with the open top-right corner. You know it from the night of your accident – and you know you've seen it before on Minsøy too.

But where? That particular detail remained stubbornly elusive, as if her memory was shrouded in dense fog.

Jasmin dried herself off. Out in the corridor, the air was thick with the smell of smoke from the fires she'd lit in the house's two wood burners.

She checked on Paul, who was sleeping peacefully. The small waxing moon was shining through his window, bathing the astronauts and rockets on his duvet in a faint silver light. The book she'd been reading to him over the last few days was lying on the bedside table: a story about a boy called Max who visits some friends and embarks on a wild adventure.

Paul must have woken up and fetched it from the box. That was unusual.

There were three origami figures on the windowsill. A swan, another bird – maybe an eagle – and a cat.

He's really talented. My little artist.

Jasmin tiptoed out of the bedroom. Small droplets of water fell from her damp hair and dripped onto the rough floorboards. *Plop, plop.* The noise continued as she suddenly stopped.

Something had caught her attention – something that had been nagging at her all evening, although she couldn't quite put her finger on what it was.

The door of the wardrobe at the end of the corridor was still ajar.

It had been worming away at her – ticking over in her subconscious for hours – but only now did she realise it had to do with the dead fox and this wardrobe. Jasmin walked over to it. The wardrobe was made of pale birchwood, polished and cool to the touch. The door creaked quietly when she put her hand on it and there was a dark brass key in the lock.

She froze. A key in the lock . . . If the fox had been inside this wardrobe and had only been dead for a couple of days, that meant someone must have locked it in there. Or was there another explanation? Of course there was: somebody had visited the house and left the corpse here. Somebody who knew Jasmin was coming.

Are you certain the wardrobe was locked? Paul never mentioned it; all he said was that Bonnie had found the fox. Nothing about a key. But wouldn't the fox have run away if the door had been unlocked?

Did someone really put a dead fox in there?

And if they did, wouldn't that be so much worse?

Why would anybody do that?

Jasmin pulled back the covers on her bed but felt far too tense and nervous to go to sleep. Her mind kept working, as if countless gears were grinding away in there, reshaping all her thoughts.

You remembered something, she thought again. *That's why you're here: to finally shed a little light on the darkness, to finally understand what really happened on the night of the accident and to track down that triangle. And you remembered something. Only a small part of the picture – but where one fragment emerges, more will follow.*

An animal. Sven Birkeland's words sprang to her mind. They'd found clear evidence on her car: fur, blood. It was an open-and-shut case, and yet . . .

You know something isn't right. You can almost remember – early in the morning, during those moments between sleep and wakefulness, you know deep down . . .

That that isn't what happened.

That it wasn't just a deer out there on the road in the storm, in the driving rain.

It was a man.

You killed a human being that night.

Jasmin woke with a start once more, gasping for breath. Sweat lay in a cool, damp film on her forehead; her trembling fingers gripped the rumpled bedclothes.

Then she heard it.

A noise from out back. It was the narrow gate that separated her garden from the track through the woods behind the house. *You locked it behind you when you buried the fox. You definitely did.*

Jasmin threw the duvet aside and leapt out of bed. The floor was cold beneath her feet, the woodgrain rough and uneven in places, and she knew very well that she'd pick up a few splinters if she wasn't careful. The carving knife she'd taken down into the cellar earlier was lying on the bedside table. *Did you leave it there?* She couldn't remember, but she grabbed it now, took it with her and held it out in front of her, ready to defend herself. Cautiously, she pushed the blind aside and peered through the window: down in the garden, almost hidden by the tree trunks and yet treacherously illuminated in the pale glow emanating from the thin strip of moon, she saw the silhouette of a man.

Whoever it was, he was staring up at her.

She was certain of it.

Jasmin felt a cry of terror welling up in her throat. The stranger's eyes met her own, and at the last moment she managed to swallow her scream.

He can't see you. It's dark in the bedroom. You can see him, but – no, he can't see you. So don't scream, don't give yourself away. Think. What should you do?

Yet before she could stir, the silent observer turned on his heel and slipped abruptly into the woods, following the path away from the house until he disappeared from view amid the towering birch trees.

Jasmin felt a sharp pain in her right hand. In her anxiety, she'd gripped the knife slightly too far up and her hand had slipped off the handle, causing the blade to slice into her skin. Blood was dripping onto the windowsill, red on white, like the tracks of a wounded animal through fresh snow.

In the kitchen she found some bandages and sat down at the table to tend to her injury under the light of the incandescent bulb.

'You aren't ready to do this alone,' Jørgen had said.

'I'm ready. I have to be.'

'At least let me follow you up there and check up on you. You don't have to go through any of this on your own.' He'd embraced her tenderly and held her for a long time, as if he never wanted to let her go.

'I know you'd do anything to help me through this,' she'd replied. 'But there are times when we have to settle things on our own. You know me – almost better than I know myself.'

'Do you promise you'll call me if anything happens that scares you?'

She'd nodded.

Three missed calls, her mobile phone told her. She'd left it on the bedside table and, having fetched it from upstairs, she was now turning it over indecisively in her hands. Bonnie had heard her, had come out of Paul's room and followed her down to the kitchen, alert and watchful, with a look in her eyes as if she knew exactly what was making Jasmin so nervous.

You haven't even been here one day. If you call him now, he'll just think you're weak. And it'll only confirm to him what he's been thinking the whole time: that you're imagining things. Deluding yourself.

As far as he's concerned, you hit a deer that night – nothing more.

When she looked up, Bonnie was gone.

'Bonnie,' Jasmin called quietly towards the hallway. 'Here, Bonnie!'

She heard the quiet click of the Labrador's claws on the stairs. Bonnie reappeared, wagging her tail, curious to see why she'd been summoned again so late at night. Jasmin stroked her thick fur. 'We should stick together,' she told her, as Bonnie tried to lick her face. Eventually, Jasmin went back upstairs and patted the basket she'd put out in the corridor between the two bedroom doors. *So she can watch over us both.* Bonnie looked at her inquisitively before turning around in circles a few times and sinking down onto her soft bed with a satisfied grunt.

'You'll look after the three of us, won't you?'

Bonnie made no sound, but returned Jasmin's gaze with her clever, dark-brown dog eyes.

Jasmin crawled under her duvet. No sooner had she rolled over onto her side and closed her eyes than she was overcome by the exhaustion that had been lying in wait on the edge of her consciousness.

Only a few hours, she thought. *Everything will look very different in the morning.*

Cracking, rustling noises came from the walls.

There's no such thing as ghosts. This is just an old house that's getting used to its occupants again.

That's all.

Chapter 5

The thatched and red-tiled roofs of Skårsteinen glittered in the light of the morning sun. A beautiful day had broken as Jasmin, Paul and Bonnie entered the village in their rental car. There were a handful of other drivers on the road, and a few of them turned their heads as Jasmin passed, their curiosity piqued at the sight of a strange number plate – especially now the holiday season was over and the residents were left more and more to themselves. Any summer visitors who stayed on for longer were viewed with suspicion.

They were strangers. Outsiders. More so than usual, even.

Strangers stood out. She and Jørgen had discovered that during their first ever visit to the island, and although it hadn't bothered him, it had taken Jasmin a while to get used to it.

The wind last night had swept the leaden grey from the sky. Instead, fleecy clouds with frayed edges were scattered across the heavens and the sun shone like a freshly polished gold coin. It was a bright day, a cheerful day, as if it had been sent to dispel all her sinister thoughts from the night before.

But he was there. You saw him. And you mustn't forget it. Because whoever he was, he won't forget it either. He might come back.

Jasmin parked on the main street, which was home to a few bed and breakfasts, a supermarket, a tiny cinema with red seats and a small screen, and the grocery store run by Karl Sandvik and his wife. A tall apple tree stood beside the squat building and there were three bicycles parked outside the shop window, which was decorated with a display of seasonal fruit and vegetables.

The air was mild and smelled of cut grass, and Jasmin's spirits slowly began to lift. 'Let's take a look around,' she said to Paul. A bell above the door tinkled as she entered.

'Ah, our summer visitors.' Karl Sandvik was standing by a shelf and stacking some large canisters containing vegetable oil, according to the labels. It was a very good idea to buy in bulk in a place like this, she and Jørgen had learned, and Jasmin hadn't forgotten the lesson. The car had a large boot, they had plenty of space at home, and she'd brought enough cash.

For a moment, Jasmin remembered how Jørgen had reacted when he'd found out that her parents had made a fortune with their business – that thanks to the shares they'd received, Jasmin and her sister would never have to work again in their lives, and yet she kept working anyway. Because she found her job fulfilling. Because you need something to build your character as well as your bank balance, as her father had put it.

But Jørgen's initial surprise had quickly passed. *He loves you, not your money.* She felt sure of it.

And now? she thought. *Is that still true? Or did what happened change things, drive a wedge between you? Is there something behind those looks he gives you when he thinks you haven't noticed? What goes through his mind those times when he lies awake beside you at night?*

Jasmin shook her head and dispelled these thoughts. She'd done the right thing by coming here. It would settle everything once and for all.

'Can Bonnie come in too?' Jasmin held the door open while Bonnie waited at the threshold and looked up at her like the well-trained dog she was.

'Oh yes, certainly.' Sandvik put his glasses on and held his hand out to Jasmin, who shook it. 'I see you've settled in all right?'

'Not quite,' she answered with an evasive smile. 'But we're getting there. Yesterday was a cleaning day.'

'It can't be easy down there.' Sandvik bent forward to lift another canister from the pallet, groaning as he did so. 'Oof,' he said, 'my old bones. And the weather, too. It's always the same.' The face he pulled as he rubbed his hand over his back was all too familiar to Jasmin thanks to her mother's back trouble.

Bonnie sniffed at some cans filled with enticing foodstuffs – *crab meat*, it said on the label – while Paul examined a display of books on the counter. Her bookworm son and her food-obsessed chocolate Labrador. *We make an odd team.*

'Down there?' she repeated.

'At the other end of the island. The wind is like a raging beast down there. The cliffs are dangerous, and as for the ground – to call it treacherous would be putting it mildly.' Sandvik coughed and gave Jasmin a mild, paternal look. 'And then for a woman to be all alone out there. Life has always been hard here, among the untamed forces of nature.'

'I'm looking for peace and quiet.' No sooner had Jasmin uttered the words than she realised they were far too harsh and unfriendly. 'I mean, so I can sort through my own thoughts. I'll be all right.'

'I wasn't trying to reproach you.' Sandvik picked up another canister and groaned once more. 'Some of the people around these parts will have something to say when they hear about it. A young woman, all by herself, without her husband. They're still a little old-fashioned in certain respects.'

'But you aren't?' Jasmin picked up her basket and started filling it with the items on the list she'd written early that morning at the kitchen table. Light bulbs and spare batteries stood at the top.

'I try not to judge anyone. None of us has an easy time of it when the wind shifts to the north and tries to knock us off our feet. This island is a stony garden, and only the strongest can make it grow. We've had all kinds of people make their way up here in the past, you know. Like you, they were hoping to find themselves . . .' He adjusted his spectacles as if fumbling for words.

'I saw the lighthouse on my way here,' said Jasmin, changing the subject.

'That old thing? Well, I suppose you can't miss it. You should pay a visit some time. Jan Berger will be sure to give you a tour if you tell him I sent you.'

'Really? Thank you, that's very kind. I'll make sure I do, Mr Sandvik.' Jasmin glanced at her list. 'Do you sell those big torch batteries here?'

Sandvik gave her a thoughtful look, as if he knew what was going through her mind.

'We do,' said a voice from behind her. Jasmin found herself looking at a small, grey-haired woman in her seventies, who was approaching them both in a wheelchair. 'Grit Sandvik,' she said. Her hand was covered in calluses. 'Don't pay too much attention to that old eccentric. He loves boring visitors with his stories.'

'Oh, I wasn't at all bored,' she replied with a smile. 'I actually found it rather interesting.'

Karl Sandvik gave her a broad grin. 'You shouldn't flatter old men like that, young lady. We both know she's right. Old men like to talk, and occasionally the stories they tell even manage to be entertaining.' His laugh was as rough as the sea. 'But only occasionally. Don't pay it any mind if folk are a little gruff with you. The people here are hard. You can't survive in a place like this if you aren't hard. If you don't have the cold Norwegian Sea flowing through your veins.'

'All the same, I think you and I are going to get on very well.' Jasmin picked up the rest of the supplies she needed, went over to the counter and paid.

'Did you tell her about the rumours?' Grit Sandvik asked.

Her husband shook his head. 'There's no need. She's only been here a day, we should let her—'

'Are you living alone down there?' Grit interrupted.

'Just me, my dog Bonnie and my son Paul.'

'Your son?'

'Yes, he's—' Jasmin turned around. Paul wasn't in the shop, but she spotted him outside by the car, where he was kneeling in front of Bonnie and getting her to put her paw in his hand. The grey paintwork of the Volvo sparkled in the sunlight. 'He's already outside.'

'I think you ought to know,' Grit Sandvik continued. 'Especially given the circumstances. All on your own out there.'

'It's OK.' Jasmin sensed this would be an uncomfortable topic, but after yesterday's events, she was on the alert. *Better to know too much than too little. Knowing things can't hurt.* 'You can tell me. But I don't want to force either of you, of course.'

Karl Sandvik shot a look at his wife as if to say, *I told you so.* 'There's a – hmm, what should I call him exactly? A drifter. Yes, I think that's the right word. Or a vagrant, perhaps. He's been spotted in various places over the last few weeks. Jon from the boat hire place says he's been lurking around the warehouses. He carries a grey plastic bag around with him and wears a long, grey trench coat or a sort of oversized windcheater that's full of holes.'

'Oh,' Jasmin replied, thinking of the figure at the forest edge. 'It's good that you told me.'

'Like I said,' replied Grit Sandvik, 'you can't be too careful nowadays.'

36

'Boeckermann has it all under control. But what I can't work out is how he got here in the first place.'

'On the ferry, man!' said his wife, shaking her head slightly. 'You know how it goes. How easy it is to stow away on board.'

Jasmin picked up her purchases. 'Who's Boeckermann?'

'Arne Boeckermann is our policeman, the only one out here. The island constable, in a manner of speaking.' Karl Sandvik closed the drawer of the enormous cash register, which jingled quietly. It was an old till, of a kind you seldom saw nowadays, and like everything else in the shop it lent the place an old-fashioned and homely atmosphere. *Just like its owners. As if time has stood still here, in a very pleasant way*, thought Jasmin.

'You've seen him, haven't you?' Grit Sandvik leaned forward and her wheelchair squeaked softly.

'Boeckermann?'

'Not him,' she snorted. 'The vagrant. Forgive me, but you seem a little . . . hmm, nervous? Is that right?'

Jasmin closed her eyes for a moment and recalled the previous night – all those shadows and fast-moving clouds in the sky; all that darkness, which seemed so endless, as if it would never lift. But Bonnie's wet nose had woken her up early in the morning, and after breakfast, Jasmin had fetched a hammer and some boards from the shed. The door had jammed, like the caretaker had told her, but she'd solved the problem with a firm kick. Armed with nails and oak boards, she'd returned to the house and sealed the door leading to the cellar. After that, she'd felt a good deal safer.

Maybe you're overdoing things a little here, she'd thought to herself as she hammered the finger-length nails into the wall. *No, you're definitely overdoing it. A man died down there, but that's all.*

You could leave the door permanently open.

There's nothing in the cellar.

37

And yet she'd nailed board after board into place until the door couldn't open an inch.

'How will you get down there now?' Paul had asked her. She'd let him hammer in the last two nails and he'd managed it very well.

'There's still the door at the back beside the shed,' she'd replied. 'We can always clear the woodpile out of the way if we need to get in. We'll need the wood anyway – the two stoves use a lot of fuel. But there isn't actually anything in the cellar that we'll want.'

Nothing at all.

'I . . .' She cleared her throat. 'I did see somebody. There's a path behind the house that leads down to the beach, and there was a man standing there last night. He might have been wearing a coat like the one your husband just described. But I'm not sure. Not entirely, anyway.'

'Oh my dear, that isn't good.' Grit Sandvik gave her a sympathetic look. 'Are you quite sure you want to stay out there?'

Absolutely, she wanted to reply, but then changed her mind. 'It might have been a bush that looked like a man in the moonlight,' she answered instead. 'I can't be sure.'

Karl Sandvik tore a sheet of paper from a notepad lying beside the old cash register and wrote down two phone numbers in his large handwriting. 'You might need this. The top number is Boeckermann's, and the other one is ours – the one for our house over there. You should call us if you see anybody else.'

'Do you have a gun?' asked Grit Sandvik in a worried tone.

'My husband has a hunting gun.' Jasmin looked out at Paul and saw him pressing his nose against the window of the neighbouring shop. 'It's still in the house.'

'Do you know how to use it?'

'No,' she replied. 'That was always too . . . It was never my thing.'

'And I say it's never too late to learn something new. If you do call at the lighthouse, ask Berger to show you how it works. In fact, let me write down his number for you too. I'd show you myself, but my back . . .' Karl Sandvik muttered.

'It's never too late to learn – unless your name is Karl and you don't know how to iron your own shirts.' Grit Sandvik nudged her husband in the ribs. 'But he's right. I mean, not that I'm trying to tell you what to do.'

Jasmin tucked the sheet of paper with the phone numbers into her purse. 'I won't forget,' she said. 'Thank you very much.'

'You're a doctor, aren't you?' Karl Sandvik asked.

Jasmin furrowed her brow. 'Surely you can't tell just by looking at me.'

'No, but Jüting mentioned he'd taken some keys out to a doctor, down by the beach.'

'Village gossip,' Grit Sandvik interjected. 'The same old story.'

Jasmin felt sure Karl was asking for a reason. 'How long have you been having trouble with your back?' she asked him, but it was Grit who answered.

'It's been especially bad over the last few weeks.' She seemed relieved and at the same time extremely thankful to Jasmin for asking. 'Sometimes – sometimes it's even worse than it is today. Like rusty nails being hammered into his back.'

'I can take a look, if you like. It isn't really my specialism, but—'

'No, there's no need,' Karl Sandvik mumbled.

'Come now, I think there is.' Jasmin saw Grit Sandvik give her a thankful smile and a meaningful nod, though it was so slight that her husband didn't notice.

'It's no problem,' she added. 'How about tomorrow, what do you say?'

'He says yes,' Grit answered for her husband. 'And he's very grateful.'

'Thank you.' Karl Sandvik nodded to Jasmin as his wife wheeled herself out from behind the counter and showed her to the door. 'He'd never admit it,' she said in an undertone. 'He's such a grump and he doesn't normally listen to anyone. And then all the fuss of travelling to the mainland, just for his back.'

On her way out, Jasmin noticed a painting in an alcove. It was an atmospheric evening scene depicting the lighthouse, its bright beacon shining far out to sea, and a man standing in front of it looking out over the waves, as if waiting for a ship to return.

'Do you like it?'

'It's very pretty. I don't know much about art, but yes, it's really striking.'

'It's local, too.'

'That must be the lighthouse, right?'

Grit Sandvik pointed at the bottom corner of the picture, where there was a signature that Jasmin couldn't decipher. 'The artist has been living on the island for many years now. Up on the northernmost tip, by the big cliffs. Gabriela Yrsen.'

'Unusual name.'

'Isn't it? She's a real hermit. Yrsen doesn't spend much time around other people these days. Something happened to her that means she's not all that pleasant to look at now. She was in a fire, and she's been living alone out there in the wilds ever since. We've hung this painting up here because people occasionally come looking for her, and – well, there's still a bit of business sense left in our old heads, you know? But after everything that's happened—'

'Grit?' her husband called from the back of the shop. 'Do you have a moment?'

40

The woman turned around, her hands gripping the wheels of her chair. 'I expect he's forgotten where he put his glasses again, the blind old bear.'

'See you soon,' said Jasmin. 'It was really nice chatting with you.'

Karl Sandvik appeared behind the counter, emerging from the doorway that led to the back of the shop. 'I have something else for you,' he announced, and Jasmin stopped. She had the impression Grit Sandvik hadn't told her everything she'd wanted to as her husband had interrupted her at the wrong moment. *We've hung it up here, but after everything that's happened . . . What did that mean?* Before Jasmin knew it, a small package had been pressed into her hands.

'Two security cameras. And two motion sensors. A couple of tourists once ordered them for their holiday home and then never collected them, after I spent ages phoning around and trying to get hold of the things. I'm sure you can make more sense of them than we can. Besides, we don't need them anyway, whereas you, out there on your own . . . Well, here you go.' Sandvik waddled back into the storeroom as if he didn't want to hear any objections.

'Thank you,' Jasmin said to his wife. 'And please tell him—'

'Ach, forget it. You don't need to thank us. But Ms Hansen?'

'Yes?'

'Please look after yourself and your son.'

'I will.'

Jasmin loaded her shopping into the boot and went to buy a few crates of bottled water from the nearby supermarket. Just as she was about to put them in the car, a shadow fell over her.

'Hang on, let me help you.'

Jasmin found herself looking at a blond man with stubble on his cheeks. 'New here?' he asked in a deep, husky voice – *like a cheese grater dipped in honey*, she thought – as he took one of the crates from her.

'Is it so obvious?' She was starting to get tired of strangers striking up conversations with her every two minutes – and besides, this guy made her nervous. 'I'm starting to think it's written on my nose.'

'It's a pretty nose, though.' He put the second crate beside the first and gave her his hand. 'Jan Berger.'

'Oh, so it's you. The lighthouse keeper.' She shook his hand. Another one covered in calluses. *An island of hard workers*, she thought. *Nature makes the locals as rough as herself.*

Berger laughed and shook his head. 'I'm not the lighthouse keeper. I'm basically the local tour guide, and the lighthouse is the main landmark around here.'

'And you're an expert in firearms, from what I hear.'

Now it was Berger's turn to furrow his brow and look confused. *You've got a real knack for giving a weird turn to every conversation*, Jasmin thought, her face flaming with embarrassment. 'Karl Sandvik mentioned it.' She pointed her thumb uselessly at the grocery shop.

'Hang on a minute, are you the doctor?'

Jasmin sighed and brushed a lock of hair from her forehead. 'Yep, that's right, and I'm down there all alone with my son.'

Berger smiled and Jasmin realised he was damn good-looking. The wind tousled his hair and for a moment, she imagined what it might be like to run her fingers through it and . . .

'Don't listen to the rumours. And above all, don't worry.'

'Somebody was outside my house last night,' she replied. 'Maybe it hasn't got around the whole village yet, but actually I just want a little peace and quiet.'

'I've heard there's a stranger on the island. A stowaway on the ferry.' Berger looked north towards the harbour, his hair whipping back and forth in the breeze. 'Sandvik is right. I *am* an expert in these things. If you like—'

'Thanks for your help, but I have to go now,' said Jasmin quickly, starting to feel flustered. She walked round the car, her cheeks bright red, furious with herself, and sat down behind the wheel. Paul gave her a curious, mischievous glance before looking back at his games console, while Bonnie stuck her head out of the window.

You really botched that up, didn't you?

Chapter 6

A few miles outside Skårsteinen, Jasmin found a pleasant spot by a stream under the shade of some birch trees and stopped for a little picnic with Paul. She laid out the treats she'd bought in the village on her red-and-blue checked blanket.

'Do you like it here?' she asked him.

'It's pretty. But I miss Daddy. Why can't he be here? With us?'

It was one of those questions Paul asked from time to time that cut straight to her heart. *Yeah, why can't he? Why don't you just call him and ask him to join us?*

'There's something I need to figure out first,' she replied. 'It won't take long.'

'It's about the accident,' said Paul. He'd taken a sheet of paper out of the glove compartment and was busy with his origami again. 'You don't need to tell me any fairy tales. I know when you're doing that, I'm not a baby.'

Jasmin gave him a long look, gazing at his blond hair. 'Another few years and he'll be turning all the girls' heads at school,' her grandmother had said.

That had been five months ago.

She'd died soon after.

Jasmin still felt a wave of grief whenever she thought of Ingvild. At least Paul had met her before she passed away.

'Look, Mummy.' Paul pointed northwards along the white gravel path. Around fifty yards from their picnic spot, it curved around the foot of a finger of rock that reared up from the grass like the needle of an enormous sundial. A woman came into view, walking towards them.

She doesn't look like a local. And it's odd that there are so many people around, considering this island is so remote.

The woman was wearing a broad-brimmed white hat, a moss-green woollen cardigan and baggy cloth trousers in a dark burgundy-red. A striking outfit, if not downright eccentric. Jasmin squinted her eyes and held her hand up against the low sun, and saw that the walker was carrying an object under her arm. Was it a book? Or something else?

The woman drew nearer, and Jasmin could see that her gait was rather cumbersome, as if she had hip trouble or another injury that limited her movement. The book wasn't really a regular book either, but a kind of notepad.

Or a sketchbook, Jasmin suddenly realised.

What was it Grit Sandvik said? Yrsen doesn't spend much time around other people. Something happened to her that means she's not all that pleasant to look at now. She was in a fire, and she's been living alone out there in the wilds ever since.

By now, the woman was so close that Jasmin could see her face under the brim of her hat. It was her. It had to be.

Yrsen's face was covered with burn scars, and although Jasmin could tell she'd undergone several operations, the doctors hadn't been able to fully repair the damage. Her skin looked slightly waxy, like a mask.

For a moment, she felt as though she'd seen this woman before, in a place where she'd also seen the sign she was looking for. The upside-down triangle.

For a fraction of a second, she thought she caught a glimpse of something being carried by the wind – a kind of smoke that curled over the grass like thin fog.

'What's wrong with her face?' Paul whispered.

'Shh,' Jasmin hissed. 'Be quiet.'

The woman was now passing where they were sitting, and to Jasmin's surprise, she stopped. Her voice was quiet, a whisper, as if she didn't use it very often – or, Jasmin thought, as if she was trying not to give herself away. 'Beautiful spot, isn't it?' The brim of the hat cast a broad shadow across her eyes, but Jasmin could just make out a dark-green gleam. Like light falling through a piece of jade. Notwithstanding her injuries, the stranger looked even more unusual and eccentric from close up.

'It's a beautiful day,' Jasmin replied. She kept blinking, as the sun was shining in her eyes.

'Simply magnificent,' the woman replied. 'The whole island is.' She drew nearer once more. 'My name is Gabriela Yrsen. I haven't seen you here before,' she said.

Jasmin glanced at Paul, who was studying Yrsen with interest. He'd made a small origami figure of a four-pointed star that was lying in front of him on the picnic blanket. 'Jasmin Hansen. I think we've seen your painting. The one on display in the Sandviks' grocery shop.'

'I'm sure you have.' She extended her hand, and after a slight hesitation, Jasmin shook it. 'May I draw you both?'

Jasmin frowned.

Something had happened when their hands touched. Like a tiny electrical spark jumping between them.

'There's a burden weighing you down,' said Yrsen in her soft, smoky voice. 'I can see it. A burden you've brought here with you.'

'I don't know what you mean.'

'May I draw you?' Yrsen asked again. Without waiting for an answer, she opened her sketchbook and produced a pencil from somewhere, which now flew rapidly back and forth over the page, leaving thin lines behind it that gradually coalesced into a picture.

'I don't think—'

'Don't be afraid, Ms Hansen. You came to this place to find answers. You *will* find them.'

'But how?' Jasmin gulped, her throat suddenly very dry. 'I don't even know where to start.'

'Believe me, it will all come back. Everything you're missing, everything you've forgotten. This place' – Yrsen cast her eyes over the surrounding landscape – 'has already helped many people. It will help you too.'

How on earth does she know? Jasmin had never given a moment's thought to things like second sight – things that crossed the border between reality and the inexplicable – but here, with this woman . . . For an insane moment, she felt genuinely convinced that Yrsen had learned something about her when she touched her hand.

But that was nonsense, of course. That wasn't possible.

'Don't be afraid, young lady. People used to visit me from time to time, up by the cliffs in the north. And do you know why?'

Jasmin shook her head. She noticed Bonnie was looking attentively at Yrsen too, but without showing the least sign of defensiveness or unease. *You trust Bonnie. And if that's how Bonnie reacts to her*, she thought, *that means you can trust Yrsen too.*

Right?

'Because it was said that I could see into people's memories. Into their memories – and into the future.' Yrsen had turned away to face the sun and her hat now cast a long shadow behind her. 'People told me I could capture their memories in my paintings. Visitors would come and I would talk with them. I would touch them – not only their hands, but also their minds. Then I would begin. I didn't always understand the meanings that dwelt within my pictures. Often the person for whom the painting was intended would be the only one who could see its true significance. And it would bring them clarity. Tranquillity of mind. Inner peace.'

'I'm sorry, but that all sounds rather fanciful.' Jasmin bit her lip. *You shouldn't have said that.* But Yrsen laughed and shook her head.

'No, you're right,' she replied. 'It is a bit far-fetched, but you know what? Sometimes it really worked. Maybe it was a kind of empathic resonance between me and the other person. Maybe it was the act of looking and focusing that made them engage with their own demons once more. Maybe I just helped them find the solution themselves.' She laughed again. 'I must admit it's been quite a while since I last told anyone all this. You're the first person in many months who's struck me as possibly having a genuine interest.'

'And now? Are things different now?' *What on earth are you trying to find out here? Can't you see how weird and creepy she is? Can't you see you should grab Paul and Bonnie and go straight back to the car?* Yet something told her to stay where she was; something forced her to sit still and wait spellbound for Yrsen's reply.

'You can see my face, Ms Hansen. You can see what's happened to me.' Yrsen clapped her sketchbook shut. 'Who would want to associate with me? Of course I don't get any more visitors. The way I look now, nobody wants anything to do with me anymore.'

'It wouldn't bother me,' Jasmin heard herself reply. 'I've seen worse.'

Yrsen smiled a thin, amused smile. 'Well, have you now? And you're probably thinking I'm exactly the right person to help you with your little problem? With that burden you're carrying around

48

with you?' Yrsen shook her head, her demeanour abruptly growing cold. 'Forget it. It'll never happen if you can't open your mind to it.'

'I didn't mean to . . .' Jasmin watched as Yrsen headed off along the path, gathering pace as if she was suddenly in a hurry. 'I'm sorry! I didn't mean it like that! Ms Yrsen, please . . .'

Yrsen didn't look back – she kept walking, hunched forwards, the wind tugging at her hat so she had to hold it down.

'Don't be sad, Mummy,' said Paul softly. He looked out over the tall, windswept grass. 'You can't please everyone, you know that. It's what Grandma always used to say.'

'I shouldn't have . . . You just don't say things like that. I made a mistake.' She paused. A sudden gust of wind blew a sheet of paper towards them. The breeze picked it up, buffeted it back towards the ground and played with it.

It was a sheet from a sketchbook.

Jasmin looked up in Yrsen's direction, but she was long gone. Then she leapt to her feet and snatched the paper out of the air before it blew away. Paul clapped his hands in excitement as Jasmin nervously turned the thick paper over. There was an address, with a message underneath it.

Come and see me, if you dare.

Come and see me, once you've found your courage again.

Chapter 7

The night was a cold one, the sky covered with low-lying cloud. Rain was on the way. Wafts of mist from the nearby beach drifted up over the forest to the house. From her veranda, Jasmin heard the distant sound of a solitary car driving along the road and for a brief moment, lights illuminated the fog-shrouded bushes and shrubs by the roadside. Then everything went dark once more.

She'd set up the cameras Karl Sandvik had given her, one on the veranda overlooking the back garden and the other by the front door. They were wireless cameras, which she could monitor from her laptop via a dedicated USB stick. The two motion sensors would be triggered whenever anyone opened either the front door or the cellar door, emitting a beep. Jasmin had tested them both out on the front door before installing one of them over the entrance to the cellar.

'You don't need to thank us,' Grit Sandvik had said. Jasmin was glad she'd made a connection with the elderly couple, that someone knew she was living out here. Someone who would worry about her if anything happened. *Which it obviously won't*, she thought.

The wind coming in from the Norwegian Sea blew leaves across the ground and fine droplets of water into her face. She heard the call of an owl in the woods, and beyond it, much further away, came the deep, drawn-out rumble of a foghorn.

Paul was asleep; she'd read to him and gently kissed his forehead once he'd drifted off. For him, the last few days had been an adventure, but for her . . . Bonnie was lying at her feet, and Jasmin stroked her thick fur as she studied the edge of the forest. *Just you try it*, she thought intently. *I'm ready this time.*

Of course, she wasn't ready; she was only trying to reassure herself. *You didn't even dare to go down to the cellar to fetch the old hunting gun.*

A few minutes ago, she had taken out Sandvik's note and toyed with it between her fingers, on the verge of calling Jan Berger to arrange – well, what exactly? *What did you want to ask him? If he can show you how to use your gun? Because you're expecting the drifter to turn up again?*

And then there was Yrsen. Jasmin couldn't get her encounter with the artist out of her mind. *You'd be crazy to go and see her. You can't.*

But what if there's something to it?

What if she's right, and she can help you?

Jasmin closed her eyes and tried to relax. *Breathe*, she thought, *keep breathing evenly, it can't be that hard.*

But it was. Especially out here.

She tried to recall the night of her accident. *Think of the sound the heavy rain made on the roof and the windscreen. Think of the wet road, of the Jeep following close behind you.*

So close behind . . .

And then it suddenly vanished.

That was all.

Are you sure?

You need to be sure!

No. That wasn't all. Not yet. Something happened after that . . . There were lights. More bright headlights, only this time they came from the other way.

Directly towards you.

Her phone rang, so loudly and abruptly it made her jump. The noise scattered her fragmented memories like a strong wind extinguishing a newly lit fire. Jasmin swore. She so desperately wanted to hold on to those snippets; she sensed that she'd finally been on her way to remembering.

'Shit, who could this be?'

It was Jørgen.

Her phone display listed seven missed calls.

When she looked back up at the edge of the forest, she realised the darkness had already advanced much further than she'd expected. The night had draped itself over the property like a heavy cloth, as if it were trying to smother every sound. She felt cold; goosebumps crawled up her bare arms and down her back. *How long have you been sitting out here? Why didn't you notice the time passing?*

She was alone. Bonnie was gone, and Jasmin couldn't say whether the dog had wandered down into the garden or headed back into the living room through the French windows, which were slightly ajar.

'Bonnie?' she called quietly, and her words drifted into the air like white fog blown onwards by the wind.

Her phone was still ringing. The ringtone was a Mozart piano concerto, which echoed through the blue-tinged night.

Jasmin answered the call.

'Hey, Minnie.'

Minnie. He'd only recently started calling her that and she still hadn't got used to the name. 'You let him treat you too much like a weak little woman,' her mother had told her from time to time. Jasmin hadn't argued with her.

In fact she'd never really argued with her.

'Hi,' she replied. As she spoke, Bonnie nudged her hand – she'd just emerged from the garden and was standing on the veranda wagging her tail, leaving earthy footprints on the spruce decking. 'Stay outside,' she cautioned her dog.

'Are you talking to me?'

Jasmin brushed a lock of hair from her forehead. 'No, that was for Bonnie.'

'Have you settled in OK?'

'Yep, everything's great,' she replied, realising how feeble it sounded. *You asked him to let you and Paul come out here on your own*, she thought. *And now you're trying to act like everything is all right – as if Jørgen's only nipped out to buy a few sandwiches.*

'Is it really?'

'No. No, I'm not sure it is.'

'What's up? Should I come over?'

Jasmin shook her head. 'There's no need. I've got everything under control. Honestly. It's better this way.'

'What's happened? Tell me.' There was a radio playing in the background on Jørgen's end of the line. Jasmin wondered if he was in a bar – and if so, who he was there with.

At the same time, she wondered if she could bring herself to care.

'There's somebody here. On the island. The locals are talking about him, some kind of drifter. By the way, did you leave any ammunition in the house?'

'Ammunition?' Jørgen suddenly sounded very distant, but his voice abruptly grew louder again when he next spoke, as if he'd held the phone away from his face for a moment. Seriously, where was he?

'For your hunting gun. It's still down in the cellar.'

'Oh, that old thing. There should still be a few bullets down there.'

'There aren't, though.'

'What do you want with the gun anyway?'

'Aren't you listening to me?' Now she felt sure she could hear another person in the background – a female voice that she definitely didn't recognise. 'There's somebody here.'

'Should I come over?'

'No. I can handle it.' She tried to sound as confident as she could.

'I really should come over.'

'Honey, I'll tell you if—' Jasmin paused. Was that a movement on the edge of the forest? Was that a silhouette looming over the shrubs beneath the poplar trees? A tattered coat, like one belonging to a vagrant?

She blinked. No. Nothing.

'Just give me a little time. Like I told you, all I need is a bit of peace and quiet to finally make sense of that night. To remember.'

'Jesus Christ, it was a fucking deer!' Jørgen yelled. 'That's all. You've got some other story into your head. A ridiculous bit of nonsense.'

'You don't know that.' Jasmin closed her eyes, but only for a moment. 'We've had this discussion so many times already. And you know what? That's the precise reason why I'm out here. So stop saying that. You know it wasn't a deer. And now . . .' She sighed. 'Now I'm going to hang up.'

'Jasmin—'

'Good night. Don't call me again until you've calmed down.' She put the phone to one side. It felt good to have cut him off like that. It felt right.

I'm not going to have people tell me what to do and what not to do anymore.

Once again, Bonnie nudged her hand with her cold nose. Jasmin realised her dog had brought something with her: a rat with a long, thin tail that she'd laid nearby on the veranda.

'Oh Bonnie, there's no need for that. You shouldn't go hunting, don't you know that by now?'

Bonnie looked up at her happily, her tail thumping against the decking.

Jasmin sighed. 'All right. Let's get rid of it and then we'll go to sleep. That includes you, my little hunter.'

Bonnie followed Jasmin as she pulled on her thick work gloves, picked up the rat and carried it into the garden. 'You just found it, didn't you? Surely you wouldn't have caught anything like this yourself?'

Bonnie's eyes glittered in the light of the thin moon, which shone mistily through the veil of cloud.

'Hmm, I don't know. You might look innocent, but I expect there's a hunter hiding in there somewhere.'

Jasmin opened the low garden gate that led onto the narrow path through the woods and down to the beach. 'Stay here,' she said, before following the path a little way into the forest and tossing the rat into the undergrowth.

'And don't you dare bring it back again,' she admonished Bonnie as she led her into the house. Bonnie woofed quietly.

The rain-slicked road. The steering wheel vibrating under her fingers. She hadn't had anything to drink, she remembered. She never drank if she knew she'd have to drive afterwards. All the same, the party to celebrate her boss's fiftieth birthday had been long, loud and very lively.

The Jeep's headlights, burned onto her retinas.

Then it overtook her.

The sense of relief that briefly washed over her when she thought it was gone.

But the lights soon reappeared in the distance, like the eyes of a predator. They drew nearer. First on the opposite side of the road, then in her lane.

Nearer, inexorably nearer – like a light at the end of a narrow tunnel that turned out to be a freight train hurtling towards her.

Jasmin heard her tyres screech as she wrenched the wheel to one side.

In the glow of her own headlights, she saw a man on the side of the road. She looked into his panicked face and saw a pair of ice-blue eyes, like cold, lost, distant stars. On his coat, which hung from his tall, scrawny body like a shroud, there was a symbol: an upside-down triangle. He screamed as her car struck him with full force, and she felt the steering wheel jolt back and forth beneath her hands.

Jasmin woke up. She was breathing rapidly, erratically, with drops of sweat on her forehead and on the skin under her thin T-shirt.

The same old nightmare once again.

And once again she'd managed to remember a little more.

You weren't mistaken, she thought, throwing the covers back and planting her feet on the cold floorboards. *There was somebody there that night and you hit him with your car.*

You killed a human being.

It wasn't an animal, and it definitely wasn't a deer, like everyone keeps telling you.

It was a person.

Jasmin went over to the window, pressed her forehead against the cool, smooth glass and looked out. The clouds were still there, hanging low in the sky and concealing the crescent moon. The outlines of the poplars and birches looked like they'd been cut out of a sheet of paper by a child.

You know what happened.

And yet everyone says it was an animal.

Why? What were they trying to achieve? Sven? Jørgen? The police officers who examined the scene of the accident and her car? What on earth was everyone hiding from her? Why did they want her to forget what happened that night?

Jasmin couldn't see any answers.

She ran her fingers through her limp hair and shook her head. *Whoever was in the Jeep, he knows what happened. And he deliberately ran you off the road.*

He was there. You saw him.

If only you could remember!

Concentrating hard, she tried to play the dream back in her mind, like a film she could pause and resume whenever she liked. The Jeep had come back. The driver had switched to her side of the road like a suicidal madman who wanted to end both their lives, and she'd swerved to avoid him. Panicking, she'd swerved to the side, lost control and hit a vagrant who was unlucky enough to be in the wrong place at the wrong time, in the middle of the night.

And then . . .

Nothing.

She simply couldn't remember.

Jasmin swore quietly.

Just then, one of her new motion sensors gave a beep.

There was something downstairs.

Chapter 8

Jasmin tiptoed down the corridor, her hands clenched into fists, her fingernails digging into her palms. The floor squeaked like a rusty old door hinge and try as she might, she couldn't reach the staircase without making any noise. Her whole body felt like a tightly coiled spring, her movements awkward and panicky.

The air smelled of the persistent cold rain that had fallen outside for hours on end and was still falling now. It smelled like damp earth and death.

One step at a time, she thought. *Quietly, very quietly, not a sound.*

She could feel her heart racing as if it was trying to find an entirely new rhythm. *It's a false alarm – there's no other explanation.*

And if it isn't?

Then you run. As fast as you can. Grab Paul and run.

Please. Let this be a mistake.

On reaching the stairs, she cursed herself for not having fetched the gun from the cellar, or at least a sharp knife from the kitchen. But those thoughts were washed away by her rising panic until there was scarcely anything left beyond a desperate urge to flee. From her basket, Bonnie watched Jasmin go past and jumped to her feet to follow her. The dog's claws clicked quietly on the floor as a deep growl emerged from her throat.

It was so dark that a man could have been standing at the foot of the stairs looking up at her and she still wouldn't have been able to see him. *Can you hear someone breathing down there? Or is it just your own frantic panting and the rush of blood in your ears?* Jasmin groped nervously for the switch that turned on the lights down in the hallway.

It gave a quiet click.

Nothing.

Was that one of the shutters swinging in front of the windows? Were those damp footprints she could see on the floorboards?

As if crossing an invisible barrier, she placed her foot on the top step. She felt nauseous, but she gathered herself, moved slowly down the stairs and peered at the front door. Completely overwhelmed with panic by now, she reached out her hand.

Locked.

So it wasn't the front door.

That left only one alternative.

A breath of cold air caressed her neck. She whirled around and gave a weak cry as Bonnie barked and jumped up at her. The other end of the hallway was empty too, the boards on the cellar door still firmly nailed in place, just as she had left them.

'But that's impossible . . .' Jasmin whispered to herself. 'I heard it.'

She tugged at the boards and examined the nails. Solid and sturdy, as they should be, and hammered deep into the wood. The status light on the motion sensor mounted between the door and the frame was green.

You heard it, she told herself again. *You heard it, you aren't— You didn't imagine it.* Even in her own thoughts, she was reluctant to utter the word: *crazy. You aren't crazy. You aren't going crazy, either.*

Not even a little bit.

She was forgetting something. Her laptop, where she'd installed the camera software. It was on the sofa in the living room, plugged into the charger.

Jasmin sat down cross-legged beside the laptop and pulled it onto her lap. Bonnie hopped up onto the couch beside her. Jasmin stroked her thick fur; that always calmed the dog down straight away.

'I'm so glad you're here with us,' she said softly. 'I don't know what we'd do without you.'

The laptop was still switched on, the screen half-closed, a blue glow illuminating the floor. Jasmin opened the program and studied the footage for a while. There was nothing to be seen beyond the rain and the wind sweeping through the grass and buffeting the birch trees.

A false alarm.

'Maybe it was Lenny,' came a voice. Jasmin saw Paul looking in at her from the hallway. He was carrying a stuffed toy lioness under his arm, which she'd given to him years ago. Sinta, he'd called her – and Lenny was Paul's invisible friend, as Jasmin knew all too well.

Her son hadn't spoken to him since April, hadn't mentioned him in months. 'Lenny,' she replied. 'Is he back?'

Paul nodded. His eyes gleamed blue in the light from the laptop; his skin looked pale. Jasmin patted the space on the sofa between her and Bonnie.

'Come here.'

Paul sat down beside her.

'I woke up,' he explained, dangling his legs over the edge of the seat, 'and I couldn't get back to sleep again. There's something banging against the wall.'

'I know. A branch.'

'It sounds like . . . I don't know.' Paul rubbed his eyes with his knuckles. 'Like a person knocking. Like there's a person out there who wants to get in.'

She put her arms around him and hugged him tight. 'You mentioned Lenny,' Jasmin said softly. 'How come?'

'He just turned up again. You know he went on a long journey. But now he's back. Isn't it great?'

Jasmin looked at her son for a while before nodding cautiously. 'Of course it is.'

'Lenny says there's something here. Something that shouldn't be here.'

Jasmin felt her throat contract. 'What – what does he mean?'

'A secret. It's a secret, he didn't want to tell me. Not yet.' He gave her a kiss on the cheek and slid off the sofa.

'I don't find that very funny, Paul. If it was meant to be a joke.'

Paul waved at her. 'It wasn't. I'm going back to bed.'

Jasmin blinked. Her son was gone. She jumped up and peered into the hallway, but there was no sign of him. There was no way he could have climbed the stairs so quickly! Jasmin rushed up the staircase and into his room. Paul was sleeping soundly under his astronaut duvet.

You're seeing phantoms more and more often, she thought.

Then Bonnie started barking – and this time, Jasmin instantly recognised her warning tone. This time it wasn't a game.

She dashed back downstairs, grabbed the long carving knife from the kitchen and sprinted into the living room.

Bonnie was standing by the French windows and staring out into the garden, her fur standing on end. She barked again.

On the veranda, Jasmin saw large clumps of soil, with footprints pressed deep into the mud strewn over the decking. The tracks vanished into the garden. Was she imagining it, or could she see the gate swinging back and forth in the wind? It was hard to make out through the curtain of rain.

'You piece of . . .' She pulled on her boots, threw on a coat and put Bonnie on a lead. *Just as far as the fence*, she thought. *But you aren't going to scare me in my own back garden. I won't allow it. Not here. This is my house.*

Jasmin opened the French windows and Bonnie dragged her outside, tugging at the lead, sniffing at the tracks and straining to go further, down the creaky wooden steps into the garden. The air was cold and the rain that instantly came pouring down on her soaked her to the skin.

Bonnie pulled at her lead again and barked, and Jasmin followed her.

The gate was open. Jasmin could see deep boot prints in the muddy patch directly behind the fence, which continued down the narrow woodland path and vanished into the trees beyond.

Bonnie tugged and strained.

Up to this fence and no further, Jasmin thought. *You really shouldn't risk it. That wouldn't be courage – it'd be sheer madness.*

Bonnie barked, but when Jasmin looked down at her, she saw the Labrador was wagging her tail. *The threat has passed*, she seemed to be saying, *so how about a little walk instead?*

Jasmin shook her head. 'No,' she said. 'We definitely aren't—'

But Bonnie leapt forward abruptly, wrenching the lead out of Jasmin's hand, and disappeared through the open gate. Jasmin swore and dashed after her, following the path into the narrow strip of woodland. The ground was sodden underfoot and smelled of rotting leaves and birch bark. An earthworm was crawling over the path, and Bonnie, who had stopped ten feet or so ahead, picked it up in her mouth. Yet instead of swallowing it, she carried it placidly in her jaws as if she wanted to take it to the edge of the forest, where she perhaps thought it belonged.

'Bonnie! Here, girl!' Jasmin got hold of the lead, but Bonnie made no attempt to follow her.

The footprints were still there, sometimes on the path, sometimes beside it, as if the man – she guessed it was a man from the size of the tracks in the mud – had veered back and forth between the tree trunks and the path.

How odd. Was he drunk? Or is this a feint? An attempt to trick you?

The roar of the waves falling ceaselessly onto the beach grew louder with every step. Bonnie pulled her onwards. The tracks were now running in a straight line – directly towards the shore.

Then the forest was behind them. They were on a gentle, sandy incline, and beyond it lay the beach, dotted here and there with rough rocks and boulders. The pounding waves, the spray glittering in the moonlight.

The Norwegian Sea.

The tracks turned sharply left and continued along the beach, but Bonnie pulled Jasmin on towards the water.

'Surely you don't want to play in the sea?' she called – but as she spoke, Bonnie made another leap forward and wrenched the lead from Jasmin's hands again, the grip sliding through her fingers with a jerk. Bonnie ran onwards, Jasmin sprinting after her.

She's seen it. So did you, though a few seconds later. Driftwood, she thought, but her subconscious intervened with an urgent warning: *Driftwood doesn't look like that in the moonlight.*

What you're looking at is skin.

Pale human skin.

It was a dead body, washed up from the sea. The water seemed to be reaching for the man's dark hair, lapping at his sunken cheeks, his long, tattered grey trench coat.

The soles of his shoes were completely smooth.

Jasmin stared at the corpse, stared at its face, and her legs threatened to give way. While Bonnie sniffed at the man's dark woollen jumper, Jasmin gasped for breath.

'This is impossible,' she heard herself say. 'You can't be here – not *here*!'

The driving rain ran down the collar of her coat, over her forehead, her cheeks; it clouded her vision. *You must be mistaken, you must be . . .*

She managed to grab the end of Bonnie's lead before slipping over and falling headlong onto the hard sand. It stuck to her clothes as she clambered back to her feet and dragged Bonnie away from the body.

'That's enough!' she cried. 'Leave it alone!'

Under the light of the moon, Jasmin ventured another look at the corpse's bloated face. The man's eyes were open; they were blue, ice-blue, as if they'd absorbed the chill from the waves that had washed him ashore. Part of his nose was missing, part of his top lip was gone – picked away by crabs, no doubt. His skin was pale and waxy and she could make out the blue lines of his veins beneath it.

But those eyes.

Jasmin hauled Bonnie away from the corpse with all her strength and started to run, back to the path, back up to the house, the rain growing ever more intense, the wind howling after her as if trying to chase her – to mock her, even.

She'd recognised the body.

By God, she'd recognised it.

Jasmin sprinted across the veranda, slammed the French windows and locked them, sobbing, trembling, beside herself with horror.

Impossible, impossible. The words rattled through her panicking mind, and yet she could still feel his ice-blue eyes staring at her, as if he was lying right there on the floor and steadily gazing up at her.

That night, when the Jeep had forced her off the road, it wasn't a deer that died. An animal, they'd told her. But that wasn't the truth.

Something here feels very wrong. Something about this place doesn't add up. Something connected to your memory – and to the dead body out there.

Jasmin realised she'd been right the whole time: she *had* run over a man that night. *He looked at you, and that look – that look – you saw it again just now on the beach.*

It was reproachful.

Accusatory.

The homeless man she'd killed that night had finally returned after all.

He'd turned up – been washed up on the beach – right here on Minsøy, though she didn't understand how.

He'd found her.

Chapter 9

The hissing of the rain woke Jasmin up early the next morning, and when she opened her eyes, the light falling through the curtains was grey and murky. Drops pattered against the window, sounding like bony fingers tapping and drumming on the glass. Jasmin shivered. Her memories of last night's events felt like they were etched deep into her bones.

Her pillow was wet. She'd been crying in her sleep.

And why wouldn't she? It was like she'd stumbled into a bad dream. The dead man on the beach. None of this was possible, and yet she'd seen him.

Are you going crazy?

Or is there something else going on here?

And isn't this exactly what you came for? Didn't you want to understand? So why are you lying in bed feeling sorry for yourself?

Jasmin clambered groggily to her feet and stretched. An unfastened shutter was banging against the outside wall, and whenever it stopped, the silence was broken by the branches of a tree scraping against the plaster on the north end of the house. She walked to the window to look at it. *That bloody thing*, she thought. *You need to find a long enough saw. Maybe there's one in the village. Or maybe you can reach it from up here.*

The garden was shrouded in mist, making it hard to see the beach, but through gaps in the fog she could see silhouettes moving around down there.

Jasmin gave a start. *Your footprints! You're standing here daydreaming, and all the while your tracks are still out there, running from the house down to the beach and back!*

If anyone found the body . . .

'Paul,' she called as she hurried over to her son's room. She found him sitting on the floor, building a spaceship out of Lego under Bonnie's watchful eye. 'I just need to pop out for a bit. Down to the beach. You stay here, OK? No going outside, not even into the garden.'

She put on her coat and boots and stepped out into the pouring rain. Her footprints had washed away, to her relief. The path behind the house had transformed into a dark-brown, muddy soup.

But what about the beach?

She *had* to see for herself.

Jasmin ran headlong down the path, sending mud and rainwater spraying outwards every time she lifted her feet. The wind buffeted the tops of the poplars and birches, and at one point a branch crashed down right in front of her.

At the edge of the forest, she stopped.

She wasn't alone.

A man in a blue raincoat with the word *Police* on its back was walking down the beach. His hand was held to his ear; he was on the phone.

Jasmin's heart started to race.

A policeman. What had Sandvik said his name was? Boeckermann, that was it. Arne Boeckermann, the only policeman on the island. And here he was, on the scene. He'd already found the body. Jasmin squinted; yes, the corpse was still there, close to the spot where she'd found it.

'Shit,' she said quietly. 'Shit, shit, shit.'

If Boeckermann already knew about the body, that meant he would be looking for possible tracks to follow. And that meant he might find her footprints.

What were you doing out here in the middle of the night?

And why did you run away in such a panic?

Why didn't you notify anyone as soon as you got back to your house, like you were supposed to?

'Shit, fucking shit,' Jasmin whispered. She retreated a few steps into the woods, hoping the rain had hidden her from Boeckermann's inquisitive gaze.

You need to think very carefully about what to do next. Should you go down to the beach and confess everything? Tell him you were the first person to find the body, and that you recognised it too?

That a homeless man who you ran over hundreds of miles away and possibly killed has suddenly turned up here, of all places? Washed up onto the beach with mud in his hair, drowned, dead as a doornail?

Nobody will believe you.

They'll all think you're completely insane.

So what now?

Think, Jasmin. Goddamn it, think!

Her every instinct screamed at her to flee.

So she fled. Jasmin sprinted up the narrow path back to the garden, slammed the gate and rushed back up to the house. Her boots were covered in mud and seemed welded to her feet – it took what felt like an eternity to pull them off again.

'Paul? Bonnie?' she called. She was standing in the living room, which was as she had left it, her laptop on the sofa, one of the colourful cushions on the floor. The green light on the camera flashed at her insistently until she reached up and switched it off.

'Paul?'

It was Bonnie who came bounding into the room, giving an exuberant bark. 'Where is he, girl?'

Of course the dog didn't answer; she merely wagged her tail even more enthusiastically – though perhaps that was just as meaningful a reply as far as Bonnie was concerned. From upstairs came a loud clatter that made Jasmin jump. It didn't sound like it came from the first floor. It sounded like . . .

She headed up the stairs, the old spruce steps creaking under her feet. Somewhere out there she could hear the shutter clapping against the side of the house again; perhaps somewhere out there the island constable had stumbled across her footprints too.

Jasmin suddenly felt overwhelmingly giddy, so much so that she had to reach her hand out to the wood-panelled wall and lean on it, closing her eyes and breathing slowly.

More clattering. It was much closer this time. Nervously, Jasmin entered Paul's room and saw that the ceiling hatch leading up to the attic was open and the ladder was lowered.

'Paul?' she called again, peering upwards. The rectangular opening at the top of the ladder was dark and the air emanating from it smelled old and stale, full of dusty, cobwebbed memories.

Bonnie nudged her hand with her nose, as if urging her to go up.

Jasmin put her foot on the bottom rung. 'Paul? If you're up there . . .' The ladder creaked alarmingly. It was nothing more than a set of thin wooden rungs mounted on two long beams, and God knew how long it had been since they'd last taken any weight. Jasmin dimly remembered Jørgen going up there to clean the attic and store away a few boxes; for her own part, she'd only been up there once or twice.

Why had Paul opened the hatch? And more than that – how had he managed it? Halfway up the ladder, Jasmin took another look around the room. *The bed*, she thought, *that's how he did it.*

He climbed up on the bed, even though he knows perfectly well he isn't allowed.

At last, she reached the attic and climbed in. It was dark and the boxes stacked under the eaves cast shadows in the blue light from her mobile phone display. It felt like the lair of a large animal. Maybe a monstrous spider.

'Paul?' Jasmin suddenly realised how nervous she sounded. *Oh Jesus, what are you doing up here? Why would he want to come up here when it's so dark?*

Something rustled at her feet under the shadow cast by two large boxes. Jasmin leapt to one side as a rat scurried past and disappeared through a vent at the other end of the attic.

Behind her, an object fell to the floor with a quiet rattle and rolled towards her across the wooden floorboards.

Jasmin stared down at it, holding her breath. The object gave a red gleam in the light from her mobile phone – it was a Christmas tree bauble.

'What on earth—?'

'Boo!' The lid of the box beside her fell to the floor and Paul leapt out. Jasmin took a step backwards and gave a low cry. Yet when she realised what Paul was wearing on his head, she couldn't help but laugh.

It was a red-and-white striped Santa hat.

'You cheeky little . . .'

He jumped out of the box and dashed past her. Jasmin lunged for his arm, but she couldn't quite catch him. He quickly disappeared down the ladder.

'We'll talk about this later, young man!' she called after him. 'You can count on it!'

Jasmin raised her phone a little higher and looked for the light switch. There! A small light bulb illuminated the room, revealing the neatly stacked secrets hidden in the shadows: the boxes filled with old holiday decorations, the Christmas tree ornaments, the wreaths. She and Jørgen had once spent the festive season on Minsøy. It felt like an eternity ago.

'And I expect we'll never come back here again,' she said to herself softly. For a moment, she thought she saw a gift wrapped in colourful paper that had been left up here on top of a dusty box, but it was just torn-up fragments of wrapping paper.

Torn up. Seems apt.

In the far corner, she saw a tall object covered by a grey cloth. It was rectangular, about the height of a man. *Was that there the last time I came up here?*

No, definitely not. What is it? Maybe a big mirror?

Jasmin threw the cover aside to reveal an oil painting. Under the wan, yellow glow of the light bulb, she saw a large burning building that looked like a manor house. Thick clouds of smoke were rising above it and orange flames were shooting from the windows. A crowd of people had gathered in front of the main entrance and were waving their arms at the conflagration, but none of them seemed to be trying to do anything about it.

She instantly recognised the signature: *Yrsen*, it said. *Like on the painting in the Sandviks' grocery shop*, she thought. *Gabriela Yrsen – the artist you met yesterday.*

Her mind went to the torn-out sketchbook page with the message encouraging her to come and visit, if she felt like it.

That'll never happen.

All the same, what was this picture doing up here?

As if fated to do so, Jasmin lifted the heavy painting from the wooden stand it was resting on and turned it over. There was a slim booklet tucked into the back of the frame.

Jasmin pulled it out, opened it and began to read. Yrsen's handwriting was clear and precise, but the more she wrote – the text filled five of the small pages – the shakier and more hesitant her

71

hand became. The paper was covered with stains; Yrsen might have been crying as she wrote it.

They come.

Time and again, they ask for my help.

They come and demand things I can't deliver. It's like a wildfire burning out of control, and I can't stop it.

They say I can help them, but isn't what I'm trying to do against nature?

I talk to them. I let them give me their hands. And occasionally, nothing happens. They're disappointed then; some of them swear at me and call me a liar before they leave.

But that's rare. Usually it works.

I can't explain how, but there's something there. Second sight? Visions that run through my mind like fragments of memory, at night, when I'm struggling to sleep. When my easel and paints are the only things that stop me from losing my mind.

Second sight. Yes, that's what they call it.

And they ask questions.

Questions I can't answer.

But I can create images for them. Thoughts set down in oil on canvas for all eternity. I can do that.

And they understand. By God, they seem to really understand what I create, even though I often don't understand it myself.

Because these are their pictures, not mine. They're meant only for others, not for myself.

It isn't a gift. It's a curse.

If that's what it is – if that's how I have to spend my life

The words broke off at this point. Jasmin flicked on to the end of the booklet, but aside from a large ink blot there was nothing else to be seen.

'Second sight,' she said to herself quietly. 'Yrsen had clients who asked her for answers as if she were a – a clairvoyant. Except she gave them her answers in her paintings . . .' Jasmin gently ran her index finger down the old, worn leather binding of the small book. 'Is that possible? And if it is, can she still do it?'

She looked at the painting again. The fire, the onlookers. Was this also a work Yrsen had created for one of her visitors? Was this painting meant to reveal something to someone? A truth, from the past or the future, meant only for them?

Memories.

A way to break through, to reveal her secret.

Come and see me, if you dare.

Come and see me, once you've found your courage again.

Jasmin knew what she would do next.

73

Chapter 10

'OK, Paul,' she called as she climbed down the ladder and shut the hatch. 'You and I are going to talk now. Frightening me like that . . .'

Paul had retreated to his bed with his games console. He didn't look up when she sat down beside him.

'Paul?'

'You don't want him to come here. It's true, isn't it? You don't want Daddy to live here.'

For a moment, Jasmin was speechless. 'What? What makes you say that?'

'You only ever think of yourself!'

'Paul—' She didn't get any further, as the sound of the doorbell interrupted her.

Paul had tears in his eyes.

'You know that isn't true,' she replied gently. 'If you'd rather he was here, I'll tell him to come.'

Paul wiped his cheek and nodded. 'I didn't mean to scare you up there, Mummy. I just saw the hatch and . . .'

'You wanted to try it out.'

'Yeah,' he answered, drawing the word out defiantly. 'And?'

'Less of that attitude. You knew perfectly well you weren't allowed in the attic. You don't know how rotten the floorboards are up there. Nobody does. You could have fallen through, and God only knows what might have happened.' Jasmin held out her hand. 'Give me that thing.'

'What?'

'No computer games for a day.'

'Because of the stupid attic? That's so unfair!' Paul shoved the Nintendo into her hand and stormed off.

'Oh, man,' said Jasmin quietly. 'I only wanted to—' Then the bell rang again and she went down to the front door, her anxiety and unease suddenly returning. She opened the door, but left the security chain done up.

Better safe than sorry, she thought. 'This island is a stony garden,' Karl Sandvik had said, 'and only the strongest can make it grow.'

'Ms Hansen?' The man peering at her through the gap in the door was wearing a checked blazer under an unbuttoned Barbour jacket, a pair of jeans and dark-green wellington boots. He had silver-grey hair that was dishevelled from the breeze outside, and his eyes were equally grey and bright. Jasmin guessed he was in his early fifties.

'Yes?'

'Am I in the right place?' He ran his hand through his wet hair, making it stand up even more wildly from his head, and looked a little uncertain – no, not uncertain, she corrected herself instantly, but a little distracted.

'What do you mean by the right place?' she replied.

'I mean, at Jasmin Hansen's house. The caretaker told me you were living out here—'

'I'm Jasmin Hansen,' she cut him off. 'But I can't help but wonder,' she added in a brief moment of pluck, 'why he would tell you who was living here. That's – well, it's private.'

75

At that, the stranger smiled and began fumbling through his coat pockets. 'Where did I—? Ah, yes.'

Jasmin found herself looking at a form of ID that she had only ever seen twice before in her life – once in theatre, after she and Sven Birkeland had stitched up a badly injured bank robber, and the second time after her own accident, while she was still lying in her hospital bed.

It was a police warrant card.

Henriksen, Hendrik, it said. *Detective Inspector.*

Jasmin felt her courage dissipate as if scattered by the wind. Her stomach sank to her knees. 'The police?' she asked hoarsely, before clearing her throat. She felt utterly foolish and certain that she was coming across as suspicious.

You're the worst actor in the world. You couldn't even lie to save your own life. Though maybe you're about to find out if that's really true.

'That's right, the police.' Henriksen put his pass away after she'd spent a few moments staring at it – though in truth, she'd barely taken anything in. The panic that filled her mind suppressed all rational thought. 'Can I come in? It's rotten weather. Don't worry, this won't take long. We're interviewing all the homeowners in the area in relation to a certain unpleasant matter.' He shivered as if he was cold and ran his hand through his hair again. *Is he really distracted?* she thought to herself. *Or is he pulling a kind of Columbo act to lull you into a false sense of security?*

Is he actually watching you very carefully? Studying your tiniest reactions? Every gesture, every revealing look? And fuck – did you remember to clean up? Did you put your dirty boots away?

'Sure,' she heard herself say. 'Of course. Come on. In, I mean, come on in.'

'Great. Those were the exact words I was hoping to hear in this weather.' Jasmin stood to one side as he stepped over the threshold and closed the door behind him. 'That's what you call a storm. Absolutely horrendous. The ferry from the mainland—'

'You've come from the mainland?'

Henriksen nodded as he took off his coat. 'Indeed I have. They asked me to come over first thing this morning. I suppose somebody's got to do it, right?' He looked around. 'Could you . . . ?'

Jasmin went to take his coat before realising she was still holding Paul's games console in her hand. She placed it on the sideboard near the front door where Jørgen had always kept all the keys and notepads.

'I suppose that's one way of passing the time while it's raining,' said the detective, pointing at the Nintendo 3DS.

Jasmin hung up his coat. 'It belongs to my son, Paul.'

'I see. Yes, the caretaker told me you didn't come here on your own.'

'We also have a dog . . .'

As if on cue, Bonnie came hurtling down the stairs and started barking at Henriksen.

The detective took a step back while Jasmin grabbed Bonnie by the collar. 'I'm sorry,' she apologised. 'Off upstairs with you!' she called, pointing at the staircase. Bonnie obeyed, but she turned around again halfway up the steps and growled.

Jasmin led Henriksen into the kitchen and made some tea.

'I won't beat about the bush, Ms Hansen. A man was found dead on the beach this morning.' The officer sat down and accepted his tea with a nod, but didn't touch it. 'His body was discovered by a walker who reported it to the police station on the island. Constable Boeckermann went through the standard procedures before notifying my colleagues on the mainland, and – well, here I am.'

'Here you are.' Jasmin had remained standing, her fingers wrapped around her mug, which was almost burning her hands.

She glanced at the long carving knife gleaming on the counter. 'A dead body . . . That sounds awful. It is awful, I mean.' She cleared her throat again and cursed herself for her untrustworthy voice. 'Did he drown?'

Henriksen raised his eyebrows. 'What makes you say that?'

'You said he was on the beach,' Jasmin retorted. *You don't get me that easily.*

'Of course.' Once again, Henriksen gave a glimpse of his gentle smile, but he still didn't touch his cup. 'The man hasn't been identified yet, but we're working on the assumption that he drowned and was subsequently washed ashore.'

Jasmin tried not to give anything away, even though this information surprised and shocked her every bit as much as if Henriksen had told her he was placing her under arrest right there and then.

The tracks have all been washed away, she thought. *He can't possibly know. And even if he does, you haven't done anything wrong.*

Unless . . .

Suddenly, the bright lights of the Jeep from that disastrous night reappeared in front of her, blazing harshly, dazzling her. Jasmin shook her head and sighed. 'And you've come to see me because . . . ?'

'Because we're hoping one of the neighbours might perhaps have noticed something.' Henriksen looked around the room. 'You have a first floor and an attic, I assume?'

'Yes.' *But there's nothing up there*, she added inwardly. *Just a sulky five-year-old and a strange picture in the loft. And a bizarre notebook that you might not want to look at.*

'Can you see the sea from up there?'

'Yes,' Jasmin repeated, feeling like a talking doll. 'You can, and I understand what you're getting at there too, but no, I'm afraid I have to disappoint you. There was no boat. Nothing anyone could have shoved the body into the water from.'

'You know that for a fact, do you?'

'Paul had trouble sleeping. I read to him and then I stood for a while by the window in his room. It looks out to the south, towards the beach.'

'I understand,' said Henriksen, though he looked as though he didn't understand a thing. Yet Jasmin felt sure by now that this was an act. He knew exactly what he was driving at – which direction he needed to steer the conversation in.

And there was barely anything she could do about it without calling herself into suspicion.

Just tell him. Say you saw the body and recognised it. That it reminded you of a homeless man. No, not reminded – that a homeless man you ran over a long way away has suddenly, unthinkably, turned up here on Minsøy.

'It's possible it wasn't a ship. We're looking at what currents might have driven the body to precisely this spot, but that'll take time.' He reached for his tea, but once again he didn't take a sip. Instead, he pensively turned the cup back and forth between his hands. 'And time is something I don't have. The most important evidence will disappear over the first twenty hours.'

'Sounds like you have a stressful day ahead of you. I don't want to keep you from your work.'

'I'm sure you don't.' Henriksen pushed the mug across the table. 'Have you left the house at all today?'

'No,' Jasmin replied. 'You know what the weather's been like.'

'And yet there's one thing that doesn't make sense to me. The dead man – he was dressed like a vagrant. What I don't understand is . . .' His grey eyes fixed on her own and Jasmin had the feeling he knew more than he was letting on. 'You weren't down on the beach last night?'

Jasmin took a deep breath. 'Why would I have been down there?'

'Perhaps because you saw something that shouldn't have been there.' Henriksen pulled the cup back towards him and finally took a sip. 'This is very good tea,' he declared, before putting the mug back down on the table. 'You know, Ms Hansen, when my ferry arrived this morning, Constable Boeckermann wanted to take me straight to the place where the body was found, but first I asked him to take me on a small . . . detour, let's say. Arne Boeckermann took me to the village grocery shop, where I bought a bite to eat. But you know what? The owner, a certain Karl Sandvik, already seemed to know what had happened. Now, I'm sure you'll tell me news travels fast in places like this, and that in a close-knit village it's hardly unusual that the owner of the local shop would have already heard about the incident. But then Sandvik mentioned a person who I only had time to call in on after I'd visited the beach.'

'After you'd . . . ?' Jasmin furrowed her brow. 'I don't quite understand.'

'You. He mentioned you. Sandvik knew the area where the body was found and he mentioned that the nearby house had recently been reoccupied. He mentioned a certain Jasmin Hansen, a stranger, an outsider, who happened to have arrived here shortly before the incident was reported. And now here I am.'

Jasmin had to compose herself. 'What are you insinuating? Yes, it's true that I've only recently arrived on the island, but I'm just as shocked as anyone that there's a . . .' She fell silent. Had she given herself away with her response?

'You *were* down there on the beach, weren't you? The rain has washed away a lot of evidence, but Boeckermann is positive he saw a figure on the edge of the woods early this morning. If I were to look at your shoes or boots, would they be clean?'

Jasmin felt nauseous; her throat had closed up. 'I – I thought . . .' She turned around, rushed into the hallway, opened the cabinet and pulled out her wellington boots.

'Here,' she said, throwing them onto the floor at Henriksen's feet. 'My boots. Nobody would go outside wearing any other shoes in this weather. They're clean. Will that do?' She tried not to show how heavily her heart was pounding – how treacherously it was beating.

Henriksen smiled again. 'Yes, that'll do.' He got to his feet. 'If you remember anything at all—'

'I'll let you know.'

'I didn't want to put you under pressure, but sometimes it's necessary. People react differently under pressure. They give themselves away.'

'Then I guess I passed the test.'

No sooner had Henriksen left the house and shut the door behind him than Jasmin sank to the floor. She had to bite her fist to suppress a scream.

Once she'd recovered herself, she dashed up to her bedroom, where she'd left her dirty, mud-covered boots. She carried them into the bathroom and put them in the bathtub before placing the spare pair she'd shown Henriksen back in the cabinet.

That was close.

Seriously close.

But now—

Just then, the doorbell rang.

◆　◆　◆

The doorbell rang and Jasmin reached out nervously to open the door. *It's him. It has to be.* And while the noise of low-volume music and lively conversation rang out behind her from the rest of the house, a smile crept over her lips. *You're acting like a teenager*, she thought. *And yet tonight is basically a work party, albeit a slightly bigger one than usual.*

Sven Birkeland was standing in front of her. His coat was wet from the rain, his hair plastered to his head, and yet in the warm light illuminating the driveway and the ivy-covered stone walls of the Brechts' house, he looked unbelievably handsome.

'Jasmin!' he said, sounding not quite like the colleague she knew from the hospital. 'Looks like this evening just got a lot more interesting.'

He embraced her, and Jasmin helped him take off his coat. 'Is our consultant surgeon giving speeches again? I suppose Brecht has already shown you his alcoves. You wouldn't believe how tedious he can be about all the design features in his house.'

Jasmin couldn't help but laugh. 'He hasn't mentioned them yet, but the night is still young.'

'Well, let's dive in, shall we?'

'Let's,' she agreed. 'And no talking shop, now.'

And then, as she followed Sven Birkeland, the memory vanished . . .

Chapter 11

All of it vanished: the party, the night when she would go on to have her accident. Why had it sprung into her head now, of all times? With a trembling hand, Jasmin reached for the handle and opened the door a crack. 'Did you forget something?' she asked bemusedly, feeling her heart race faster than it had ever done before. Henriksen was standing in front of her, as though he had returned to finally reveal the true reason for his visit.

What's he doing now? Is he reaching for his handcuffs?

'Not as such, no. Just this.' A slender business card appeared between his fingers, as if he were a magician who could conjure objects out of thin air. 'I thought you might need it. Please call me right away if you notice anything that seems threatening to you, no matter how trivial. You'll find my mobile number on the card.'

'Thank you.' Jasmin realised she was gripping the door handle so hard it hurt, but luckily Henriksen couldn't see her hand.

He turned to go, and it occurred to Jasmin that she could ask him about the drifter – whether there was any news on that front, whether he'd already heard about him. But in the end she merely watched as Henriksen got in his car and drove off.

Only then could she breathe freely again.

That was really close. Fucking close.

She spent the next hour cleaning the sand and mud off her dirty boots before placing them next to the other pair in the cabinet.

Paul was still in a bad mood.

'You'll have to come downstairs if you want something to eat,' she said when she looked in on him. 'I'm going to cook myself lunch, anyway.'

Jasmin sat down on the sofa and rested her plate of spaghetti with tomato sauce on her knees. She didn't want to stay in the kitchen; Henriksen's aftershave was still hanging in the air.

As she ate, she went over her plan in her mind. She had to visit Yrsen, that was obvious. She had to ask her to hear her out. Maybe it would help; maybe this would be the crucial spark, the moment of impetus, that would let her finally remember *everything*.

And after that . . .

You have to find out whether it's true.

Whether you really did see him.

If Henriksen wasn't lying and the man really did drown then maybe you were imagining things after all.

Under the light of the moon last night, maybe you saw what you wanted to see in his face. Maybe you imagined it. Maybe it wasn't him.

Jasmin could think of only one way to resolve her doubts. She had to find out where they'd taken the body. If it had been removed from the island then she had a problem on her hands – but she didn't think that would have happened yet. No, she felt sure they'd keep the corpse here on Minsøy, for now.

So find out where it is.

Easier said than done.

'That's enough sulking now,' she said to Paul. 'We're going to take a little trip into the village. What do you say?'

'What for?' He looked up from the book he was reading and Jasmin realised he was only pretending to be mad at her. Not for the first time.

'We're going on an adventure,' she answered. 'Like Max and the boys in your book. Only we're going to be detectives.'

Jasmin found a small, charming cafe on the main street in Skårsteinen and sat with Paul by the window, which looked out on to the road. The cafe stood directly opposite the only bookshop in the village, and next door to that was the police station.

The first time she'd come here in search of Sandvik's grocery shop, she'd seen a police car parked outside the station – a Volkswagen that had seen better days.

This time, Boeckermann's car wasn't there.

'I'll be with you shortly,' the waitress called over to them. She was wearing a floral-patterned apron and wiping one of the tables down with a cloth. Jasmin got up and approached her. Once out of Paul's earshot, she asked, 'Have you heard?'

The woman looked at her warily. 'Heard what?'

'I'm new here. My husband and I own a small holiday home down by the beach.'

'Oh.' The waitress nodded sympathetically. 'Of course. And now you're worried. That's understandable.'

'I've just been to the police station,' Jasmin lied, 'but there was no one there. Is that normal?'

'No, it's not. But to think of a dead body turning up here, of all places.' The woman hesitated. As though she'd already said too much. 'Well, you know how it is in a small village like this. News travels fast.'

'Do you mean to say they're all out right now? That the station is empty?'

'They're down at the coast. So I heard.'

Jasmin sighed. Then she looked at the menu and thought carefully. She wouldn't get anything else out of the waitress here, but Karl Sandvik might know more. 'I'll take two hot chocolates,' she said.

'Two?'

'Please.'

She took the drinks and went back to the table where Paul was sitting. 'I need to pop over and see Mr Sandvik. You remember him, don't you? There's something important I want to ask him. Wait here for a second with Bonnie, OK?'

'OK, Mummy,' Paul replied sullenly.

Jasmin shot a warning look at Bonnie, who was lying under the table, before heading out and crossing the road. The shopkeeper was alone and reading a book. Homer's *Odyssey*, Jasmin saw from the cover.

'Ah, hello there,' he greeted her. 'How are you settling in, Ms Hansen?'

She frowned. 'That looks like rather heavy going for this time in the afternoon.'

Sandvik shut the book and placed it carefully on the counter. 'A good book is never heavy going. I expect you've already heard the news. I can tell by looking at you.'

'Mr Sandvik, could you do me a favour?' Jasmin tried to flash him her most engaging smile, but found it a challenge. *You're getting rusty*, she thought. 'I can't find any police officers in the station up the road.'

'Oh no?' Sandvik scratched his chin with his thumb. 'They're all in a bit of a flap at the moment. Boeckermann was never going to cope with anything like this on his own, and as for the new chap and his team – well, I'm not quite sure what to make of that lot.'

'He's called Hendrik Henriksen and he's come from the mainland.' Jasmin noticed how eagerly Sandvik took in the new information. Henriksen's name would probably be all over the village before long, which meant he'd be recognised before he could introduce himself to anybody he wanted to interview. 'He's already asked me a few questions, but I've remembered something I didn't tell him, so I need to know where I can find him.'

'They were all at the ferry terminal just now. Down by the Bakke warehouse.'

'Bakke?' Jasmin hadn't heard the name before, and she couldn't remember seeing any warehouses down there either.

'The fishing company,' Sandvik explained. 'From what I've heard, the man wasn't killed on land.' He lowered his voice to a conspiratorial whisper. 'So it makes sense that they'd want to start by interviewing the people with the biggest boats who sail the furthest offshore.'

Did that mean the corpse had been disposed of from a trawler? Jasmin blinked. It didn't seem to ring true. 'And you saw it for yourself? I mean, that Henriksen and Boeckermann were down there?'

'I went for a stroll, like every morning, and I saw them and their police van with my own eyes. I wouldn't send you off to the other end of the village for no reason, young lady.'

Jasmin laughed. 'No, I'm sure you wouldn't. You're one of the good guys.' Then she grew serious once more. 'I . . . There's another thing I wanted to ask you, about a subject that's kept coming up ever since I got here.'

Sandvik smiled encouragingly. 'Go on.'

'There must have been a fire here at some point.' She thought of the painting she'd discovered in the attic. 'A serious fire. An incident people don't like to talk about. I'd be interested to know what happened back then, and when exactly it was.'

And what the deal with Yrsen is – whether that was when she suffered her burns. Could that be possible? She kept those thoughts to herself, though. Jasmin had the impression that the lines around

87

Sandvik's mouth had grown harder, but he sounded as laid back as ever when he spoke. 'There was a fire once, out on the western end of the island. But that was another era. And not one I care to remember.'

'I—'

'Sometimes the past should stay in the past. Sometimes people should let things lie.'

'I understand.' She wouldn't get anything more from him on this subject, however hard she tried. She could see it in his eyes. Besides, she'd never been very good at getting strangers to reveal their secrets.

She said goodbye to Sandvik, who waved at her as she left the shop before returning to his book. Back in the cafe, Jasmin noticed Paul hadn't touched his hot chocolate yet. He was looking out of the window, lost in thought.

'Give it a try, it's very good.' Jasmin dabbed her lips with a napkin.

'I've been thinking,' said Paul, 'that there's something going on here.'

'What do you mean?' Jasmin scanned her surroundings, but the waitress was elsewhere. That was just as well. Paul's words made her feel a little nervous.

'It's all fake,' he said. 'It feels off.'

'Don't say things like that. This is a nice little village.'

'When I was in the attic,' Paul went on, 'I didn't just find the old Christmas things. I saw that painting too, the one with the cloth over it. I looked under the cover.'

The fire, Jasmin thought. *The old building in flames, the onlookers in front of it. Yrsen's scarred face and her diary. How are all those things connected?*

'And?' she asked cautiously. 'Quite apart from the fact that Daddy and I told you—'

'That I'm not allowed up there.' Paul shook his head. 'I don't know. When I saw it, I felt funny. Like there's something here, inside the house, down on the beach – everywhere on the island. And it doesn't want us here. It doesn't add up – it feels very, very wrong.'

Jasmin felt goosebumps creeping down her arms.

Paul abruptly stood up. 'Can we go, Mummy?'

'Of course.' Jasmin paid and put Paul's untouched hot chocolate back on the counter. 'Sorry. I enjoyed mine, anyway.'

As she left the cafe, she noticed the waitress give her a bemused look.

After a short stroll through the centre of Skårsteinen and down to the harbour, Paul and Jasmin found themselves standing outside the warehouses Sandvik had mentioned. Seagulls screeched and bickered in the distance. It smelled of fish and the sea, and the wind blowing in from the water was as cold as the touch of an early frost.

There was a man loitering by a jetty nearby who embodied every cliché of a sailor. Jasmin asked him if he'd seen the police officers.

'They were here,' came the gruff reply. 'And then they left again.'

'So they didn't interview anybody?'

'Nope.' He scratched his chin. 'Just dropped off a package. And you can probably guess what it was, can't you? Bakke owns the only big cold storage shed on the island.'

'The only . . .' Jasmin realised what he meant, and the realisation felt good and terrifying at once, like a hot-and-cold shiver running down her back. 'Thank you. Thank you very much.'

'For what?' He pointed along the road heading north. 'They drove off that way.'

There's something going on here. Paul's words echoed through Jasmin's mind as she headed north in her rental car. *And maybe more people know it than you would like. How else did that old painting get into your attic? Did the caretaker put it there? Or somebody else? Were they trying to hide it?*

Did they know Jasmin had found it?

Were they watching her?

What about the drifter everyone kept mentioning?

'Where are we going, Mummy?' Paul was sitting on the back seat and scratching Bonnie between the ears while the dog gave out low grunts of satisfaction. 'It's nice here. Nicer than the other way, somehow.'

'Nicer than the south, you mean.' Jasmin kept glancing at the rear-view mirror, but there was nobody following her. The road was completely empty.

No Jeep chasing after you with blinding headlights.

'Do you remember the piece of paper that blew over to us on the wind?'

'You caught it in the air. That was pretty cool!'

'Well, I think we should go and talk to the artist again. I mean, partly because I want to apologise to her for the things I said.'

'And also because you think she'll help you.'

'What makes you say that?'

Paul shrugged. 'Just a hunch. Daddy wouldn't like it.'

Daddy isn't here, Jasmin thought. But Paul was right: Jørgen definitely wouldn't like it, what with his aversion to the occult.

A woman with second sight, a clairvoyant? It's complete nonsense, barely more than a con.

But she knew things she shouldn't have known, even though all she did was touch your hand, for the briefest of moments. And everyone in the village knows about her. Think of the picture in Sandvik's shop, and the one in the attic too. Her story must be true. She really must have drawn people to the island in the past who believed she could help them – and who she really did help.

Until the fire.

'The way I look now, nobody wants anything to do with me anymore,' Yrsen had said.

How sad. How lonely she must be, out there on the northern tip of the island.

'We'll pop in for a quick visit,' said Jasmin. 'That's all.'

'Are we going to have something nice for dinner tonight?' Paul asked enthusiastically.

Jasmin had to smile. That was the Paul she knew. 'We will, I promise.'

And then you're going to call Jørgen and settle everything with him. Ask him to come out here. As soon as he can.

Not for your sake, but for Paul's.

That's your priority.

Chapter 12

The house Jasmin's satnav directed her to stood at the northern end of the island, close to the clifftops. Yrsen's house was set back from the road and hidden behind a sandstone wall, a scanty hedge and a fence. Clad in burgundy-red wood, it had a thatched roof from which two chimney stacks protruded. Jasmin took Paul by the hand and together they walked over to the fence securing the edge of the cliff in order to look down at the sea. The waves rolled against the blue-black rocks, their crests capped with foam.

'Wow,' said Paul in awe.

'Yes, nature is truly powerful,' said a quiet voice behind them. Jasmin turned around and saw Gabriela Yrsen shuffling towards them, leaning on a walking stick. She was wearing a white scarf that fluttered in the wind, but no hat this time. Her hair was dark, almost black, without a single strand of grey, and it gleamed in the light of the low sun. *A wig*, thought Jasmin. The fire had taken so much more from her than she'd thought.

The thundering and crashing of the waves was deafening, so Yrsen gestured for them to follow her back towards the house.

'People have been telling me for so long now to sell up, pack my bags and leave, but no. I simply can't leave it behind.'

'That's understandable,' replied Jasmin feebly. 'It's a very impressive place.'

'Nature takes whatever she can. The ground is fragile, and according to a geologist who came here a few times to take measurements, it's very possible it might all suddenly collapse and that my little house could end up in the sea. It might be better if I wasn't around when it happened, he said . . .' Yrsen looked out to sea. The endless volumes of water, the low grey clouds – it was an atmosphere like something from a painting by a tortured artist. 'Then again, maybe it'd be better if I was.'

'You shouldn't think like that,' Jasmin replied.

'Tea?'

'Yes, please. Can Bonnie . . .'

'You can bring her inside as long as she doesn't chase my cat.'

'She won't.'

They followed Yrsen past a metal sculpture that was rusting away by the front door. The salty air had corroded it badly, but you could still see what it was meant to depict: a sailor gazing northwards, as if keeping an eternal lookout for things only he knew about. He had a telescope in his hand which he held up to his eye, and the perforated metal cylinder was specially designed to catch the wind, making an eerie howling noise.

Yrsen noticed Jasmin's look. 'The sound makes your hair stand on end at first, but it grows more familiar over time.'

Jasmin couldn't imagine ever getting used to it.

The house was more spacious than it looked from the outside and was filled from top to bottom with prints, sketches and paintings that covered the walls and lay in piles on the floor. The air held a mild odour of incense; by the windows, pale curtains drifted in the wind, while a fire burned in a small stove. Just as Yrsen offered her a seat on the sofa, a log broke apart with a loud crack that made Jasmin jump.

Jesus, you've been so on edge the last few days.

Paul sat beside her and Bonnie lay down at her feet on the carpet, not letting Jasmin out of her sight. She'd caught the scent of the cat but didn't give chase, as if she knew she wasn't at home here and therefore had to behave herself.

'I hope you like my herbal blend,' said Yrsen, placing a tray laden with cups and a teapot on the table before sitting down in a tall wingback chair. Jasmin noticed the sketchbook in front of her. The last thing Yrsen had worked on seemed to be an outdoor scene – a mother and son enjoying a picnic. It looked very familiar.

Jasmin took a sip of her tea. 'It's good. Really good.'

'So you came after all.' Yrsen gave her a penetrating look. 'You changed your mind.'

'I'm mainly here to apologise. For what I said. It was inappropriate and hurtful.'

'Apology accepted,' Yrsen replied unhesitatingly. 'Now stop skirting around the issue. Tell me why you *really* came.'

This wasn't a question she could avoid, Jasmin realised. *If you really want her to help, you need to give her an answer.*

'Because I need your help.' She struggled to get the words out, but as soon as Jasmin had said them aloud, she felt better. It was a relief, as if she'd shaken off a heavy burden. 'Because I'm really worried. And because I feel certain we didn't cross paths by coincidence.'

'I don't know if I can still do it.' Yrsen reached out her hand and her sudden gesture took Jasmin by surprise. 'But it's worth a try.'

'How does it work?' Yrsen had got down to the real reason for her visit so quickly that Jasmin felt unprepared. 'Can Paul be here?'

'Maybe he'd like to go out and play with the dog.' Yrsen locked eyes with Jasmin.

What are you doing here? Are you really planning to . . . ? The warning voice in her head reminded her of Jørgen, and Jasmin chose to ignore it.

'It's all right, Mummy,' said Paul. 'Bonnie and I will be outside. Come on, Bonnie!' He jumped to his feet, but Bonnie refused to stir at first. Yrsen opened a door leading out to a small, fenced-off garden beside the house with a birch tree whose branches rustled and swayed in the wind, and Jasmin led Paul and Bonnie outside.

'Don't go near the cliffs!' she called after him.

'I won't!'

'He's a good boy,' she said to Yrsen. 'He has a good heart. Sometimes I wonder if I'm really the mother he needs. One who's always there for him.'

'You're caught up in old memories,' Yrsen declared. 'I think it's time you pushed them aside once and for all. It'll liberate you, and you'll feel better for it.' She lowered her voice. 'And I think there's something you urgently need to acknowledge. A truth you've suppressed. One that you desperately need to make sense of.'

Jasmin took a deep breath. 'Something on this island isn't right. It's strange, but it feels like there's been a cover-up of some horrible past event. And I can't shake the feeling that it's connected to the accident – to *my* accident.' She looked down at her hands, at her fingers, which were drumming nervously against her teacup. 'A dead body was found today, down on the beach. Not far from my house.'

If Yrsen was surprised to hear that, she didn't show it. 'I didn't know. What with my isolated existence, it takes a long time for news of that kind to reach me. Often I only hear it when I take one of my rare trips into the village.'

'It scares me.' Jasmin watched as Paul threw a stick and Bonnie fetched it for him. 'It's – I thought . . .' She fumbled for words, but couldn't find any that really expressed how she felt. The wide, ice-blue eyes of the corpse kept following her, haunting her deep-est dreams.

In her nightmares, the corpse would sit upright.

In her very worst nightmares, it would speak to her. *It was you, you murdered me. Can't you hear my bones crunching under the wheels of your car? Can't you still hear me screaming? Have you forgot-ten what you saw?*

'Ms Hansen,' said Yrsen softly. 'Would you give me your hand?'

Jasmin didn't move. 'I found your diary. Or maybe it was more a sort of notebook.'

'I'm sorry?' Yrsen's voice was now cool and distant, like a mountain stream washing over a bed of gravel. 'I don't understand.'

'In the attic of my house – which my husband Jørgen and I haven't set foot in for years – among all the boxes of junk we stored up there, I found a painting. It had your signature on it, and on the back, tucked under the frame, there was a small, thin notebook.'

Yrsen nodded thoughtfully. 'Do you have it with you?'

'No, it's back at the house. I'm sorry, I didn't think to bring it.'

'And you're certain the painting was by me?'

'I just told you it has your signature on it,' Jasmin replied, more sharply than she'd intended. 'It shows a fire, a huge building in flames, and people in front of it. A crowd of people jeering.'

The artist gave a quiet sigh that sounded like old, painful memories. 'I know what you mean now. Oh yes, I remember it very well.'

'You remember?' asked Jasmin, raising her eyebrows. 'How did it get into the attic of our house?'

'That painting was stolen, Ms Hansen. A long time ago. I didn't know . . . Oh my God.' Yrsen clearly didn't want to say any more, and because she looked shocked – close to tears, even – Jasmin didn't want to probe any further either.

'I'm sorry. Whatever happened in the past, I didn't mean to be rude,' she answered cautiously. 'I thought you might be happy that it's turned up again. Though I found it really disturbing, personally.'

'Happy? Most certainly not.' Yrsen shook her head. 'And yes, I understand your reaction. I'm probably the only person who truly understands it.' Yrsen waved these thoughts aside, and as she did so, the sleeve of her cardigan rode up. Jasmin noticed there were burns not only on her face, but on her arms too. She recognised the signs of a skin graft.

For a moment, she saw the harsh headlights of the Jeep from that dreadful night in front of her eyes, a flash of light, and there was a strange smell too – an odour of . . .

'Maybe I should leave.'

'You're saying that out of politeness,' Yrsen replied. 'Deep down, you want something altogether different.'

'I want the truth. That's all.' Jasmin looked out at Paul, who was still playing with Bonnie. 'That night, when I had my accident . . .'

'Yes?'

'We're similar, you and I,' said Jasmin softly. 'Maybe that was partly why I came back. Why I'm here.'

'We're survivors, you mean. The two of us.'

'Exactly. I don't know what your story is.' Jasmin lowered her eyes. It felt good to say this out loud, despite everything. 'But with me – I haven't only been unhappy since the night of the accident. Even before that, I'd been feeling like the whole world could go to hell and I wouldn't care. What happened that night – it was just the final straw, the icing on the cake, so to speak. Except the cake was rotten.'

'What happened?'

'Jørgen and I . . .' Jasmin found it hard to continue. 'We were expecting a child. Our second. That was two years ago – and I lost the baby. A miscarriage in the third month. After that – ever since that day – everything went downhill.'

'I'm so sorry, Ms Hansen.'

Jasmin felt a tear trickle down her cheek. She'd tried to suppress the loss, to erase it, because she knew she had to be there for Paul – that she had a son who needed her strength and love and attention – and she'd succeeded, she felt sure of it.

You need to keep going, she'd told herself time and again.

'It was a little birthday party. A few of my colleagues from the unit were there – our consultant Brecht was turning fifty. I didn't have anything to drink, not a drop.'

'And yet you had an accident.'

'Because somebody ran me off the road. There was another driver, a big Jeep. My car didn't stand a chance against it.' Jasmin could hear her voice trembling and felt ashamed. *Pull yourself together. Be strong, for Christ's sake.* 'There was a man standing on the side of the road, a – a homeless man, I think. My car hit him, must have injured him badly, but beyond that I don't remember anything. And then . . .'

Yrsen held out her hand. 'Have courage.'

'How does it work?'

'Nobody knows. Very few people possess the gift, and very few of those can truly *see*.'

'But—'

'There are no buts. No explanations. Either you believe in it, or you might as well leave, Ms Hansen. I'm afraid I can't put it any other way.'

Jasmin reached for Yrsen's hand. As she did so, Yrsen gave a shriek that echoed through the whole house. She slumped backwards, staring into space. The teapot fell to the floor and shattered. Jasmin shrank back.

'You've seen him again. You've . . . What have you done?'

'I've done nothing!' Jasmin replied. 'Nothing at all.'

'You've killed a man and looked him in the eyes, Jasmin, you're – you're cursed! Can't you see there's a shadow lying over you? You brought it here with you. Darkness is never far away on this island and you're drawing it in. It's been dormant for so long, but you—'

'That's enough!' Jasmin leapt to her feet. 'I never should have come here.'

'Ms Hansen!'

Jasmin blinked. When she opened her eyes, she saw Yrsen standing in front of her, the sketchbook in her hand.

'What happened?' Jasmin murmured.

'We talked for a while, and you apparently nodded off.'

Jasmin shook her head. Something was clouding her thoughts, preventing her from thinking clearly. 'Did you hear a scream just now?'

'No, of course not.'

'Are we – are we done?'

'Yes.'

Yrsen looked unmoved as Jasmin called for Paul and Bonnie. 'So should I paint it for you?' She'd reverted to the same tone of voice as before. 'The picture. The solution to your problem?'

'Do whatever you want.' Paul came inside and Bonnie followed him. 'We're going now.'

Yrsen followed them to the door. A gust of wind buffeted against them, so strong that it almost knocked the car keys out of Jasmin's hand.

'I'll do it. One last time. For you, Jasmin Hansen.'

Jasmin reached for the car door handle and tried to put the key in the lock, but her hands were shaking so violently that it took her several attempts.

'Four days. Then it'll be ready. I hope when you see it, you'll finally understand what happened. It's meant for you, not for anybody else. And, Ms Hansen?'

Jasmin stopped and turned around to look at the artist. 'Yes?'

'Let's hope it will bring you peace.'

Chapter 13

Jasmin was far too agitated to drive straight back to her house on the coast, so she made another stop in the village instead. After their visit to Yrsen and all the fresh air he'd had, Paul was in high spirits and not a bit tired – in fact, he seemed hungry for new adventures.

The ornate, bronze-coloured lettering on the sign over the front of the bookshop said *Proprietor: Veikko Mattila – 1978*. A little bell tinkled as she opened the door. Paul entered the shop ahead of her, but Jasmin left Bonnie in the car as she felt sure a dog with muddy paws wouldn't be welcome here.

The bookshop was very small, with a low ceiling and full-height shelves that were crammed with books and groaning under their weight. It was a place where every sound was muted and everything seemed tranquil, secretive and mysterious. Jasmin used to love places like this when she was a child, and Paul loved them too now.

An odour of yellowing paper hung in the air. Jasmin could almost hear the quiet creak of leather book-bindings, the whisper of heavy pages being carefully turned.

A figure appeared from behind one of the shelves – a short, grey-haired man in a brown blazer and yellow bow tie who wore a pair of round spectacles on his nose. He sized her up. 'Yes?'

'I'm Jasmin Hansen,' she introduced herself. 'We're just having a look around.'

'If you're looking for something in particular, I can order it in for you. It takes a few days, but it's always reliable.' His voice was soft, like the rustle of paper. 'My name is Veikko Mattila. I'm the proprietor.'

'Actually, I'm new here – *o*n Minsøy, I mean – *and* I'm looking for books on local history, about the village and the island as a whole. Do you have anything like that in stock?'

His eyes lit up. 'But of course. If you're interested in history then you're in the right place.' Mattila started pulling books out from a high shelf, muttering to himself and pushing them back into place. He laid out a few titles on the counter before turning back to face her and adjusting his glasses.

'I have here a comprehensive history of the island, written by an academic who still lives locally. Johann Larsen, a Danish man. You ought to find everything you're looking for in there.'

'He lives here on the island?' Jasmin flicked through the book. It was a bulky tome, full of pictures and text in small print, and it weighed nearly as much as a brick.

'That's right. But he *never* accepts any visitors. History is something of a hobby for me too, you know, and I once tried to get in touch with Larsen myself. But he never replied to any of my letters.'

'You aren't Norwegian.' Jasmin could tell from the man's accent. 'Are you from Finland?'

'Well spotted, Ms Hansen. But I wouldn't chalk his lack of response up to that. No, he just doesn't like people.'

'There must have been a major fire here at some point,' said Jasmin. 'I've heard about it in a few different places now, so I was looking for . . .' She thought of the tears that had welled up in Gabriela Yrsen's eyes, of how lost for words the artist had been. Whatever had happened, it must have been terrible.

'A fire? You must mean *the* fire. The big one.'

'Meaning?'

Mattila tapped his fingers on the book. Jasmin saw there were traces of nail polish on his index finger – or was it a bruise under the nail? Had he slipped while using a hammer? 'It's all in there,' he explained, seeming not to notice Jasmin staring at his hand. 'But if you want a summary: it was sixty years ago now. Sixty years to the day, in five weeks' time. It happened on the last day of October. They'd built a sanatorium up in the north and it burned down to the ground.'

Jasmin felt her throat go dry. 'A sanatorium?'

Mattila clasped his hands behind his back and began to pace back and forth like he was giving a lecture. 'About seventy years ago, when the science of psychiatry was still in its infancy, the Norwegian government came up with a plan – admittedly a rather foolhardy one, by modern standards. Out here, in this remote spot, they decided to set up what we'd call a *pilot project* these days. An institution – a sanatorium. For traumatised people coming back from the world war. Victims of the occupation. Untreatable patients. The operation expanded; there were some early successes. Lessons were learned. And then it all burned down.'

'I didn't know that.' Jasmin blinked. For a moment, she thought she could see the walls moving, the books rattling around on their shelves, as a rushing, hissing noise emanated from the back of the shop and the lights grew dimmer and redder.

'Ms Hansen?'

Jasmin blinked and shook her head. *You're overtired. Not enough sleep and too much bearing down on you in too short a time.*

Once again, she saw the ice-blue eyes of the dead vagrant in front of her. Saw him lying there on the beach, his lips eaten away. Saw him standing terrified on the edge of the road, frozen in her headlights.

'I see,' she said hoarsely. 'Do you know anything else about it?'

'About the fire in particular, you mean? No. That's a point in the island's history the tourist brochures tend to skip over, for obvious reasons, and the locals keep quiet about it too. As for Larsen – he might know more, and perhaps he could even share his knowledge with us, if he had any sympathy for the curious.' Mattila gave a brief, forced laugh that sounded like a metallic snort. 'I'd say it was a dark time on the island. But of course, we often get visitors who take an interest in it.'

'Often?' Jasmin pricked up her ears. 'Do you mean other people have been asking about the sanatorium lately?' *Should you mention Yrsen to him now? Should you ask him about her?*

'But of course.' Mattila seemed unmoved at her excitement. 'Someone came along very recently, in fact.'

'Who was it?' Jasmin knew she was acting suspiciously and asking too many questions, but she couldn't restrain herself.

'Well, he didn't introduce himself – not like you – and he also seemed rather short-tempered in general, so . . .'

'So you don't know? What did he buy? Can you describe him to me?'

Mattila studied her with an amused expression. 'You aren't from the police, I'd have noticed that. You're playing at detectives a little, aren't you?'

'I need to know who was asking about the sanatorium. It might be important. Please, tell me as a favour, if you remember him. Describe him to me.'

Mattila closed his eyes and frowned as if he was thinking carefully. 'He looked a bit dishevelled, somehow. Like he was on the run. He had a scar on his face and a tattered old coat that looked like it was only being held together by all the patches on it.'

That sounded like the homeless man's coat. But did he have a scar on his face? Jasmin tried to call the figure she'd seen last night to mind, but all she could really remember were his strange blue eyes.

Those eyes. Like they were reflecting the North Star itself – cold, piercing and emotionless. Had he been here, in the shop? Were the drifter who seemed to keep turning up around the island and the dead vagrant on the beach one and the same person?

'And then he bought the book and left. That was the last I saw of him.'

'The book? This book here? Larsen's history?'

'I had two copies in stock. He bought one, and you're thinking about purchasing the other.'

'That's right,' said Jasmin thoughtfully. 'I am.' She made her decision. 'Yes, I'll take it. And there's another thing I'm going to do too. I'm going to talk to Larsen. It's about time someone shed a little more light on all this.'

◆ ◆ ◆

Jasmin spent the rest of the day with Paul and Bonnie. Only in the evening, once he'd fallen asleep and Bonnie had settled down at the foot of his bed, did she find time for her book.

It mentioned the sanatorium – there were even pictures of it – and after a quick search online she managed to find out where it was located too: on the western end of the island, near a small bay and next to a long line of jagged rocks where the land fell steeply away to the sea far below and it was impossible to get to the foot of the cliffs without breaking your neck. All that remained there now were the ruins of the sanatorium, a handful of houses and a hydroelectric plant. Johann Larsen lived a little further to the north in another remote spot – almost as remote as Gabriela Yrsen's house.

How did all this fit together? Was there any connection?

Jasmin had put new batteries into the large torch and fetched a screwdriver from the toolbox, and both items were now lying ready on the coffee table.

Do you really want to do this? It might be dangerous to leave Paul here on his own, but you can't take him with you either. Bonnie will stay with him. She'll watch over him, and you'll be as quick as you possibly can, won't you?

Are you really sure?

She didn't know the answer. All she had was a vague sense that she needed to bring light into the darkness, to achieve clarity at long last – and yet the feeling clashed so violently with her instinct not to leave Paul alone that it made her heart ache.

Forgive me, Paul, she thought. *Forgive me for leaving you on your own for a while.*

She went back into her son's room once again and kissed him gently on the cheek, at which he sighed in his sleep and rolled onto his other side. Then she tiptoed back to the door. The torch and screwdriver disappeared into her coat pocket. She put on a brown woollen hat and pulled it down low over her face.

The drive back into the village was long, her headlights scarcely able to penetrate the darkness on the road. The rain had set in again and the radio was playing a song by a local band that Jasmin hadn't heard before. Yet the music managed to calm her nerves. *If the headlights of a Jeep suddenly appear in the rear-view mirror now,* she thought, *then everything will repeat itself.*

Then you'll scream.

Skårsteinen came into view, the buildings on the outskirts of the village dotted at random over the landscape like building blocks scattered by a child. Nobody was about, nobody saw her.

She turned off towards the harbour and followed the road until the grey building belonging to the fishing company came into view, along with the towering chimneys of the smokehouses and the white lorries with *Bakke* written in blue lettering on the sides. Jasmin parked the car a short distance from the road, got out and looked around. The area was deserted; there was nothing but darkness behind the windows of the old brick warehouse. A quiet rushing noise came from the sea as the waves crashed against the nearby quayside.

This is where they brought the body. And if he hasn't been collected yet, he must still be here. He has to be. And you're going to find him, look into his face one more time and figure out if he was really there on the night of your accident. If he has a scar like the bookseller mentioned. If the body in the warehouse is the drifter.

A chain-link fence blocked her way onto the premises, with a set of large crates labelled *Parkov International* stacked beside it. Jasmin looked around. There was still nobody else about.

Now or never.

Go through with it or turn back. Once you're over the fence, it'll be too late to change your mind.

Jasmin climbed onto the crates and reached for the fence, placing first one foot onto the wire, then the other. The mesh rattled and jingled; it was much noisier and more strenuous than she'd expected.

Somewhere in the distance, a dog started barking. The noise was loud, a warning call. It was on the alert.

Jasmin froze. Her heart was pounding; her hands shook as they gripped the fence. She felt her courage draining away, felt the wire cutting into her skin.

Up or down.

This decides everything.

You haven't come all this way only to turn back now, she thought. *Come on!*

Jasmin roused herself, gathering all her courage, before climbing upwards and lowering herself down on the other side. Her feet landed on the concrete with a thud.

It was loud, far too loud, but she couldn't do anything about it now. Under the light of the moon, Jasmin crouched down and crept forwards, keeping one hand on the grey wall of the fishery building so as not to lose her way. Ahead of her she saw the cooling units, humming quietly in the night, and to her right was a door. The coolant lines disappeared into the same building. This was the place she was looking for. *With a bit of luck . . .*

The door was locked. Jasmin took the screwdriver from her coat pocket and tried to insert it between the door and the frame, but it wasn't as easy as it looked in the movies. However much she threw her weight behind it, the door didn't budge an inch.

It's no good. Turn back, drive home and forget this whole stupid idea. You're trying to play at detectives, just like Veikko Mattila said, but you're in way over your head.

Jasmin turned around, her shoulders sagging. Failure.

In the silvery moonlight, she caught the gleam of a window that had been left ajar.

As if the finger of fate were pointing towards it.

She and Jørgen had locked themselves out of their apartment in Oslo once. Jørgen had managed to get hold of a screwdriver and then, with a simple little trick, he'd managed to pop the kitchen window, which they'd left open like this one.

Jasmin had watched him do it and remembered.

Maybe you'll get lucky. Maybe it'll work here too. But before that . . . She looked around for another crate and found an empty one that was evidently waiting to be filled. It scraped quietly along the concrete as she braced herself against it and pushed it over to the wall, so she could climb on top and reach the open window.

After that, Jasmin got to work with her screwdriver. Jørgen had pushed down sharply in the spot where the window met the frame, then tugged on it and rattled it back and forth. Jasmin swore quietly when nothing happened after her first attempt.

Again.

It has to work.

The screwdriver slipped, but Jasmin composed herself and tried once more.

Stay calm. It must be doable somehow.

And eventually she managed it. The window gave way with a quiet jolt and swung wide open.

Jasmin tucked the screwdriver back into her coat pocket and reached through the opening. The brickwork surrounding the window offered her a handhold as she pulled herself up and clambered into the building.

You've done it.

On the other side, she hopped down quietly, dropping a few feet to the tiled floor. She found herself inside a kind of factory where the fish from the trawlers were processed. Long rows of gleaming stainless-steel tables lay spread out before her, along with a conveyor belt covered with large hooks for transporting heavy fish. There were knives stored in huge blocks, electric saws and drainage channels along the floor.

To her left, she saw a curtain of heavy plastic strips covering the entrance to a corridor. Jasmin pushed it aside and peered through the doorway. The gleam of her torch was the only thing penetrating the thick darkness. A gurgling noise came from one of the drains, and the air smelled of fish, blood and the acrid odour of cleaning agents.

The temperature started to drop.

You're on the right track. She followed the coolant lines that wound their way along the ceiling far above her head like lifeless snakes, and they eventually led her to the refrigerators. Huge steel doors blocked her way, sealed shut with a locking system operated by a lever on each door. Jasmin passed her torch to her left hand and pulled the first of the levers downwards. The door unbolted itself with a quiet hiss and Jasmin hauled on the handle with all her strength until it stood open. Ice-cold air poured out in thick clouds of fog and she instantly started to shiver.

If you go in there and the door closes behind you then you'll be a block of ice by the time everyone comes back in the morning.

No, she couldn't risk it. Jasmin cast her eyes around for an object heavy enough to keep the door open, but she couldn't see anything in the processing halls that she could easily move.

But inside the refrigerator . . .

One of those big boxes of fish might do.

Jasmin pulled up the hood of her coat and stepped inside, holding the door open with one arm and hauling one of the big red boxes off the shelf with the other. It fell to the floor with a bang and a clatter, and she managed to drag the container full of frozen fish towards her and position it in the doorway, where it blocked the door from closing.

Now for the important part.

Jasmin followed a route marked with yellow arrows that led deeper into the refrigerator. Amid the endless shelving that reached all the way up to the ice-encrusted ceiling, the clouds of icy fog and the frost-covered floor and windows, she found it difficult to keep her bearings. The inside of the vast refrigerator felt like a frozen labyrinth of death.

She peered to the left and right, but she couldn't see anything anywhere that resembled a human corpse.

They were here, she thought, as the cold gradually robbed her of all rational thought. It ate away at her, making each breath more uncomfortable than the last, sinking deep beneath her clothes and into her body.

Henriksen had been here, Boeckermann too, and they'd had a van with them. This was the only place on the island where they could temporarily store a corpse before transporting it to the mainland.

It has to be here.

Jasmin walked a little further into the freezer and felt herself hunching forward with every step, as if her body were responding instinctively, struggling to protect her from the cold.

Jesus Christ, you need to get out of here. Whatever they're storing in here, they've set the temperature far too low.

Jasmin was on the point of turning back when she saw it: an empty shelf with no red crates on it. No fish, not here. Instead, there was . . .

She could hardly believe her eyes. Was this a hallucination, conjured up by her brain as it slowly froze?

Don't be absurd, she scolded herself. *Take a closer look.*

There, in the darkness, on one of the lower shelves, lay a large black body bag like the ones used by the police. *You've seen those things before at the hospital. You've found him.*

Now all she needed to do was open the bag and look at his face once more.

Jasmin reached for the zip.

Chapter 14

The headlights of the Jeep in the rear-view mirror were blindingly bright. Jasmin felt herself reach out with sweaty fingers to turn off the radio. She fumbled for her phone.

Someone's following me.

Someone's coming for me.

Those two thoughts pushed all others from her mind, but then the Jeep accelerated and overtook, speeding away until its tail lights – like the eyes of a snake – disappeared into the distance.

Jasmin lowered the window a little. Fresh, cold air blew into her face. It felt invigorating, exactly what she needed.

She put her foot down once more. Another few miles. *You're nearly home. As for Jørgen – he'll understand. That you needed an evening to yourself, for once. That you wanted to clear your head.*

And what he doesn't know can't hurt him, right?

Jasmin looked down at her phone and opened WhatsApp to send him a message, but there were no bars on the display. She was too deep in the forest to have any reception, too far from the nearest mobile phone mast.

When she looked up again, the dazzling headlights were back. She felt hypnotised, like a terrified deer, the seconds rushing onwards, as if there was no avoiding it, no way of escaping from the two tonnes of iron and steel hurtling towards her – until she yanked the wheel to one side with a scream.

Too far.

Too *fast*.

The car swerved out of control; there was a smell of burning rubber, a horrible stench and . . .

There he was.

His old moth-eaten coat covered in patches, his shoes worn, ready to fall apart as soon as he took another step. His eyes ice-blue, staring, reproachful.

Accusatory.

Jasmin heard the dull thud as her car hit the man – heard snapping and cracking, the shock absorbers screaming as the stranger disappeared – and then the bonnet was doused in blood and the windscreen shattered as the low-hanging branches of a pine tree smashed through the glass as if it was made of paper.

But this time there was more.

She remembered something. Another fragment emerged from the fog and re-entered the conscious part of her mind.

The Jeep pulled up nearby. She heard its tyres screeching to a halt on the wet asphalt. Jasmin felt blood flowing down her face, dripping onto her lips. It tasted of iron and copper and felt warm – hot, even.

The driver's door of the Jeep swung open. She heard the sound of footsteps drawing nearer. Jasmin tried to turn her head towards the window, but a wave of agony flooded through her body. She couldn't do it, her neck felt . . .

Please don't let me die, don't let me be paralysed, please no . . .

More and more blood flowed over her nose, her cheeks.

Somebody opened the door of her car.

A pain in the crook of her neck, like the prick of a needle.

As Jasmin lost consciousness, she thought she could see strange things playing out in front of her. A figure in a black raincoat, the hood drawn down low over their face, dragging an object along the ground. It was some kind of animal, with four hooves and thick fur.

Something like a deer.

The beep of the freezer's temperature alarm roused Jasmin with a start and she gave a low cry. Her hand was still resting on the cold metal of the zip as if it were frozen to her skin, and she was staring into the face of a corpse.

Ice-blue eyes.

Lips eaten away.

But no scar on his cheek that she could see.

The body from the beach is the same man you saw on the night of your accident – but he isn't the drifter with the scar on his face who you keep hearing about.

They're two different people.

She zipped up the body bag and whirled around. The cold had seeped through to her bones; her coat was filled with crystals of ice. She hurried to the door, afraid that somebody might shut the heavy steel colossus from the outside and lock her in.

When she reached the exit, she pushed the box she'd left in the doorway to one side and stepped out into the corridor.

She'd never been this cold before in her life. It was hard to breathe; her cheeks and lips were numb, as if she'd spent hours in there with the corpse, staring at its face.

Now you know what you wanted to find out.

It's him.

You weren't mistaken.

Jasmin searched for a way out, hurrying through the darkened corridors and the tiled processing halls, until she found a door a few minutes later that was only bolted from the inside. She pulled the bolt back, threw the door open and sprinted towards her car. And all the while, the same thoughts echoed through her mind on a loop: *Someone made the body disappear and then brought it to Minsøy. Someone on this island means nothing but evil.*

And you're the only one who knows what's really happening.

Jasmin got in her car and took several deep breaths. By the time she started the engine and turned the heating up, she'd managed to compose herself enough to be able to drive – to move her fingers and grip the wheel. She steered the car back onto the main road through Skårsteinen, heading out of the village and towards the south, as distant stars glimmered icy blue in the cold night sky above her.

You know there's something going on here. You know that better than Henriksen, better than Boeckermann.

Only one person knows it as well as you.

The driver of the Jeep.

If he was acting alone.

Chapter 15

The house stood before her, dark and silent, as she steered the Volvo onto the drive. Rain had started falling again, wetting the grass and making it glitter under the headlights.

A nocturnal bird called softly as Jasmin walked over from her car to the front door. She could control the motion sensor with her phone, and she now opened the app to switch it off temporarily before entering the house.

Everything was quiet and cloaked in deep darkness.

Not even Bonnie stirred.

Was that a creaking noise she could hear from the steps down to the cellar?

Jasmin flipped a switch and the hallway filled with light. First she checked the boards nailed to the cellar door, then the windows. Everything was as she had left it. The hands on the clock over the kitchen table pointed to quarter past eleven.

She tiptoed up the stairs. Bonnie had noticed her by now and trotted over quietly to nudge her with her nose and wag her tail. Paul was lying on his side, fast asleep.

Jasmin felt tears well up in her eyes as she looked at him, slumbering peacefully, breathing softly.

Where have I brought you to? What on earth is going on here? Wouldn't it be better if we left first thing tomorrow?

These thoughts governed one part of her mind, but the other urged her to stay and shed light on the darkness. *Whoever was driving the Jeep that night, he's here. Here on the island. And he isn't done with you yet. What is he planning?*

Who could harbour such hatred that he'd do something like this?

I don't know, she thought. *There's nobody.*

Jasmin stepped into the shower to rid herself of the cold that had taken possession of her body under the warming jet of water. Then, wrapped in a fluffy woollen dressing gown and with thick socks on her feet, she made some tea and sat down in the living room to look at the book she'd bought, which she hoped would tell her more about the history of the island. She placed her mug on the coffee table next to the book and the old metal bowl she always used to keep fruit in – an heirloom inherited from Jørgen's mother. Paul had left Bonnie's dog chew on the table too, and Jasmin pushed it to one side.

Good girl, she thought. *She never takes anything off the table.*

The fire that had destroyed the sanatorium was mentioned only in a brief aside. An inglorious end, the historian called it – an unsolved crime, in the wake of which the facility was never rebuilt. A few culprits had been rounded up and sentenced: teenagers from the village, supposedly on a dare that had got out of hand. Two of them had arranged to break into the building to cause trouble. They'd started a fire. People had got hurt.

But was that really what happened?

You have to talk to him. To the historian.

Jasmin thought of Karl Sandvik and his words of warning. Maybe it would be a good idea to call up Jan Berger and have him teach her how to use her gun after all.

She flicked onwards, and on another page featuring a glossy photograph – an aerial view of the fjord – she found a yellow sticky note.

Remember: seven, not two, it said.

What's that supposed to mean? The handwriting – doesn't it look familiar somehow?

Jasmin rummaged through her purse for the receipt Mattila had issued to her, but she couldn't find it. *You must have left it in the car.* She pulled on her boots and went back outside. The silhouettes of the trees were towering, restless guardians flanking the house, and at this time of night they seemed even more threatening than usual. The receipt from the bookshop was in the glove compartment, as she'd expected.

Beneath the light over the kitchen table, she compared the lettering – *forty-nine krone*, Mattila had scribbled on the receipt – with that of the note in the book. *Remember: seven, not two.*

The handwriting wasn't the same.

But what if . . .

She flicked onwards through the book and found the historian's signature at the end of the afterword. *Jesus, it must have been him.* That angular S – it was the same as the one on the note.

How is this possible?

Jasmin searched the cabinet in the corridor for the phone book and looked up the number of the bookshop.

'Mattila?' answered the proprietor. He sounded like he'd been drinking.

From the corner of her eye, Jasmin briefly saw the blinding flash of the Jeep's headlights in the window at the end of the kitchen – but when she looked up, there was nothing to be seen but the darkness beyond the glass. She smelled petrol, smoke – and alcohol.

'This is Jasmin Hansen,' she said quietly. *You need to be careful what you say. They might be listening in.* 'We spoke earlier today. I bought the last copy of—'

'I know. I remember.' Mattila's voice sounded very far away, as if there were more separating them than just a few miles. 'I remember it very well.'

'Somebody left a message in the book. "Seven, not two" written on a sticky note.'

'Did they really?'

'It wasn't you?'

'Most certainly not,' the bookseller replied. 'And I happen to know that your copy was hand-delivered to the store by Larsen himself.'

'Larsen personally gave it to you?' Jasmin gripped the receiver with all her strength. 'But that would mean—'

'I don't know what it means,' Mattila cut in, 'but don't you think . . . ?'

Jasmin caught a glimpse of a movement down by the edge of the woods. As if a strange force had assumed control of her body, her fingers loosened and the telephone fell from her hand, landing on the sofa with a quiet thud.

Without stopping to think, she switched off the light, scurried over to the French windows and peered out, her heart beating faster.

He was down there.

He'd returned. Under the light of the moon, Jasmin recognised his coat, which was blowing gently back and forth in the wind. On his cheek – yes, if she squinted, it was just possible to make out a scar running from his eye down to his chin. It looked like a knife wound that hadn't been stitched up properly, because he'd never gone to hospital or visited a doctor who might have wondered how such a serious injury could have happened.

You need your gun. The words flashed through her mind. *You can't go on like this. If you want to stay here and keep playing at detectives, you need to be able to defend yourself.*

In a surge of courage – or possibly recklessness – Jasmin opened the French windows. If the intruder wanted to get in, he'd simply break the glass and nothing would be able to stop him. Apart from Bonnie, perhaps.

But Jasmin doubted her Labrador would be able to hold out for long against a big man like him. 'What do you want from me?' she yelled down at the forest. 'What do you want, you piece of shit? Leave us alone!'

The stranger lifted his hand. At first, Jasmin thought he was greeting her, but then she saw he was pointing west. The realisation sent hot and cold shivers through her body.

Just a few moments later, the drifter turned on his heels and vanished down the narrow path.

The west.

Out where the island became ever more barren and unpopulated. Out where the sanatorium had been built, and where the old historian had taken refuge.

All the evidence was pointing in the same direction.

Slow down, she cautioned herself. *It might be a trick. Maybe he's trying to lure you there. Maybe he only wants you to leave the house.*

The most important clue was the dead body in the cold storage unit.

How was it possible to transport a corpse all the way out here and leave it down on the beach?

There must be more than one person involved. No one could have managed it on their own. That was her starting point. That was how she was going to get to the bottom of all this. Jasmin felt certain of it.

If you have the courage.

Jasmin picked up her phone and scrolled to Jørgen's number. Her finger hovered over the call button – and yet she didn't press it.

Tomorrow you're going to talk to the historian. Or try to, at least. And after that you're going to visit Hendrik Henriksen. It's time you came clean to him. You need to tell him you recognised the body on the beach; that somebody on the island is playing a wicked, wicked game; and that the drifter has turned up at the bottom of your garden once again.

She put the phone back down on the sofa and glanced over at the window. What if the stranger came back? Wasn't it high time she brought the gun upstairs?

But the gun was still in its cabinet, which meant she'd have to go down into the cellar, and she didn't want to do that.

No way.

A man died down there.

All the same, Jasmin got to her feet and approached the cellar door. The boards over it were still every bit as secure as when she'd nailed them up. Gripping the screwdriver, she levered the planks out of the doorframe one by one.

It was much easier than she'd expected.

That wasn't good at all, and only strengthened her resolve to arm herself.

Eventually, she managed to remove all the boards and open the door. The air that blew into her face was cold and musty, like an old grave.

Jasmin flicked on her torch and went down the steps.

Downstairs, the door to the back room was standing ajar – but then again, that was how she'd left it the last time she'd come down here. She saw the red rowboat, the gas central heating in the corner. The pipes gurgled quietly and eerily as if a slimy creature was squirming around inside them.

Jasmin opened the gun cabinet, the unoiled hinges squeaking noisily. The gun lay before her – dark steel with a walnut stock. And just as Jørgen had said, a small box of ammunition was standing next to it.

You didn't notice it when you last looked. That must be what happened.

It had been here the whole time. There was no other rational explanation.

At least, not one she could accept without losing her mind.

Jasmin put the ammunition in her pocket and lifted the gun. It was heavier than she'd expected. She looked over at the door leading to the back of the cellar again. It was open a crack. Behind that door was where they'd found the captain, dangling from one of the ceiling beams on a finger-thick length of rope.

Something was drawing her towards the back room. She could sense it.

You need to look inside.

Put it behind you.

Overcome your fear. It's only a room in a cellar – empty, dusty, maybe with a few cobwebs.

Jasmin had taken a step towards the door, deeper into the cellar, when her ears caught muffled noises from upstairs.

It sounded like voices. Two people talking to each other – and one of them, she realised with mounting horror, was Paul.

Oh God.

No, no, no.

Jasmin dashed up the cellar stairs, ran like she'd never run before, and the treads creaked and groaned as she stormed up the main staircase to the first floor. The door to Paul's room was ajar. She reached out and pushed it open, lifted the gun to her shoulder and—

Paul was sitting upright in bed, staring at the wall. He was alone.

'Who were you talking to just now?'

He didn't reply. His eyes were fixed on the wall and aside from his heavy breathing, he didn't move an inch. Jasmin wasn't even sure he knew she was there.

Was this a nightmare?

'Paul?' she asked timidly. 'Paul, who were you . . . ?'

She took a step forwards, moving a couple more feet into the room. Paul still didn't respond. It was unusually cold in there, and only now did Jasmin notice the ice crystals that had formed on the inside of the window.

There was frost on Paul's duvet too, in his hair, on his skin.

He was pale and so cold, so horribly cold.

He turned to look at her, and Jasmin thought she heard his vertebrae snapping. 'He's in the wardrobe,' said Paul in a voice that sounded chill, like the crackle of ice, and his breath felt every bit as cold as the air in the room as it brushed against her cheek like the grasping fingers of a corpse.

Jasmin spun around towards the wardrobe, which stood in the corner behind her. Her muscles were close to giving out, her legs on the verge of buckling under her. She felt ready to collapse on the spot.

Run, while you still can. The words shot through her head, yet the dreadful chill in the room seemed to freeze her to the spot, even more so than the cold she'd felt in the refrigerator a few hours before.

The wardrobe door swung open with a screech.

The homeless man emerged. His piercing, ice-blue eyes glittered as he reached out his hand.

He was pointing not at her, but at Paul.

'They're going to come for him,' he said in a hoarse voice. 'They're going to take him away from you.'

Jasmin whirled to face Paul. Her son was gone.

Then she woke with a start and everything vanished. Jasmin heard the echo of a scream and realised it was her own.

Her neck ached. Outside the window she saw the pale light of the morning sun, but it seemed wan and strangely discoloured, like it was shining through a soot-streaked pane of glass.

You fell asleep on the sofa. It's ten o'clock in the morning already!

Jasmin looked around for the shotgun but she couldn't find it. The floor lamp by the French windows bathed the living room in a dull, buttery yellow light. Her book was lying on the coffee table, along with the fruit bowl, the dog chew and, in its shadow, two strange origami sculptures Paul had made: a kind of geometric figure – something like a triangle, if she wasn't mistaken – and a deer. When Jasmin checked the cellar door and found the boards still nailed into place, she realised that too had only been a dream.

Just a horrible nightmare.

You should go back to the cellar tomorrow, she thought. *But I bet you won't find any ammunition down there. In other words, everything is as it should be.*

She checked the windows, doors, motion sensors and cameras before heading upstairs, her newly purchased book tucked under her arm. The steps squeaked softly under her feet.

Maybe if you read a little it'll help you calm down from your dream. Or you could rip out a page and make an origami sculpture like the ones Paul left downstairs . . .

The book nearly slipped from Jasmin's fingers.

With a sudden chill sense of horror, she realised the sculptures in the living room hadn't been there when she'd come downstairs after her shower.

No sculptures. Not before she'd dozed off. And that meant they must have been left here while she was asleep.

Somebody had been in the house.

Jasmin dashed up to Paul's room.

The door was shut.

She hurled it open and barged inside.

What she saw there made her heart stop in her chest. The window was shattered, shards of glass strewn all over the rug. Bonnie lay motionless on the floor. Her son's bedding was rumpled, the duvet thrown to one side, and Paul was nowhere to be seen.

He was gone.

PART TWO

FIRESTARTER

Chapter 1

You've seen it before, Jasmin realised. *The upside-down triangle with the open top-right corner.*

It's wrong. It shouldn't be like that.

There's only one way to put it right.

You need to turn it over.

Turn everything on its head.

You're going to find it out there. You've seen it before, the first time you and Jørgen came to Minsøy.

And you saw it again too, later on. After your accident.

If you can connect the two places you saw it – which is what you came back to the island to do – then the triangle will make sense once more.

'Ms Hansen, did you manage to recognise the driver of the Jeep that was pursuing you?' The words of the detective who had interviewed her as she lay in her hospital bed echoed through her mind.

'No. I didn't have the chance.'

'You mentioned a woman named Hanna Jansen earlier. Who is she?'

'Just an old, painful memory. She's the woman Jørgen once cheated on me with. The woman who wants me out of the way.'

'Do you think Ms Jansen could have been driving the Jeep?'

'Maybe. Maybe she's still out there somewhere. Waiting for her chance – waiting to finally take me out, once and for all.'

And then her memory shifted, the detective and her hospital bed disappeared, and Jasmin's thoughts took her to a different day, to a different place, where . . .

Chapter 2

'I've already told you not to worry,' said Jasmin as she flicked on the indicator.

'But we both know how they're going to react when they find out about everything,' replied Jørgen, who was sitting beside her on the passenger seat. 'You know what your father thinks. That you'd be better off—'

'Enough, now.' Jasmin steered the SUV, which they'd bought two years previously, onto the broad drive leading up to the property of Marit and Stale Adamsen. Jasmin's parents lived in a neighbourhood full of enormous mansion houses next to the Frognerparken in Oslo.

'That maybe you should have married someone else,' Jørgen went on. 'Someone better at business. It's the same story every time.'

Jasmin glanced at the rear-view mirror. Bonnie was sitting in the boot and pressing her nose alternately against the security grille and the rear windscreen, looking back and forth restlessly out of excitement at the prospect of bounding around in the garden. Meanwhile, Paul was oblivious to everything that was happening since he was sound asleep in his child seat, which was gradually getting too small for him. He was nearly five, after all.

'I know,' she replied. In front of them, a tall curlicued metal gate swung open automatically. Beyond it, the drive led up to the house. 'And *you* know my father only says it to wind you up. That's just his – well, his particular sense of humour.'

'His sense of humour.' Jørgen snorted.

'Don't be so grumpy. We're only staying an hour.'

'A whole hour, yes.' Jørgen pulled an ostentatiously pained face which Jasmin couldn't help but laugh at, and Bonnie barked as if she wanted to join in the fun too.

Her parents were waiting for them on the veranda in front of the house. It was a mild spring day in Oslo and the March sunshine felt good after the long, cold, grey winter that had held the city in its grip for several months, bringing unusual quantities of snow.

Jasmin embraced her mother and father. Later on, as they sat on the veranda, Marit watched Paul playing with Bonnie in the garden. 'He's starting to get properly big,' she said. 'It's so good to see you all again. You know how I always say—'

'That we don't come to visit anywhere near often enough.' Jasmin finished her mother's sentence and cast a quick glance at Jørgen. 'Yes, I know.'

'Well, boy,' said Stale to Jørgen after a while. Jasmin noticed Jørgen purse his lips. 'How's business?'

'Do we really need to talk about this right now, Dad?'

'I think we should,' answered Stale obstinately.

So Jørgen told him the truth. 'Business isn't very good at the moment. To be honest, I'm not sure how long I can keep the company afloat.'

Paul and Bonnie made a sudden dash towards the open gate and Jasmin leapt to her feet. 'Excuse me. Paul!' She hurried down the veranda steps and her mother followed her, catching up just as she reached her son. 'Don't go onto the road,' she scolded him, before looking up at Marit. 'Well? Yet another sermon?' Jasmin tried to stay calm, but on the inside she felt tense.

'You know you're free to do whatever you like with your own money. But how often have you helped him out already? And how much of that came from your shares in your father's company? From us?'

Jasmin ran her hand through Paul's hair. 'All right, off you go,' she told him, 'but stay with Bonnie.' She and Marit watched as Paul picked up a small, unripe apple from the grass beneath one of the trees and threw it for Bonnie to fetch. 'Some of it came from there, you're right,' she answered her mother quietly, 'but that's *my* business.'

'Your father isn't happy that his youngest daughter is so careless with her money.'

'Just say what you really mean. He still can't stand Jørgen, that's what it boils down to.' Jasmin folded her arms. 'And I'm tired of having this conversation.'

'Don't take that tone, Jasmin. It is what it is. You can't change your nature. Nobody can. Jørgen simply isn't very successful. One day perhaps you'll understand our concerns.'

'One day?' She snorted. 'That'll never happen.' Jasmin turned her back on her mother and ran after Paul and Bonnie. She could hear raised voices from the veranda; it sounded like they were arguing up there. *Your concerns*, she thought. *You have no idea. Money isn't everything.*

Paul. Bonnie. Jørgen. They were all that mattered. If anyone ever took Paul away from her, she thought as she felt the spring breeze brush over her skin, she'd move heaven and earth to get him back.

And Jørgen would do exactly the same.

Chapter 3

Jasmin didn't notice the tears trickling over her cheeks as they mingled with the rain that was now pouring down in torrents, washing away any footprints the kidnapper might have left behind. The sky had taken on an indigo colour and looked like an old wound. An omen of the coming autumn storm that reflected the mounting panic and tumult in her mind.

After she'd found the window shattered and Paul missing from his room, Jasmin had knelt down beside her unconscious Labrador, who was lying on the floor at the foot of Paul's bed.

Bonnie was alive, but breathing slowly and unevenly. Jasmin's trembling hands had found blood on her fur. The kidnapper must have struck her down in order to get her out of the way, as otherwise she would have given her life to defend Paul.

'Bonnie,' Jasmin had whispered. 'Come on, don't do this to me.'

The dog blinked. Her tail flapped gently against the floor, but other than that she'd refused to move. Jasmin didn't know what she should do next, couldn't get her thoughts straight – Bonnie, Paul, the window, the footprints. She'd rushed out into the driving rain and run in circles, staring at the ground. Her panic felt like a veil that had fallen before her eyes, stopping her from seeing the kidnapper's tracks on the lawn. The garden gate was ajar, and there were clumps of soil on the roof of the veranda and the white wooden posts that held it up. Footprints, which the rain was rapidly washing away.

Somebody had climbed up there to get to Paul's window, which opened on to the veranda.

Eventually, a scream fought its way up her throat; she screamed her fear and desperation into the rain until her voice was hoarse and she could scream no more.

Now completely soaked, she ran back into the house and scrabbled through her purse to find Detective Inspector Henriksen's business card. For a moment she was afraid she'd lost it, but then she found it tucked behind her driving licence.

Jasmin dialled his number with trembling fingers. She felt nauseous, hot and cold at the same time; she wanted to weep, to beat at the walls.

You should have seen this coming. The words ran through her mind over and over again. *The moment you first spotted the drifter, you should have taken Paul and gone back to the mainland. But no, you had to play the detective.*

'Henriksen.' His voice emerged quietly from the speaker and Jasmin could hear noise in the background. It sounded like music and the clink of glasses.

'This is Jasmin Hansen,' she said. 'My son has been abducted.' She blurted the words out so quickly and hurriedly that she wasn't sure if Henriksen had even understood her.

'Hold on, did I hear that right? Your son has—'

'Disappeared.' Jasmin finished his sentence for him. 'He's been kidnapped.'

'Kidnapped?' Henriksen repeated. 'Are you sure? He isn't just outside playing with the dog?'

'No, Bonnie was knocked out cold. Someone broke in through the window of Paul's room – there's glass everywhere.'

'I see. Ms Hansen, are you sure you're alone in the house?'

Jasmin glanced down the hallway at the cellar door. The boards were still nailed firmly to the doorframe. 'Yes, I'm sure.'

'We're on our way. Stay at home if you think you're safe there, but if not then please leave immediately the moment you realise you aren't alone. OK?'

Jasmin felt her phone almost slip out of her trembling hand. 'OK. Please hurry.'

'Give us fifteen minutes. We'll be right there.'

'Wait! Do you know a vet?'

'A vet? For your dog? Of course. I'll ask around.'

After hanging up, Jasmin remained standing in the middle of the living room. She was unable to take so much as a step; fear had paralysed her whole body, from her head to her feet. *Paul is gone. He's gone.* The thought took hold of her, circling endlessly through her mind. Only after a few minutes had passed did she manage to head back upstairs to check on Bonnie. The dog was standing upright and shuffled towards her, unsteady on her feet but obviously not seriously injured.

Jasmin carried her carefully downstairs, laid her on the sofa and waited for the police to arrive.

Henriksen was true to his word. They arrived fourteen minutes later: the detective inspector himself, Arne Boeckermann – whom she'd only seen from a distance before now – and three other colleagues Henriksen must have brought with him from the mainland. These were a woman with short red hair, who fixed Jasmin with a curiously scrutinising look, and two men who pulled on white overalls and started searching the house and the surrounding area.

Meanwhile, Henriksen's first move was to head into the kitchen. To Jasmin's surprise, he set about making her a cup of tea. 'Ms Hansen,' he explained as he handed her a mug, 'this is Margret Gundersen, the village doctor.'

'What about the vet?'

'Margret can help with that too – she's trained in human *and* veterinary medicine.'

Only now did Jasmin realise why the red-haired woman had been looking over at her so oddly – she'd been observing Bonnie, not Jasmin.

'Now, why don't you take a deep breath and tell me what happened while Dr Gundersen looks at your dog?'

'Yes, of course.' She followed Henriksen onto the veranda and told him everything as the inspector closed the French windows behind them, walked up to the wooden railing and looked out over the garden.

'We'll find him,' he said quietly and confidently. 'We're on an island. There aren't many places to hide, and our colleagues from the marine police and the coastguard are checking every boat that leaves.'

'But what if he's hidden an inflatable dinghy in an out-of-the-way cove?' Jasmin asked. Her heart thumped against her ribs as if it were about to leap out of her chest.

'He wouldn't make it to the mainland on something like that. Besides which, my colleagues will be patrolling the area. We're taking this incident very seriously indeed.'

'That doesn't mean we'll find Paul though.' Jasmin lowered her head as her grief overwhelmed her. Tears flowed down her cheeks and she couldn't even lift her hand to wipe them away.

Henriksen gently touched her shoulder; his hand was warm and reassuring. One of the forensic technicians approached, leaned over to Henriksen and whispered something in his ear that she couldn't hear. Jasmin could see one of the police officers shining a torch around the garden. The beam cast a silvery gleam on the drifting wafts of fog, making them glitter like billows of dry ice.

'My colleagues have found fingerprints and hair samples, which we'll send straight to the lab.'

'We have to do something,' Jasmin heard herself say quietly. 'We have to look for him.'

'And that's exactly what *we're* going to do.' From the way he emphasised the word, she realised he wasn't including her. '*You* should wait here.'

'I can't.' She finally wiped the tears from her cheeks. 'No, I want to come with you. I want to help, not just sit here and wait. That's more than I could bear.'

Henriksen studied her carefully. 'Will you be able to handle it?'

'Yes. Absolutely.'

He nodded. 'Then you can come with me. But call your husband first. He needs to know what's happened.'

Jasmin pointed at the origami sculptures on the coffee table. Through the blur of her tears, the folded paper looked like it was melting onto the woodgrain, as if it was made of water.

'Those sculptures,' she said. 'Paul didn't make them. He does a lot of origami, but those were left by the kidnapper.'

Somewhat awkwardly, Henriksen pulled a thin latex glove over his right hand and picked up the sculptures. 'A deer and a triangle,' he said thoughtfully. 'Why a deer?'

Because you killed a deer that night. Only that isn't what happened. Tell him. Come clean.

'He was here again last night – the drifter everyone's been talking about. I saw him down in the garden. Then I fell asleep on the sofa. I had a nightmare, and when I woke up, Paul was gone.' Jasmin looked up at Henriksen. The lump in her throat had subsided but she still felt so helpless. It was a feeling she wanted to shake off as quickly as possible. *You have to take action. You can't let them hurt Paul.*

'Something on this island doesn't add up.' Jasmin looked out into the pouring rain. Silhouettes moved back and forth through the grey: faceless figures in coats who resembled the drifter. 'They're hiding something.'

'Who? What do you mean by that?'

'I don't know yet. A terrible event – a fire everyone knows about, but nobody ever discusses. There's a historian I wanted to visit . . .' She broke off as she realised how trivial her little investigation had suddenly become.

Paul had disappeared and she had to find him and bring him back. Nothing else mattered now.

But what if those two things are related? What if it's all connected? Yrsen. Paul. The fire. The historian, the drifter, my accident, the body on the beach.

'Ms Hansen?'

'We should dig deeper,' she said. 'I don't know exactly who is trying to hide the truth, but they might be behind the kidnapping.'

'Do you have any evidence for that assumption?' asked Henriksen with interest. 'Have you seen anybody? Has anyone threatened you or your son?'

'The drifter, but . . .' She thought of the gesture the stranger had made to her, how he had pointed towards the west. 'He never actually came near us.'

'But you don't know for certain.'

'No.'

'We'll find evidence, assuming the rain hasn't washed everything away.' Henriksen didn't sound particularly confident. 'Every criminal leaves evidence behind. We always find *something*.'

'But that won't help Paul. Even if we find out who the kidnapper is, he could be hiding anywhere. How big is this island?'

'Around twenty-five square miles. We'll leave no stone unturned.'

'We? You mean, you, Boeckermann and the handful of colleagues you've brought here? Is that all?' Jasmin snorted. 'It won't be enough.'

'I'll do my best to get reinforcements, but it'll be tricky.'

'Tricky?' asked Jasmin sharply. 'My son is missing.'

'There are several other cases on the mainland that are taking up our resources. Paul has only been gone for a few hours.'

'So? Do you really think he's just gone for a walk and will be back any minute? That he broke the window for fun?'

'Of course not. Please try to stay calm, Ms Hansen.'

'I will not!' It felt good to get angry, much better than sitting around ineffectually. 'And if you aren't going to take the initiative—'

'Ms Hansen—' Henriksen raised his hand as if to hold her back, but Jasmin shoved it forcefully aside. She left Henriksen on the veranda and stormed into the house, almost stumbling over the vet, who was giving Bonnie an injection. The Labrador's tail thumped against the sofa and she lifted her head when she saw Jasmin. She had a white bandage over her ears.

'How is she?' Jasmin asked softly. 'Will she pull through, or . . . ?' Jasmin didn't want to say the word out loud; she felt as though that would give it power somehow – too much power.

'She'll be back on her feet soon enough. Maybe in the next few minutes, even. I've given her something to stabilise her. The bandage needs to stay on for at least three days, and you should bring her to see me again after that. My surgery is on the way into the village, you can't miss it.'

Jasmin nodded thoughtfully as she stroked Bonnie, running her fingers through her thick, chocolate-brown fur. She'd seen the veterinary practice from her car yesterday; it had a distinctive sign featuring a floppy-eared dog.

'Thank you,' she said quietly. 'If Bonnie were to die . . .'

'Stay strong,' Gundersen replied, squeezing Jasmin's shoulder. 'You'll see your son again.'

With that, the vet nodded to her and left the room. Jasmin remained sitting by Bonnie's side, stroking her. She didn't look up when Henriksen came back in; instead, she watched his sturdy boots move over the floorboards and disappear towards the hallway.

A few minutes later, she heard a rattle at the cellar door.

Jasmin leapt to her feet.

Henriksen had already removed the topmost board.

'What are you doing?'

'I'm wondering who might have put up these boards,' he replied, as if he'd been expecting her reaction. 'It looks to me like it was done in a hurry. An emergency measure.'

'I didn't want any rats or anything to come up from downstairs. One of the windows down there doesn't close properly. Bonnie would have got skittish if she'd smelled any animals creeping into the cellar or crawling up here through some little gap.'

'So you found something down there?'

'I don't know,' answered Jasmin evasively. 'I've only been in the cellar once since we got back.'

Henriksen looked at her with a strange expression. 'Would you mind me taking a look for myself?'

Jasmin shrugged. 'Feel free. There's nothing worth seeing down there. The boiler, the gas heating. And our old hunting gun.'

'Were you planning to use it?'

Only in my dream. 'Maybe,' she answered truthfully. 'I don't like guns. But out here, on my own with just a dog and a child, I found it reassuring. After the drifter reappeared, I wanted to go and fetch it, but then I noticed Paul was gone and . . .' Her voice broke; she couldn't say anything more. Henriksen fetched a heavy screwdriver and prised the wooden boards out of the wall one by one until the door could be opened once again. The stairwell was dark; the odour of mould and decay that wafted up towards them was stronger now than before.

A spider skittered away into the darkness as Henriksen pointed his torch at the wooden steps. The sound of falling rain seemed to be emanating from the very walls. *There's something inside them*, Jasmin thought, although she knew how insane it was. *Something is living in these walls, and at night, when everything falls quiet and the only thing you can hear is your own heart beating, it makes rustling, scuttling noises.*

Something is living here.

Something very old.

And it isn't happy that you've disturbed it.

Henriksen descended the first few steps before turning back to look up at her, as if he'd realised she wasn't following him. 'Are you coming with me, Ms Hansen?' His voice sounded dull, as if the darkness was absorbing it and on the verge of swallowing it altogether.

'I'd prefer to wait up here,' she replied.

'Are you afraid?'

Afraid. The way he pronounced the word irritated her. *Afraid? You aren't afraid. Whatever's going on here, there must be a rational explanation for it.* This new voice reminded her of Jørgen. She realised she hadn't called him yet to tell him about Paul's disappearance.

'Of course not,' she said, trying to sound as tough and nonchalant as she could. 'Lead the way.'

Together, they descended the staircase until Jasmin and the inspector found themselves looking at the boiler. The gas burner ignited with a quiet rumble before they could take a step towards it. Jasmin noticed Henriksen give a start.

'It's only the heating,' she said quietly. 'Nothing out of the ordinary.'

Henriksen took a long look at the red rowboat before turning to the gun cabinet. The door squeaked softly. He reached for the shotgun and took it out. 'You do know cabinets like this one should always be kept locked?'

'Yes. But I knew Paul wouldn't come down here. Not with the door nailed up – though he wouldn't even if I left it open. He was a good boy, he always did as he was told.'

'Was?' asked Henriksen sharply.

'Is,' Jasmin corrected herself. The thought that her subconscious was already strangely preparing itself for the possibility that she might have to talk about Paul in the past tense made her shudder. 'Slip of the tongue. As for the gun cabinet,' she sighed. 'I'm sorry. I was a little distracted when we got here.'

Henriksen didn't put the gun back. He pointed towards the door at the end of the cellar, which stood slightly ajar. 'And what's through there?'

'An old storage room full of all kinds of junk. Jørgen wanted to renovate the whole cellar, but—'

'Jørgen? Your husband?'

Jasmin nodded. 'That's right. But something got in the way of our plans.'

'Something bad?'

'I don't think that's relevant, is it?'

'Not yet, it isn't,' said Henriksen. 'But I think we'll need to talk in more detail over the next few hours, Ms Hansen.'

'I can't think what about. Besides, I don't have time for anything like that right now.'

'You will, though.'

'Excuse me?'

'I've just told you that you can come with us and help. We can continue the conversation then.'

Jasmin didn't reply and watched as Henriksen reached for the handle of the door at the end of the dark, musty cellar. It creaked quietly as he pushed it open. He cast his eyes slowly across the room before turning back to her and shutting the door behind him.

'Just an old storage room, like you said.'

'A man died down there,' Jasmin explained as they climbed the stairs back up to the house. Henriksen was still carrying the gun. 'He hanged himself from one of the beams because he couldn't go on.'

'The previous owner?'

'The one before that,' Jasmin corrected him. 'The seller told us the story, otherwise we'd never have heard about it. It's creepy, but at the end of the day it's only a memory. A tragic memory. An old man who killed himself after losing his wife and son at sea.'

'A *lasting* memory.' Henriksen closed the cellar door behind them. 'That's how it is with these old houses. Something always gets left behind. *Always.*'

Chapter 4

'He doesn't have his coat with him,' said Jasmin sadly. She and Henriksen had gone back into Paul's room. 'He'll catch his death of cold. The temperatures last night – we *have* to find him.'

'What do we have?' Henriksen asked Boeckermann. The island constable was standing by the broken window and looking out into the sodden garden. The wind carried the sound of the breaking waves up to them and blew fine, salty mist into their faces. The glass that framed their view out into the cold, hostile world was sharp and jagged-edged, like a wound. Jasmin wrapped her arms around her body – she felt so cold, so horribly cold, as if the icy Norwegian Sea itself had soaked deep into her bones.

Something had changed the moment Paul went missing.

The people here, Sandvik's voice echoed through her mind, *are hard. You can't survive in a place like this if you aren't hard. If you don't have the cold Norwegian Sea flowing through your veins.*

'Not much,' Boeckermann replied. Before he turned to face Henriksen, Jasmin noticed him give her a thoughtful look, as if to say he didn't think it was very wise to speak openly in front of the victim's mother. *Do they think you might be behind all this?* Jasmin wasn't sure if she found the idea ridiculous or if it made her furious instead.

'Are there any footprints? Whoever did this, he must have climbed out of the window onto the veranda roof and jumped down from there into the garden with Paul in his arms. The extra weight would have driven his shoes deeper into the muddy ground.' Jasmin looked from Boeckermann to Henriksen. 'There must be footprints. I'm right, aren't I?'

Henriksen nodded. 'You have good instincts, Ms Hansen.'

'We found two footprints,' Boeckermann confirmed. 'The rain has largely washed away the pattern of the treads, but the measurements and photos the forensic team managed to take are better than nothing, I think.'

Better than nothing? Jasmin snorted.

'It looks like it was a man to me, and based on the depth of the footprints . . .' Boeckermann glanced across at her, but only for the briefest of moments, as if he was afraid of making eye contact with her for longer than a fraction of a second. 'I reckon he weighed about two hundred pounds, factoring in the boy.'

'Great. So pretty much every man on the island is a suspect, right?' Jasmin shook her head. 'That gets us nowhere.'

Henriksen gave a brief laugh that instantly died away when he saw Boeckermann's sharp look. The floorboards creaked behind them.

'Hendrik?' It was one of the policemen who had arrived with the detective inspector on the ferry. 'We've found a few footprints with traces of sand in them leading from the beach up to the house. Smaller ones.'

'Those are mine,' said Jasmin instantly. 'I was down on the beach.'

You have to tell him, urged an inner voice, one that sounded considered and rational. *You have to tell him you found the body. That you lied to him.*

146

'That's not all,' the officer continued, before leaning closer to Henriksen and whispering in his ear.

Henriksen raised his eyebrows. 'Really? Well, that is a surprise.' He looked at Jasmin with an astonished expression that she couldn't quite place. *What did the man just say?*

'So what do we do now?' she asked. 'And I don't mean putting up posters or making an appeal on the radio, as it won't be any use. Not if the islanders are working against us. If there are people out there with something to hide—'

'We're going to keep looking for evidence,' Henriksen answered evasively. 'But I've just learned of another incident last night. There's been a break-in, and the body from the beach has been stolen.'

Jasmin was thunderstruck – she couldn't have been more surprised if Henriksen had announced to her that they were calling off the search for Paul right then and there.

You saw him. And when you left the freezer, he was still lying exactly where you found him.

Somebody was there after you.

She felt hot and cold at the same time. Sweat beaded on her brow. *Why is Henriksen telling you this? Does he know more than he's letting on? Is he gauging how you react? And if he is, did you fail the test?*

'Is everything OK, Ms Hansen?'

She swallowed to dispel the unpleasant sensation in her throat – a dryness, as though her vocal cords were wrapped in sandpaper. *You were there, and now the body is gone. And after all that's happened, there's a pretty good chance they're going to blame you for it.*

You've landed squarely in the trap.

Jasmin cursed silently, furious with herself.

'I'm just surprised something like that could happen.'

'I think we all are,' said Boeckermann, shooting her a penetrating look. She noticed his hand wandering towards his belt, where he kept his handcuffs, and she could almost see in his eyes what he was thinking.

He doesn't trust you.

He knows something.

Or maybe he knows everything.

'I'll go and take a look. Everyone else stay here.' Henriksen went to the door and Jasmin followed him with trembling knees and a pounding heart, unsure what to do next.

The historian who lives on the island. You should talk to him.

'What are you planning?' asked Henriksen. 'Are you going to look for Paul on your own?'

'With all this rain . . .' Jasmin shook her head. 'As much as I feel an urge to run outside and scream his name, to search the area, it would be pointless. If he was still near the house then you'd have found him by now. He isn't hiding – he's been taken away from me, and the kidnapper won't be keeping him anywhere nearby.'

Henriksen took a step towards her. 'And you're positive you don't know anything – anything at all – that might help us in our enquiries?'

'No,' Jasmin lied, surprised at how easy she found it by now. 'Nothing.'

'That's a pity,' Henriksen replied. 'I hope you won't disappoint me.' With those words, he went out to his car and drove off without looking back.

Chapter 5

The rain grew more intense by the second as she drove along the country road. Vast quantities of water were pouring down onto the woods and the narrow grey strip of asphalt winding through them. The wipers were working at maximum speed but still failed to make any headway against the deluge. Jasmin was heading west, her satnav directing her towards Larsen's house. She'd found the address online.

'He *never* accepts any visitors.' That was the warning she'd been given by Mattila, the odd little bookseller. *We'll see about that.*

The radio was playing a song by a local band. 'And things are really going to liven up this weekend when the boys and girls come to play in Skårsteinen,' said the presenter afterwards. Jasmin spotted a poster on the side of the road. The wind and the rain hadn't been kind to it – the paper was badly frayed around the edges.

Would the concert still go ahead once the news got out about her son's disappearance? The man on the radio didn't seem to have heard about it. What would happen when he did? Should she ask him to make an on-air announcement urging his listeners to look out for Paul?

The car passed over a dip in the road where a deep puddle had formed and started to skid. *Aquaplaning*, thought Jasmin, gripping the wheel. *The tyres on this rental car might not be in the best shape.*

Jasmin was so lost in thought, she'd hardly noticed the speedometer creeping over sixty.

You're driving far too fast. In this weather, that's dangerous.

Lethal.

A bright flash in front of her eyes, like the headlights of a Jeep on a cold night. A smell of burning penetrated her nostrils, making her gag.

For the tiniest fraction of a second she was there again, back on the rain-slicked road that night. The piercing eyes of the homeless man – his scream as she ran him down.

Jasmin's hands were shaking. She gripped the steering wheel so hard that the skin over her knuckles turned white.

The screech made by her shock absorbers as her car rolled over the man's body had branded itself into her soul forever. But that burning smell – she hadn't noticed it last time. What did it mean?

Whatever it was, it couldn't be good.

The road grew narrower and after a few hundred yards, a side road appeared on her left – barely more than a muddy track, but her satnav told her to take it. The pine trees loomed up into the grey sky and swayed back and forth in the wind. Small branches on the road snapped and cracked under her wheels.

'Well, this is just great.'

Jasmin slowed down and turned onto the side road, holding the steering wheel steady as the trees surrounding her reared up ever higher towards the dark rainclouds. It felt as though the shadows cast by the dense forest were creeping into the car. Jasmin turned her headlights on. Rugged rock formations towered around her: mossy crags that had been weathered by the rough sea wind. Banks of fog hovered between the trees. Everything was drenched and dripping with water.

A small house with a gabled roof came into view, along with a grey fence and a gate flanked by two massive pillars with fire bowls burning on top of them. Despite the heavy rain, they were giving off gouts of flame and casting thick clouds of smoke into the air. The sight of those blazing columns made Jasmin think of a beacon, but they also called to mind a certain aesthetic from a dark era in history when people marched in processions past fire bowls like these.

'You stay here, OK?' she said to Bonnie. Her dog had curled up on the passenger seat and was making it very clear she didn't want to brave the rain. 'I won't be long.'

Jasmin got out and pulled her hood up. The rain pattered sharply against her head and shoulders. The freshly mown grass strewn over the drive was now soaked with water and threatened to swallow her shoes up as she walked over it.

She walked through the open gate, past the fire bowls, which popped and crackled. Whatever was burning in there, the rain seemed to have no effect on it. The grey granite gateposts resembled columns flanking the entrance to a pagan temple, while the fire bowls were made of dark stone which looked as smooth as marble.

A cold shiver that had nothing to do with the rain or the chill ran down Jasmin's back. This place seemed so strange, so unnatural, as if it belonged to another time.

This is all so crazy.

Are you sure you really want to talk to this man?

You have to.

There must be a connection with what happened back then.

At the solid oak front door, Jasmin reached up and beat the bronze knocker, which was shaped like a hammer – Thor's hammer. A dog started barking inside the house. It was loud, deep and threatening.

Bonnie would have instantly barked back, had she been at Jasmin's side. She heard footsteps, saw a silhouette moving around behind the frosted glass window next to the doorframe.

'Who's there?' said a gruff, muffled voice through the door. 'Make yourself scarce.'

'Mr Larsen, my name is Jasmin Hansen. I'd like to—'

'I couldn't care less who you are. Get lost. I don't talk to visitors, and especially not to nosy reporters.'

'That's not why I'm here.' Jasmin struggled to make her voice sound calm, yet resolute. 'I'm here because my five-year-old son has been kidnapped. It happened a few hours ago. I know there's been a cover-up on the island. I also know you have information about it, and that you're afraid of something – whatever that might be. But I'm not one of them. The *others*, I mean. I'm new here.'

For a few moments, everything in the house fell silent. Then a chain rattled and the door opened a crack. Jasmin found herself looking at a locked security chain, at a short man in a woollen jumper with thin blond hair and a pipe in his mouth from which a puff of smoke was drifting upwards – and also down the barrel of a shotgun.

'What the—? You're insane!' Jasmin took a step back. 'You can't—!'

'I *can*, if you choose to enter my property without permission.' Now that she was face to face with him, the man's voice sounded like the dry, smoky crackle of a log on a fireplace. 'I can call the police any time I want.'

'So why don't you?' Jasmin had curled her hands into fists. *If you let him scare you then you might as well turn around and leave right now.*

'Because what you just said wasn't altogether untrue,' the man replied. 'Who are you? Jasmin Hansen, what kind of name is that? What are you doing here?'

'I read your book.' Larsen was staring at her with such suspicion that Jasmin cursed herself for not having brought it with her.

'I'm trying to find out what happened here. You wrote a book about the history of the island, and I stumbled across it and bought it, only to find that you have as little to say about the fire as everyone else I've asked so far.'

Larsen didn't move, though the curls of smoke continued to emerge from his pipe. 'So you've read my book. You and several thousand others.'

'I met Gabriela Yrsen. The marks left on her body by the fire were unmistakable. Somebody out there thinks I'm getting too close. They threatened me, and as if that wasn't enough, they kidnapped my son.'

'That sounds like a rather fanciful story.'

'It's true. All of it happened, I swear. Please, help me.'

'The kidnapping isn't necessarily connected to everything else.' The barrel of the shotgun dipped slightly and Jasmin was relieved to see his reaction. *He trusts you a little more*, she thought. *You're on the right track.*

'Not necessarily,' she answered, 'except for one clear link. The kidnapper left something behind. A reference to the thing I'm looking for.'

'Shit,' she heard Larsen mutter. He reached up and undid the security chain. 'I hope you like dogs. They're my only friends out here.'

'Absolutely – I have a Labrador myself.'

'Good. That's good.' A fleeting smile passed over his wrinkled face. 'Animal lovers are very welcome with me. Come on in, if you like.'

He moved to one side, clearing the way for her, and Jasmin stepped through the door. The interior was furnished in dark wood, with panelling on the walls and art nouveau cabinets from the nineteen thirties.

'Do you like my ornaments?' He gestured briskly at a space on the wall between two cupboards where a large number of medals were hanging.

Military medals.

But it wasn't possible – he wasn't old enough. He must be a collector.

'They aren't what I was expecting.'

'A little hobby of mine,' he said. His eyebrows contracted, almost meeting in the middle. 'It's not a crime, Ms Hansen.'

He led her into a small, overheated room that evidently served as both an office and a lounge. At the back it led into a conservatory where several broad-leaved plants stood in large pots. Music was playing softly in the background, and in the back of her mind, Jasmin identified it as Wagner. Larsen's desk was covered with folders, books and newspapers. It looked as though he was searching for something he hadn't managed to find yet.

'The islanders have always been experts at keeping secrets. They store them up, guard them carefully. That much is immediately obvious to us outsiders, but few people manage to get to the bottom of it.'

'Did you manage?'

'Maybe. What do you want to know?'

Jasmin didn't take her eyes off Larsen for a second. 'What went on back then? What's the deal with the fire and the sanatorium? What happened exactly? And why does nobody talk about it?'

'A terrible crime was committed here,' said Larsen, and as he spoke, puffs of smoke escaped from his lips and his pipe and drifted towards the ceiling. 'A sin against human nature.'

'And that means?'

'Death! It means nothing less than death, Ms Hansen. There was a sanatorium, there were patients. Then there was the incident.

That's all.' Larsen removed his pipe from his mouth and pointed at the window. The rain was hammering against the glass and Jasmin felt very glad to be inside, although the room was uncomfortably warm. 'A man from the institution attacked a teenage girl, raped her and killed her. And the islanders took their revenge.'

'Revenge?' Jasmin shuddered at the word. 'They turned vigilante and lynched the patients, you mean.'

'Indeed they did. Men from the village – the victim's father, her brother, her friends. But the interesting thing, Ms Hansen, is that they didn't care about the consequences. All the collateral damage, all the pain. All those innocent people who had to suffer.'

'What did they do?' Jasmin asked, though she felt sure she already knew the answer.

'They started a fire. They *killed* people. The murderer, yes, but many others too.'

Another flash appeared before her eyes. Jasmin felt her knees grow weak; she tottered on her feet, grasping at the walls for support. *A fire*, she thought. *A fire in an institution.*

'What's the matter, Ms Hansen? Don't you understand? They killed indiscriminately, heedless of the deaths of innocent victims, simply to have their revenge – and they all knew what they were doing! There never were any teenagers acting on a dare. The islanders set the sanatorium alight and burned it to the ground, along with everyone inside it.'

'But there's no way they could have kept an act like that secret for all these years.' Jasmin could hear how hoarse her voice had grown. The heat in this confined room was suddenly unbearable. 'The police—'

'The police,' Larsen repeated scornfully, shaking his head. 'The police looked the other way, like they always did. Like they still do today. That's why you aren't going to find your son. Not like this.'

'Excuse me? You can't possibly mean that.'

'I always mean everything I say. If I don't mean it, I don't say it.' Larsen took a step towards her and for a moment, Jasmin wondered if she'd made a mistake by coming here on her own. For a moment, she was afraid he was about to grab hold of her. 'You should take care, Ms Hansen. These people aren't to be trifled with. They'll do anything to keep their secrets.'

'You mean there's more?'

Larsen laughed – a malicious, gloating laugh that bubbled up from the depths of his throat. 'So much more, Jasmin Hansen. So much more.'

'Seven, not two,' she said. As she spoke, she took a step towards Larsen, prompting the historian to move backwards in turn. 'What does that mean?'

'I don't know what you're talking about.'

'I think you do.' Jasmin stared at him, searching for signs that he was lying. 'I've read your book, like I told you. And I know you personally delivered it to the bookshop over in Skårsteinen. I found a note inside it yesterday and I'm sure the handwriting is yours. *Seven, not two.* What does it mean?'

Larsen merely laughed, blowing smoke into the air. 'Was that all you found?'

A triangle. A paper sculpture of a triangle. She decided to tell him. Larsen walked over to the far wall and took a folder down from an oak dresser that reached almost up to the ceiling. He blew away the dust that had gathered on it.

'A sign like this one here?' He held a photo up in front of her. 'This was taken inside the sanatorium. Back before it burned down.'

Jasmin stared at the picture. It showed a man in white clothing sitting at a table with his back to the photographer, and on the table in front of him lay a handful of origami sculptures that he'd made.

Jasmin could scarcely believe her eyes when she saw one of them was a triangle with an opening at one corner. The man had placed it between the other figures – a deer and a swan spreading its wings.

'That symbol – I need to know what it means,' said Jasmin urgently. She felt droplets of sweat trickling between her shoulder blades. *Jesus, why is it so hot in here? And why are you reacting like this? Something doesn't add up – something about this place is so wrong, so screwed up, but you can't quite put your finger on it.* 'What about Gabriela Yrsen? Was she there? Was she a patient at the sanatorium? Was that why she barely survived the fire? Why did she never tell anyone what really happened?'

'Yrsen?' Larsen laughed again. The smoke rising from his pipe drifted silently towards the ceiling. His tobacco smelled like dried herbs and the inside of a whiskey barrel. 'Tell me, Ms Hansen, doesn't all this strike you as a little too *convenient*? A woman with burns on her face? A dead body on the beach? Seven, not two? And you, right in the middle of it all? The old sanatorium, the fire – doesn't it *remind* you of anything?' He gestured to a shelf on the wall that held a bottle of spirits and a few glasses. 'Would you like a drink?'

Jasmin stared at him. 'What – what do you mean? What's supposed to be convenient about all this? What exactly should it remind me of?' Once again, a bright flash appeared before her eyes, like a line of fluorescent lights mounted on a bare ceiling, racing over her head. Was this the hospital they'd taken her to after her accident? That smell hanging in the air – it reminded Jasmin of petrol and fire.

She rubbed her fingers over her palm, and for a hideous moment, it felt as though they were sticking to her skin. She forced herself to keep breathing and brushed her hair away from her face. 'I don't know what you're talking about,' she replied, once she'd composed herself slightly. 'But I'm not going to let anyone pull the wool over my eyes. Either you tell me everything you know right now, or I'll find it out on my own.'

'Oh, you will, Ms Hansen. I truly hope you will.' Larsen pointed to the north. 'The victims were all buried in absolute secrecy. But the graves still exist.'

'Where?'

'I can't really explain it to you. But I can show you.' Larsen rummaged around on his cluttered desk in search of a map of the island and eventually produced one from underneath a pile of thick, leather-bound books. He picked up a biro and drew a circle around the spot on the map. It was in the north, not far from Yrsen's house.

'And what will I find there?'

Wordlessly, he pressed the map into her hand – but now that he was close to her, he also leaned forward towards her ear. A shudder ran down Jasmin's back as she smelled his breath, which stank of alcohol and tobacco.

'You need to be careful,' Larsen warned her in a barely audible whisper. 'They're going to test you. The whole time. This might be your last chance.'

Jasmin recoiled. Her heart was pounding. 'I don't understand—'

'None of this is what you think it is. But I feel confident you'll pass the test. Oh yes, I'm sure you will.'

'Who are you?' Jasmin almost screamed. She staggered backwards, bumping into a bookshelf, and a few folders tumbled to the floor. Swastikas gleamed in the flickering light of the fireplace. 'You're insane. It's true, isn't it? You're playing with me – you're taking pleasure in tormenting me.' She kicked one of the folders across the floor. 'All this disgusting memorabilia – you make me sick. Fuck you!'

Through the window, Jasmin saw a car pulling up in front of the house. It was Henriksen's. *What is he doing here? How did he find me?*

'Ms Hansen!' Larsen called after her. 'You have to stay on the right path, do you hear me?'

'Leave me alone!'

She ran to the door and hurled it open, nearly colliding with Henriksen. 'Ms Hansen,' he said in a quiet, sonorous voice. 'I thought I might find you here.'

'Oh, how nice!' she yelled sarcastically. Pushing past him, she sprinted through the driving rain towards her car. Bonnie looked up as she got in and turned the key in the ignition. The engine screeched in protest, the starter howled, yet the car refused to start.

'You fucking piece of shit!'

She stared out into the torrential rain. Then she put Bonnie on the lead and got back out of the car.

'You need to take me with you,' she yelled at Henriksen. 'Before we both get washed away!'

CHAPTER 6

'How did you find me?'

Jasmin peered out into the rain as Henriksen drove. Bonnie was curled up on the back seat. If the inspector was annoyed that her dog had left wet pawprints on the upholstery, he didn't show it.

'It was easy,' Henriksen answered. 'I found your book. The one about the history of the island. I'd heard the author lived here on Minsøy so I assumed your next step would be to pay him a visit.'

'You think too much,' Jasmin retorted, and felt surprised at her own audacity. 'That isn't always a good thing. Why did you even bother looking for me?' She glanced over her shoulder at the road behind them. Nobody was following, but she wanted to be sure. 'You know, Larsen says the islanders burned down a sanatorium some years ago. An act of revenge. They let innocent people die and hushed everything up. Apparently there's an old graveyard hidden in the north of the island.'

'Do you believe him?' Henriksen was concentrating fully on the road, but Jasmin knew he was listening carefully – that not a word escaped him.

'He's an old Nazi,' she replied. 'His house is full of medals and all kinds of German army junk, and I don't even want to know what he's got in his cellar.'

'Is that so?' Henriksen raised an eyebrow, which arched over his high forehead in a fine black line.

'But whoever he is and whatever he's collecting, I think he was telling the truth. Something happened here and certain people want to cover it up. We should look for the graveyard. And if you don't want to help me – well, I'll have to do it on my own. Just like everything else.'

'You're a strong, independent woman, there's no doubt about it. But I'll come with you.'

Jasmin thought of Jørgen and the panic she'd felt when she'd had to go down into the cellar again, after all that time. How her instincts had told her to grab Paul and Bonnie and flee.

But that's not what you did in the end. You stayed and set about shedding light on the darkness. You're brave enough to get through all this. She took the map out of her coat pocket and showed Henriksen the circle that the old historian had drawn on it. 'It should be a few hundred yards down this road,' she said. 'Then left.'

Henriksen muttered something she didn't understand, but he steered the car in the direction she wanted. The noise of the tyres on the asphalt mingled with the drumming of the rain on the roof had a soothing effect on Jasmin. It had an even rhythm that made her feel drowsy. *The few hours' sleep you had on the sofa last night weren't enough; you feel weary deep in your bones. If you really want to see this through, you need to make sure you stay fit and get enough sleep.*

'Did you call him?' Henriksen asked after a while. 'Your husband?'

The words took a while to penetrate the fog in her brain. 'No. I forgot.' Jasmin fumbled through her coat pocket for her phone. There were over thirty missed calls. She felt the blood rise to her cheeks. 'What with all the excitement . . .'

'It's perfectly understandable.' Yet the look Henriksen gave her told a different story. It was searching, maybe even distrustful.

Because he thinks you're a suspect?

Just then, her phone rang again. She answered straight away. Jørgen was beside himself with worry, and when she told him about Paul's disappearance, he fell silent for a long while, as if his pain and fear had rendered him speechless.

When he finally spoke, his voice sounded old and brittle. 'Paul? You say he's . . . ?'

'He's disappeared.' At that moment, she despised him for his weakness. 'You aren't here, so don't start making accusations. I couldn't have done anything to stop it.'

'I'm not accusing you of anything,' Jørgen replied gently. 'Jasmin, are you sure he isn't—'

'Hiding somewhere and treating the whole thing like one big game? Yes, I'm sure. He would never do that, and you know it.'

Jørgen made a noise that sounded like desperation. 'What are you going to do now?'

'I'm going to find him. Along with the people who kidnapped him. The police are here, so I'm not on my own.'

'The police?' Jørgen's voice had an undertone of incredulity, but Jasmin ignored it. *He didn't think you were capable of that. He thought you'd bury your face in your hands and hide.*

Like you used to.

'Maybe you should ask him if he wants to join you out here,' Henriksen interjected. 'It might be good for your emotional stability.'

'Was that one of the police officers?'

'Hendrik Henriksen,' Jasmin replied. 'He's leading the investigation.'

'You mean . . .' Another pause. Then: 'Wait, the investigation? But Paul isn't—'

Dear God, no. And you shouldn't even think about it either.

'That's not all that's happened. There are strange things going on out here – mysterious things connected with Paul's disappearance. Someone is hiding the truth.'

'You mean, Paul was kidnapped because you—'

'Maybe.' Jasmin looked out into the pouring rain, the rising fog, the tall grass on the side of the road that swayed back and forth in hypnotic waves under the wind. 'Maybe we should never have come here. But maybe it was also fate. Maybe I had to come to this place to finally put an end to it all. To finally understand—'

A burst of static came down the line and Jørgen was gone. Jasmin was out of signal range. Henriksen shot her a sharp glance. 'To finally understand what, Ms Hansen? Is there something you want to tell me?'

Jasmin shook her head. Her thick, blonde plait bounced from side to side. 'No. I was going to say that I might finally understand the meaning of that terrible night, but it's all too crazy. None of it makes any sense.'

'Perhaps you should fill me in on what happened.' Henriksen turned the car onto the side road and followed it until the satnav told them they'd reached their destination. A birch forest. The wind rustled through the branches and leaves on the trees, making a sound like that of the waves on the shore.

Everything here sounds like the sea, thought Jasmin. *Except for the sea itself, which sounds like icy chill. Like death.*

'Fill you in?' The words tasted like bitter medicine on her lips. But of course Henriksen assumed she was talking about Paul's abduction when she spoke of 'that terrible night'. He didn't know anything about her past. 'There's nothing I haven't told you already.'

'Nothing, Ms Hansen? Are you sure?'

She looked away as she replied. 'Yes. I'm sure.'

Chapter 7

They got out of the car. Jasmin put the dog on the lead and Bonnie sniffed inquisitively at the grass and undergrowth as if nothing had happened. Henriksen opened a large umbrella that offered them some protection from the rain and the droplets rattled on the dark fabric in an even, clockwork staccato.

A weathered wooden sign with a scarcely decipherable inscription stood forlornly on the side of the path, overgrown with dense, spiky vegetation. 'Are we in the right place?' Jasmin asked. Her words were drowned out by the rain and it felt like the day was growing colder with every step she took, as the water seeped through to her skin in spite of her winter coat and Henriksen's umbrella.

Jasmin sneezed. Bonnie looked up at her and wagged her tail before turning back to the grass, where she'd found an enticing trail that led deeper into the undergrowth. 'This must be the place, assuming Larsen wasn't talking rubbish,' said Jasmin in an effort to pluck up her courage. 'It must be here somewhere.' She tried to keep walking but Bonnie was tugging at the lead again.

'I think she's picked up a scent,' Jasmin explained. 'Maybe someone else was here recently. She wouldn't be acting like this otherwise.'

'Someone else was here? Bonnie can smell that in this weather?'

'Maybe they knew I'd be coming here. Maybe they're watching my movements. And yes, she can.'

Henriksen glanced at her briefly and a grin played over his lips. 'Why do you think they would be watching you so soon after the abduction? Given how recently it happened, wouldn't it make more sense for the kidnapper to lie low and wait until it's safe to break cover again? And then make contact with you afterwards – perhaps to demand a ransom?'

'Perhaps. I don't know what goes on inside the minds of people like that.' Jasmin pushed aside a low-hanging branch from which raindrops hung like tiny crystals. The autumn leaves covering the ground had dissolved into a damp, slippery mass that smelled of mould and putrefaction, of tree sap and the sea. 'The graveyard must be here. Larsen might be crazy, but he wasn't wrong about—'

Jasmin fell silent.

'What's the matter?' Henriksen produced a small torch and shone it into the undergrowth. He looked around helplessly, as if he regretted getting out of the car in this weather. 'You've spotted something, haven't you?'

Jasmin scratched at the path with her shoe. Here, under their feet, the ground wasn't a wet, muddy mixture of soil and leaves. They were standing on something firmer.

A stone slab, which Jasmin now unearthed.

'Look here. Granite. This footpath is laid out with paving stones.' Jasmin took a step forwards and pushed more soil and foliage to one side. 'They lead this way – there are more slabs over here.'

'So there are.'

Jasmin quickened her pace. The stones ran in a straight line, and they could still make out traces of human activity here and there where people had hacked back the trees and the vegetation in an effort to keep nature in check. That must have been many years ago now, however, as the forest had reached out to reclaim this spot once more.

Henriksen pulled Jasmin to a halt and pointed up the path. Here, beneath the branches of the birches and pines and beech trees, the rain was lighter. Bonnie looked up at them, as if to ask why they'd stopped.

'Do you see that? It's an archway.'

'And what used to be a gate.' Jasmin walked over to it and put her hand on the stone, which was damp and covered in moss. It felt like a furry hide under her fingers. The iron rods that had once barred the way were now barely more than a rusted outline. 'It's a graveyard. Out here in the forest, in the middle of nowhere.'

The three of them passed under the arch together. Jasmin spotted the gravestones, which were also covered in moss and dense vegetation. Many of them were crooked or had fallen over completely. This was a place that hadn't been visited for a long time – a place that had been deliberately forgotten and abandoned to the wilderness.

Bonnie growled. She pulled at the lead again, almost knocking Jasmin off balance; the lichen-covered paving slabs were slippery and treacherous.

The dog barked in the direction of a large grey gravestone that reared up out of the dark soil like a huge shard of bone. It was easily big enough for a person to hide behind.

Maybe this place wasn't as abandoned as she'd thought.

Henriksen's hand went to his gun. He put his finger on his lips and gestured for her to stay back.

Then he started to approach the gravestone. Bonnie continued growling and tugging at the lead.

'Show yourself, right now! We know you're there!' Henriksen drew his gun from the leather holster he wore on his belt in what

Jasmin felt was a surprisingly slow and clumsy movement. He pointed it at the gravestone, inching forwards all the while.

'Show yourself! I'm not going to say it again!'

Suddenly, something leapt out from behind the gravestone. Jasmin caught a glimpse of a dark shadow on four legs that scurried into the undergrowth at lightning speed.

A dog?

Bonnie barked one last time and fell silent.

'Just a stray dog,' said Henriksen, though he didn't sound entirely convinced.

Jasmin cleared the leaves and moss from a nearby gravestone. The rough granite felt like sandpaper under her clammy fingers.

'This place – is this really where the people who died in the fire at the sanatorium were buried? But then why are there names on the gravestones? Why create a special graveyard for them if the idea was to sweep all this under the carpet?'

Henriksen was too far away to hear her, so these words were only for the wind – and maybe for Bonnie too, though she didn't seem to take much interest in them. Jasmin watched the inspector pace up and down among the gravestones at the other end of the cemetery, shining his torch on the eroded inscriptions.

This place brought her out in gooseflesh, and not just because it was a graveyard and the people buried here might have died a terrible death. Something about it wasn't right – something felt so wrong that it made the hairs on her arms stand on end.

Had Larsen tricked her? Had he sent her here, far from any other settlement on the island, to get her out of the way? Was he in cahoots with the others?

Christensen, she thought, running her index finger over the letters chiselled into the stone. *Who were you?*

She walked over to Henriksen, who was squatting in front of a fallen gravestone and clearing the moss away with his gloved hand.

'There are forty-five graves here.' Henriksen wiped the rain-water from his face. His expression was serious. 'Forty-five, Ms Hansen.'

A flash before her eyes. Jasmin clung on to a nearby gravestone in an effort to stay upright. She raised her hand to her face and felt a warm liquid dripping over her top lip. Blood was trickling from her nose. She wiped it away vigorously, but she still couldn't shake off the burning smell or the echo of screeching tyres from that fateful night.

'Forty-five victims we were supposed to forget,' she said quietly, her words washed away by the rain. 'And we won't find any mention of this place in any official documentation. I'm certain of it.'

'I doubt that's true. We'll look into it.'

'We?' Jasmin asked. 'Since when is there a *we*? I thought you were investigating all possible leads.'

'What do you mean?' Henriksen rose to his feet, giving a quiet sigh as he braced his hand against his lower back. Jasmin stared at him. She'd seen this man before, she realised.

She'd seen Henriksen somewhere before. His gesture felt so familiar to her – for a brief moment she felt it jogging her memory.

But you can't remember where.

Henriksen gave her a penetrating look, as if he'd realised what was going through her mind.

'It means,' she replied, 'that you think I might be involved. Because that's how it always goes. You have to consider every eventuality. And you think it's odd that I came to this island on my own, with just my son and my dog, and that I didn't want my husband with me. Maybe you even think Paul's kidnapping was cleverly staged.'

Henriksen hesitated before he replied, but when he spoke, his voice was cool and professional. 'You're quite right. I'm not ruling anybody out. There are still too many variables in this case. Too much is still unclear.'

'The body on the beach. The missing corpse.'

'Precisely. That might indicate the culprit isn't acting alone.'

'Maybe. In any case, I'm glad you're going about your work so professionally.' Jasmin walked over to the next grave. 'You know what? We should take photos of all these headstones. It should be possible to compare the names with the patient records from the sanatorium, assuming they weren't all destroyed in the fire.'

'Good idea.' Henriksen reached for his phone, but it slipped out of his hand and landed in the mud.

Jasmin picked it up and handed it to him. 'Here you go, Inspector,' she said with a smile.

There was a symbol engraved on the back of the device. Jasmin caught only the briefest of glimpses before Henriksen took it from her.

It was the inverted triangle with the open top-right corner.

Why did Henriksen have that symbol on his phone? She'd seen it before, either on the night of her accident or at some point afterwards – she wasn't sure which. But she'd also seen it prior to the accident, somewhere on Minsøy.

She knew that because Jørgen had been with her when she'd seen it.

You already know this man. That gesture, the way he carries himself – and now the symbol too. Where do you know him from?

'Ms Hansen?'

She shook her head – shook off these thoughts and her sense of déjà vu. 'Sorry. I imagine it's tricky to investigate cases like this one – when people are kidnapped while their relatives are nearby.'

'Every kidnapping is a shocking event. But everyone reacts differently.'

'What about me? How am I doing?'

Henriksen wiped his phone down and put it in his trouser pocket. 'You're coping better than most. You can't bear to do nothing. That means there's a chance you might get in our way and maybe even harm the investigation, but I have to admit, I wouldn't have found my way here if you hadn't got Larsen to tell you about the graveyard.'

'I just want him back.' Jasmin felt the rain running down her face like teardrops. 'If only I could hold Paul in my arms again . . .'

'It's OK, Ms Hansen.' Henriksen took a step towards her and gently touched her arm. Jasmin clung on to him as she felt her legs start to tremble.

You've tried to suppress it. You wanted to keep reality at arm's length, but Paul has disappeared. Paul has been kidnapped, and you're doing all you can to distract yourself, but you're slowly starting to realise it's no use.

'I don't want anything to happen to him,' she whispered in desperation. 'I don't want him to—'

'Ms Hansen, we're going to do everything in our power to get him back.'

'But what if it's out of our hands? What if we fail? What if we try everything, but in the end – in the end all we can do is stand back and watch it happen?' Tears were now flowing down her cheeks – tears she'd been trying to hold back all this time, but which she couldn't hold back any longer.

Pull yourself together. You won't find him standing here crying. Whining won't help Paul.

She started taking photos of the gravestones. Henriksen did the same at the other end of the cemetery, and eventually they met in the middle.

'Somebody was here before us,' said Henriksen. 'Over there I found a series of letters spray-painted onto the headstones. Like a group of vandals were hanging around here.'

'Letters?'

'Four Ns, an H, an E, three As, an S and a J.' Henriksen showed her the photos. The letters had been sprayed on in red paint. Jasmin swallowed as she looked at the graffiti.

'I'm cold,' said Jasmin, 'and I feel like I'm never going to be dry again.'

'Same here.' Henriksen quickly shoved his mobile phone back in his pocket as if he were expecting her to try and take another look at the triangle symbol on the rear. Jasmin felt sure he'd noticed her reaction. 'What now? Should we wrap this up? Go back to the car?'

'Yes. For now. But maybe there's more,' she said, as the three of them walked back down the path towards the car. 'Maybe they killed these people to cover up more than what we know about. Larsen said an escapee from the institution murdered a young girl. What if that isn't true? Or if it isn't the whole story? What if they did things here that they wanted to keep hidden from the authorities, and that was why they started the fire?'

This thought had been nagging away at Jasmin for a while now, and she felt relieved at having shared it with Henriksen.

'Is there any evidence for that?'

'You mean, is it more than idle speculation?' Jasmin replied. She got into the car beside the inspector and held her hands in front of the air vents as he started the engine and adjusted the heating. 'It's just an idea. A suspicion, since I think this whole story is a sham.'

'Are you sure?'

Jasmin hesitated. 'No. I'm not sure.'

'You can trust me.' The car rejoined the tarmacked main road and Henriksen accelerated. The wind grew even stronger, driving the rain almost horizontally against the windows in wild gusts. The howling sounded like a child crying in the distance. Could it be Paul? When Jasmin looked back, she thought she saw two lights gleaming on the road.

They were being followed.

'I think someone was watching us. Look, there's a car behind us.'

Henriksen's eyes wandered to the rear-view mirror and his brow furrowed. 'Yes, I see them. It's probably just—'

'Watch out!' Jasmin yelled. A man was crossing the road in the downpour. Henriksen slammed on the brakes and managed to miss him by a hair's breadth. Jasmin saw a tall figure in a long grey coat disappearing into the fog – caught a brief glimpse as the tyres screeched and she lurched forward into her seatbelt.

'That was him!' she cried. 'The drifter! I'm certain of it!'

Henriksen stopped the car and turned around. The shock absorbers creaked as he pulled up abruptly on the side of the road around where they'd seen the figure.

'Stay here,' he ordered her before leaping out of the car. She saw him hurry a little way down the road and watched him draw his pistol. Again, it looked clumsy, as if the holster had got snagged on his coat. Once he finally had his gun in his hand, he vanished into the mist.

Bonnie raised her head to bark at the window, at the rain outside, and Jasmin couldn't get her to stop. 'Shh, Bonnie, be quiet!' Jasmin hissed. Her heart was racing. *You weren't mistaken*, she told herself. *It was him, the stranger you saw at the house – the stranger everyone's been talking about.*

Now he was here, which meant he might have followed them to the graveyard. Maybe he'd even listened in on them and heard what she'd discussed with Henriksen.

Bright lights in the rear-view mirror. The Jeep!

Fuck.

Jasmin opened the door and planted her feet on the asphalt. 'Wait here,' she said to Bonnie. 'Hendrik?' she called into the pouring rain as she pulled her hood down over her face. 'Where are you? Hello? Can you hear me?'

No reply. It felt like the world had been swallowed up by all the rain – everything was so quiet, as if a blanket had been thrown over the island, smothering every sound.

'Stop!' she heard Henriksen yell. 'Right now!'

Oh God. The words echoed through her mind. *Oh God, oh God, oh God.*

Then silence.

What now? Why did Henriksen shout like that? And what if something happens to him? Should you go back to the car? Find a hiding place? Call the police?

Jasmin took a few steps back towards the car and gripped the door handle. The rain ran down her face, obscuring her vision. 'Hello?' she called uncertainly. 'Hello?'

There was no reply – no sound beyond the ceaseless patter of the rain and the babble of water running down the dark asphalt.

That harsh light once more, this time accompanied by a piercing pain that throbbed behind her temples.

Jasmin took out her phone and with a chill sense of dread, she realised she didn't have any signal out here. Not a single bar.

'Hello? Inspector Henriksen? Are you there?'

You have to look for him. He should have come back by now. There must be something wrong.

Once again, Jasmin began to walk cautiously in the direction Henriksen had headed. Her right hand vanished into her coat pocket.

It is what it is, said a voice in her head that sounded like Marit and Ståle at the same time. *You can't change your nature. Nobody can.*

She stretched out her hands like a blind woman fumbling her way through the fog, feeling the rain flowing down her fingers. Apparitions darted around her, faces in the mist. Jasmin had no idea how long she spent blundering around like this. For a split second, she thought she saw the body from the beach emerging from the drifting fog – lurching towards her – and she threw her right arm up to defend herself. She heard a loud bang close by that made her jump.

Then there was somebody lying on the ground in front of her, curled up into a ball, injured. Somebody wearing not a grey trench coat, but a dark raincoat. It was Henriksen.

Jasmin knelt down beside him and felt his pulse, her hands shaking. Despite the rain running down her fingers and his neck, Jasmin managed to detect a heartbeat. He was alive. Then she saw the blood on the back of his head, as if he'd fallen over. Jasmin had seen plenty of injuries like this before, and although as an anaesthetist she hadn't been directly involved in treating them, she still knew what she needed to do. 'Hendrik? Can you hear me?'

She watched as his eyes wandered up to her face and met her own. He reached out his hand as if to grab hold of her. 'You'll be all right,' she called to him reassuringly. 'It's only a flesh wound. Do you have a first aid kit?'

Henriksen nodded and mumbled, 'In the boot.'

Finding the car keys in his pocket, Jasmin sprang to her feet and hurried back to the car. Bonnie looked up as she approached and her tail thumped against the upholstery, but Jasmin merely unlocked the boot and took out the first aid kit before rushing back over to Henriksen, where she swiftly bandaged his wound, all the while casting nervous glances into the rain, afraid the drifter might return. As soon as she'd finished, she helped Henriksen back onto his feet.

'Slowly, nice and slowly.'

He threw his arm around her and Jasmin led him back to the car, taking short steps.

'Easy now, Hendrik. Easy. You'll be right as rain, it's barely more than a graze.'

But you don't know that, she thought. *Minor wounds sometimes turn out to be worse than they first seem.*

'What happened? There was a bang?'

'It's nothing, I just tripped,' the inspector managed to say. 'All of you stay where you are. Everything is OK, there's no need to get worked up.'

All of you? He has no idea who he's talking to.

Jasmin started the car. Her thoughts turned to Dr Gundersen, the island doctor. She'd be able to tend to Henriksen's injury. Luckily Jasmin knew where to find her.

'Drive slowly,' Henriksen added as Jasmin steered the car through the rain. *You need to hurry. Whatever he says, it's important for him to get checked out and treated as soon as possible.*

So get a move on.

Jasmin raced down the wet road at top speed.

Henriksen sighed and moaned softly beside her as the car hurtled over a bump in the road. 'I'm sorry,' Jasmin said instantly, 'but we're nearly there. It was definitely him – he must have attacked you. He realised you were following him. Now we know for certain he's dangerous.'

She followed a long curve that ended in a straight stretch of road running along the clifftops. The waves crashed furiously against the sheer rock, sending spray flying upwards, and the roar of the water sounded like a raging beast.

'A storm,' Henriksen whispered, so quietly that Jasmin could barely hear him. 'There's a storm brewing, it's coming closer and closer. You need to be careful. We all do . . .'

'Why?' Jasmin glanced across at him, unsure if he was lucid or if he was seeing things. His eyes were focused on a mark on the ceiling of the car.

'Because it might wash you away, Jasmin. Because it might carry you along with it and there's a risk you might never come back, never find your way home . . .'

She swore and put her foot down again. At the same moment, the phone in Henriksen's pocket started ringing, and the ringtone sent goosebumps crawling up Jasmin's back and over her neck.

You know that music.

You've heard it before.

It was Wagner. 'Siegfried's Death'.

The same piece Larsen had been playing on his record player when she visited him.

It can't be a coincidence.

Shit, what's going on here?

The ringtone kept playing, but Jasmin drove on undeterred. Eventually she reached the sign for Skårsteinen, where she braked and turned off the road. Dr Gundersen's practice was on the edge of the village. With Jasmin's help, Henriksen managed to get out of the car and hobble over to the door, where Jasmin rang the bell. A dog started barking somewhere in the neighbourhood and Bonnie joined in from inside the car.

Then the door swung open. Dr Gundersen's red hair was hidden under a black woolly hat and her cheeks were slightly flushed.

She looked as though she'd been out for a while in the cold. 'He's bleeding,' Jasmin explained. 'We need to take a look at him right now.'

Together, they helped Henriksen into the surgery on the ground floor of the house and lowered him into a chair. Dr Gundersen removed the wet bandage while Jasmin took Henriksen's phone and wallet out of his rain-sodden coat.

Gundersen glanced at her. 'You're a doctor, right?'

Jasmin nodded. 'I'm an anaesthetist.'

'You're bleeding.' Dr Gundersen pointed at Jasmin's right hand.

Only now did Jasmin realise there was blood flowing down her fingers. It was smeared over the front of her raincoat too.

When did that happen?

'Here,' said Dr Gundersen. 'Some bandages.'

Jasmin took them and began tending to her own injury. Once her hand was firmly wrapped in gauze, Jasmin saw that the doctor was busy replacing the bandage on Henriksen's head and she took the opportunity to examine the inspector's phone. Her fingers touched the display as she looked at his list of recent calls, hoping to find out who had been trying to get hold of him so urgently during the journey.

Larsen, it said.

The historian.

Hadn't Henriksen told her he didn't know the man? So why did the inspector have his number saved on his phone?

And a few lines below it on the call list: *G. Yrsen.*

'What are you doing over there?' Dr Gundersen asked sharply. Jasmin looked up guiltily and saw the doctor giving her a penetrating look.

She doesn't believe your story. She isn't sure what to make of you.

'I'm trying to find the numbers for the officers Henriksen arrived on the island with. They need to know what's happened.'

'I understand that you'll need to contact them,' Dr Gundersen retorted, 'but this isn't the time for making phone calls. Right now' – she beckoned Jasmin over to her – 'you need to make sure he gets some rest. You're a doctor; you should look after him. It's harmless, just a minor flesh wound on the back of his head.'

'What do you mean?'

'I can't keep him here,' Dr Gundersen answered. 'Not right now, anyway. I have urgent patient visits to make. Why don't you take him home with you?'

'Oh,' Jasmin replied. She hesitated for a few moments, surprised at Dr Gundersen's suggestion, but then she came to a decision. *You owe it to him. After all, it was your idea – yours alone. He came to the cemetery for your sake. He wanted to take you straight home, and it was thanks to your detour that he ended up getting hurt.*

'OK, I'll take him with me and keep an eye on him,' she agreed. 'I'll let his colleagues know once we get to my place.'

'Your place?'

'The house on the coast,' Jasmin replied. 'Remember?'

'Oh, of course. Where they found the body. The *old* house,' said Dr Gundersen, lost in thought.

'I'm sorry?'

'Nothing. Just thinking out loud.'

Once again, those flashes of light suddenly appeared before her eyes – the smell of petrol and fire, of burning fabric and . . .

Screaming.

For the first time, she heard screaming. And it wasn't the homeless man she'd run over on that horrible night. It was somebody else.

Remember: seven, not two.

Jasmin felt like her legs were about to give way and she held out her arms in search of support. She felt the cold metal of a kidney dish that Dr Gundersen pressed into her hands.

'It's perfectly natural that you would react like this,' the doctor explained in a calming, professional voice. 'What with the shock, the journey here.'

'That's not it though! I – I don't know what's wrong with me!' Jasmin shoved the kidney dish aside, and it fell to the floor with a loud clatter that echoed painfully through her mind.

'Are you all right, Ms Hansen?'

'I keep seeing things that shouldn't be there! I can smell things I shouldn't be able to smell. I . . .' She took a deep breath and tried to dismiss these thoughts – to find her way back into the here and now.

You're standing in a doctor's surgery; you've rushed over here with a detective inspector who's been attacked by a mysterious drifter.

That's all.

But was it really all?

Jasmin's thoughts turned involuntarily to Gabriela Yrsen, the artist with the gift of second sight.

And now, as insane as it seems, you're starting to see things too.

Yes, that really is insane.

It's more than insane.

It's something you shouldn't even be thinking about.

Seven, not two.

'What if she's here? What if Hanna Jansen is here?'

'I'm sorry?' The doctor turned around to face her and Jasmin saw she was holding a dangerous-looking syringe in her hand. A drop of fluid glittered at the tip of the needle. 'Who is Hanna Jansen?'

'A person from my past. Someone we all thought we'd seen the back of.'

'Is she threatening you?'

Jasmin looked out into the rain and heard Henriksen breathing evenly behind her. 'That's what I'm going to find out.'

Chapter 8

As the hours went by, Jasmin gradually began to understand what it meant to her that Paul was gone, that her son was missing. It was a vast, gaping wound inside her, one that would never heal.

When she arrived at her house by the beach with Bonnie and Henriksen, the realisation hit her so hard that her breath caught for a few moments.

Something was urging her to run out into the rain and call his name. Some part of her wanted to believe that Paul would come trotting around the corner if only she shouted loud enough – his hair a little tousled, his coat and his knees a little dirty from where he'd fallen over, but alive, and maybe even grinning at all the fun he'd had on his adventure. And she would ruffle his messy hair and take him into her arms, tell him how much she loved him, how much she'd missed him, and that he never had to worry about her being angry with him as long as he always came back to her.

But of course she didn't go out and call for Paul, and of course when she stepped over the threshold with Henriksen she found her house cold and empty.

An old pipe gurgled inside the wall and the gas heating in the cellar sprang to life with a rumble, like a monster hiding in its cave.

Jasmin accompanied Henriksen down the hall and into the living room, where she helped him lower himself carefully into the armchair by the fireplace. The fire had almost gone out, so Jasmin added a few more logs.

'Hendrik? How are you feeling?'

'The way anyone would feel after escaping so narrowly with their life,' he said, looking up at her. 'What is it people say in situations like this? I could feel death breathing down my neck.'

'It's a minor scrape. It looks worse than it is.' Jasmin watched as Bonnie settled down onto the rug with a quiet grunt. 'I'm sorry it turned out like this though. If only I hadn't come up with that stupid idea about the graveyard—'

Henriksen shook his head and grimaced, since even that small gesture caused him pain. 'It isn't your fault . . .'

'Jasmin,' she said quietly.

'You should tell my colleagues.' He gestured at his phone, which she'd put on the coffee table. 'They need to know what's happened. Dial the most recently called number and put them on loudspeaker.'

'Sure. But after that you need to rest. I'll look after you.'

'That's good to hear.' Henriksen coughed and instantly groaned in pain.

Jasmin brought out some freshly brewed herbal tea and told him to sit as still as he could while she contacted his colleagues. Then she walked over to the French windows with his phone.

Larsen. Yrsen.

Their numbers in his list of contacts.

And between them, just like he'd said, she saw one of his colleagues. She tapped the name.

The male voice that emerged from the small speaker on the phone belonged to Arne Boeckermann. She told him what had happened to Henriksen.

'He shot at him?' Boeckermann repeated in a sharp tone. 'Madness. This is madness. Nothing like this has ever happened here before.'

'Hasn't it?' Jasmin asked pointedly. 'Hasn't it really?'

'What do you mean?'

Jasmin remembered what Larsen had told her: *The islanders have always been experts at keeping secrets. They store them up, guard them carefully.*

'You get to hear certain things, if you travel around enough and keep your ears open.'

'Put Henriksen on. I need to talk to him.'

Jasmin looked at the reflection in the glass. The inspector had laid his head on a cushion and shut his eyes.

'I can't right now,' she said. 'He needs to rest. You should launch a manhunt. Everything seems to keep centring on the same person – the drifter everyone's been talking about. It wouldn't surprise me if he was behind Paul's disappearance too. You go about your work, and Henriksen will get in touch when he's back on his feet.'

'Ms Ha—'

Jasmin hung up.

It had felt good to talk to him like that, to hear the arrogance fade from his voice, but now she felt exhausted.

Her thoughts turned briefly to Karl Sandvik, the old grocer who ran the village shop. She'd promised to drop by and look at his back, but now, under these circumstances, she barely had the strength even to call him to postpone, or to ask him to help look for Paul.

Suddenly she remembered the letters on the gravestones. Jasmin looked up the photos Henriksen had taken on his phone and went through them one by one.

N. N. N. N. H. S. J. E. A. A. A.

It was a name, she realised. It couldn't be anything else.

And the name was . . .

Jasmin's breath caught.

No, it couldn't be true.

When she rearranged the letters – and if she wasn't mistaken – she saw the words *Hanna Jansen*. Sprayed on the gravestones in red paint, the name of that woman.

The woman Jørgen had once had an affair with.

That was a long time ago, all in the past.

Wasn't it?

If Hanna Jansen was behind all this then she had to get in touch with Jørgen. *You trust him, don't you? He's the first person you should tell about this.* She put Henriksen's phone back on the coffee table and took out her own.

She needed to ask Jørgen to tell her the truth.

'Hey, honey,' she greeted him when he picked up after the second ring.

'Jasmin, what—'

She remembered the background noise she'd heard during her conversation with him on the previous evening. It had sounded like he'd been in a bar with another woman.

'Hanna Jansen,' she said abruptly. 'Does that ring any bells with you?'

Jørgen hesitated. Jasmin felt it was too long, his hesitation – too long and too guilty. 'What about her? We've already talked about this so often. I thought we'd settled everything. I've apologised so many times, for—'

'She might be here. She might still be trying to get me out of the way.' Jasmin sounded so cold that she was amazed at her own tone of voice.

'But that's impossible. She left. Moved away, to somewhere in Sweden. She's gone. For good.'

'Think about it, Jørgen. I'm begging you, please think about it.'

She hung up before he could say anything else.

'They've launched a manhunt for the drifter,' she told Henriksen, sitting down beside him on the sofa. 'Boeckermann wanted to talk to you but I didn't let him.'

Henriksen jerked his head up and looked at her through weary eyes. 'You did what?'

'Doctor's orders,' Jasmin replied with a faint smile, and was relieved when Henriksen smiled back. Her words dispelled the tension between them.

'I'll make us another pot of tea,' she said. 'You stay put.'

'Whatever you say, doctor.' He laid his head back on the cushion and closed his eyes.

Hanna Jansen.

The drifter.

Minsøy.

Jasmin entered the kitchen, the floorboards creaking under her feet. The table was bare, but the blue plate Paul ate from was still in the sink where she'd left it.

He might never use it again.

With that thought, Jasmin was overwhelmed by a feeling of desperation that passed in shockwaves through her whole body. *He's gone*, she thought, *and all you've done so far is follow a trail that seems as bizarre as it is illogical.*

You need to confront either Henriksen or Larsen with the truth. Maybe Yrsen too, if you dare to go and see her again.

But you have to do something.

Jasmin made the tea – a herbal blend she'd bought from Sandvik's grocery store – and carried the large porcelain pot into the living room along with two mugs. Steam curled in silvery spirals towards the ceiling.

Henriksen was looking out of the window. The rain was beating against the glass and the thick fog made it impossible to deploy a helicopter. 'Maybe you're right,' he said softly. 'Maybe they really are conspiring against us in this wretched place.'

Jasmin nodded, but to avoid replying, she lifted her cup to her lips and took a sip. The hot tea scalded her tongue. The triangle symbol on his phone, his contact list, the letters that spelled out the name Hanna Jansen.

It was all too much.

You can't trust him any more than the others. He might just be trying to gain your confidence.

'Maybe we should confront them with it. With the truth.' Henriksen didn't take his eyes off the window, as if there were a secret hidden out there, behind the rain.

There's only one trail left for you to follow. Into the sanatorium – or wherever the remains of it are. The picture Larsen showed you had that symbol on it, the one that matches the origami sculpture the kidnapper left behind.

But can you trust Henriksen with this information?

Eventually, she decided she could. 'The old sanatorium. The west wing is still standing.'

'And what do you expect to find there?'

'The kidnapper left that origami sculpture in the house. The open triangle. Larsen showed me photos of the old sanatorium and one of the patients' – she almost said 'inmates' – 'had made the same figure. There *has* to be something there.'

'Of course – but it's a trap. Or at least it could be one.' Henriksen touched his neck and grimaced.

'Don't scratch,' Jasmin admonished him. 'I know, but what else can I do? What if he never gets in touch or makes any demands?'

'Not enough time has passed for that yet.'

Just then, Jasmin heard a rattle that she instantly recognised. It was the letterbox in the front door.

She and Henriksen exchanged a look.

Then she hurried out of the room.

Chapter 9

A white envelope was lying on the floorboards by the front door. Droplets of rain had speckled the paper, forming an irregular pattern. Jasmin opened the door and peered out into the downpour, which cloaked the path and the road beyond it in a grey haze. Nothing.

The drainpipe running down the front wall made a gurgling sound, while water dripped from a leak in the gutter onto the paving stones that Jørgen had laid in front of the house years ago. Patches of moss had started to appear on them. Now that Paul had disappeared, Jørgen might never get around to fixing the place up.

Maybe he'll blame you.

You shouldn't have told him about Hanna Jansen.

If Paul never comes back – or if they find his body – then it won't just be your son you'll lose. You know it could come to that. You should start to prepare yourself.

She reached nervously for the envelope. The paper was wet and felt like the skin of a corpse – cold and clammy, with a repulsive waxy texture. Jasmin carried it into the kitchen and opened it with a sharp knife.

The sheet of paper she shook out onto the kitchen table was covered with letters someone had cut out of a magazine and glued into place.

I KNOW WHAT YOU ARE, it said in large, uneven characters. Some were in colour, others were black, and each one had been cut out from a different page.

Jasmin felt panic wash over her like a wave from the icy Norwegian Sea. She had to clutch the back of a kitchen chair to prevent herself from falling to the floor as all the strength drained from her legs. Slumping into the chair, she stared at the page.

Then she turned it over in the hope she'd find more on the other side, but there was nothing. Only those five words jeering at her painfully, like red-hot needles piercing straight into her soul.

'Ms Hansen?'

Henriksen had followed her into the kitchen unnoticed. He was pale, but seemed steady on his feet. It was too late to hide the threatening letter from him as he'd already spotted it on the table.

'Did that arrive just now?' he asked, his eyes opening wide.

Jasmin nodded. She felt hot tears running down her cheeks, like drops of lava. 'It must be from him. The drifter – the kidnapper. Why would anybody else send it? He's mocking me.'

It had to be from him or from Jansen – or maybe from both of them, if they were working together.

'Did you see anybody at the door?'

Jasmin shook her head. 'No. There was no one there.'

'Shit.' Henriksen took his phone from his pocket. 'I'll let my colleagues know he was here again.'

He went to the living room to make his call, and although Jasmin couldn't make out exactly what he was saying through the closed door, she had the impression he was irritated. It even sounded like he was having an argument.

Is he really on the phone to Boeckermann and the others, or is he talking to someone else? The thought sent a shiver down Jasmin's spine.

Henriksen came back into the kitchen. 'We're going to take another look around the property and search for evidence. Including on this letter.' He cast an appraising eye over the threatening message. '*I know what you are*,' he read out loud. 'I don't understand.' His eyes wandered over to Jasmin. 'But you, Ms Hansen – I think you know what these words are referring to.'

Jasmin swallowed. She wanted to deny it, but she struggled to get the words out as she couldn't bring herself to tell yet another lie. She couldn't do that to Henriksen. He'd been shot at, and all for her sake.

But the contact list, said that other nagging voice inside her. *What's the deal there? What is he hiding? Who was he arguing with just now?*

'No,' she answered after a long pause. 'I don't know what they're referring to. I'd hoped he might at least make some demands, for money or – I don't know, something connected to Paul. That he might give me a chance to get my son back.' She was on the verge of collapse; she could feel it. Her hands were now shaking uncontrollably.

'We need to check the camera footage,' she said weakly. She started looking around for her phone and eventually found it on the coffee table in the living room. The app she used to control and monitor the cameras took an eternity to load, but eventually she managed to access the recordings.

The cameras had picked something up.

Dear God. They saw you. They followed you here.

'Ms Hansen?'

Jasmin tilted her screen to let Henriksen look at the video too. Of course, the man at the door was none other than the drifter in his trench coat, with a hat pulled down over his face – and now that she could see him, she had to cling on to Henriksen for support.

In the clear light of day, the drifter looked like the homeless man she'd seen in the headlights of her car. He looked like the man she'd killed. He didn't look up at the camera, but it was in his posture, his gait as he walked up to the door and then returned to his van, hunched and limping slightly, before driving away. This was no coincidence.

The homeless man was real, and you ran him over. He was washed up on the beach – you know that because you looked into his face in the cold storage unit. And then he vanished.

If this drifter was acting like the homeless man, it could only mean one thing: he knew what she'd done. He must have left the body on the beach, and now, to terrorise her even further, he'd brought her this letter because he knew only *she* would understand its true meaning.

What was more, the vehicle parked at the end of the drive was an unmarked white delivery van – and Jasmin realised she'd seen it before.

'That van was parked outside the fishing company building down at the docks yesterday.' Jasmin ran her hand anxiously through her hair. 'I'm certain of it. I went for a stroll through the village with Paul and I noticed it there. Jesus Christ, he was watching us – there's no other explanation!'

'Calm yourself.' Henriksen studied the recording with a furrowed brow. 'Can I make a copy of this?'

'Yes, I think so. Let me fetch my computer.'

She left Henriksen in the kitchen and dashed into the living room – but instead of picking up her laptop, she charged out onto the veranda and screamed her panic, frustration and rage out into the wind.

'You won't do it!' she cried. 'You won't drive me crazy!'

Jasmin gripped the wooden railing and forced herself to breathe calmly. 'It'll all be OK. Everything will be OK.'

191

I know what you are.

A murderer.

Was that what the drifter was getting at? Did he want her to confess that she'd killed a man that night?

But nobody believed you when you tried to tell them what happened. Nobody wanted to know. They all told you it was only an animal, a deer.

Does he want you to search for proof? Proof of your own guilt? But why? What does he hope to achieve? Why is he tormenting you like this?

Hanna Jansen must be behind it all. She wants to get you out of the way. No other explanation makes sense. She might even be working with Jørgen.

Somewhere out in front of the house she heard a car pulling up, and she hurried back inside. The front door swung open – *Did you leave it ajar just now?* Jasmin wondered – and Boeckermann came storming in. His hair hung in dark, wet strands over his face and water dripped onto the floorboards from his oilskin coat, which made him look like an oversized scarecrow.

They'll warp, said a voice in Jasmin's head that sounded like Jørgen. 'The water isn't good for the wood,' she said out loud. 'We need to mop it up, the water isn't good—'

'He was here,' said Henriksen. 'You take a look around. I'll be right with you.'

Once Boeckermann had left the kitchen, Jasmin felt Henriksen's hands on her shoulders. She felt tears running down her cheeks and falling to the floor, where they mingled with the rainwater Boeckermann had tracked inside. 'The water isn't good for the floorboards,' she repeated. *Paul, my little Paul, how could this have happened? How could you leave me like this? How could I have allowed it?*

'He's gone,' she whispered. 'It's useless, there's no way to ever—'

'Jasmin,' said Henriksen gently. 'I'm going to put you to bed now. You need to sleep. The situation is too much for you, and that's understandable. It's what the kidnapper wanted. He's playing with you.'

Jasmin felt an urge to snatch up the letter and rip it into a thousand tiny pieces, but Henriksen gripped her wrist and extracted it from her fingers. 'That's not something you should do right now,' he cautioned her. 'Even if I can understand your reaction.' Gently yet firmly, Henriksen led her upstairs. The rattling of the rain against the roof made her feel sleepy. 'Why don't you put your head down for a while? Please.'

'But I don't want to,' she heard herself protest in a voice that didn't quite sound like her own. 'I have to—'

'No,' Henriksen answered. 'You don't. Not right now anyway. You need sleep, at least a few hours. After that the world will seem a little clearer.'

Jasmin fell back onto the bed. The duvet was so soft that she sank into it as though it was a cloud. Henriksen drew the curtains and the thick blue fabric dimmed the light. 'You're injured – you shouldn't be walking around so much. You know that,' she admonished him quietly.

Henriksen nodded. 'I'll be careful. Don't worry, Ms Hansen. I'll stay here until you wake up, I promise. Boeckermann and I will have a look around for evidence. After that, I'll ask my team to examine the letter for fingerprints and get an officer to bring your car back from Larsen's place.'

Jasmin nodded. She climbed under the covers, and now that she was in bed, the urge to sleep overwhelmed her. The bedroom dissolved, the walls unravelled, leaving nothing more than thin white fog – or smoke – and in the distance, the voice of a child calling to her.

Paul!

Jasmin reached out her hand, but her muscles felt heavy as lead. She struggled to hold up her arm as the fog-shrouded outline of her son groped towards her in fear, searching for safety.

'You need to come and save me!' he cried – and although Jasmin knew this was all in her imagination, she still gave a start at how realistic it seemed.

'How?' she asked him. 'Tell me how!'

'Someone on the island knows. He knows everything. You need to find him.'

With all her might, Jasmin tried again to lift her arm. Her fingers strained for Paul, but her son's silhouette drifted further and further away from her, receding into the distance. Eventually she closed her fingers, but all she could feel was cold air and fog.

He was gone.

The upside-down triangle. There it was! She could see it, right there on the wall, marked out in black paint. Jasmin felt a sense of relief well up inside her. She'd found it!

'So, are we going to finish the game, or are you going to keep staring at that NHI logo?'

Jasmin blinked. A man was sitting in front of her, smoking a pipe, and there was a chessboard between them. The white figures were on his side, while she was playing as black. He was relatively short and had thin blond hair above a receding hairline. His tobacco smelled pungent, the smoke rising to the wood-panelled ceiling above their heads. She looked around the room. A fire was burning in the hearth, which was surrounded on all sides by bookcases, while rain rattled against the window at the other end of the library. A few armchairs were positioned around the fireplace, each with an open book resting on them, and yet Jasmin and the man were alone. The door was ajar; somebody was pacing up and down outside it and talking quietly, as if to themselves. She heard a rumble of thunder, but the storm was so far away that the rain almost drowned out the noise.

'I—' she heard herself say. 'I don't know.'

The man slid his queen along the board. 'Check,' he declared. 'And mate.'

Jasmin looked down at the chess set. 'I was distracted.'

'You always are, these days. You're planning something, girl.' He puffed at his pipe again, sending another waft of smoke towards the ceiling. 'I hope you aren't going to rat on me.'

'What would I rat on you about?'

'My deliveries. I'm hiding them from the others. As you know.'

'Deliveries?'

'Special deliveries.' He leaned forwards. 'For my collection. And in return, I won't tell anybody here that you sometimes—'

Jasmin felt every muscle in her body grow tense. She felt ready to take flight. 'What?' she asked sharply.

'I overhear things, from time to time. Your conversations with him, even though you're completely al—'

'That's enough,' Jasmin cried. She leapt to her feet, retreating from him towards the window. The patter of the rain against the glass was reassuring. Hypnotic, even. She rested her forehead on the cool surface and closed her eyes. Her fingers reached into her trouser pocket in search of the object she'd hidden away there a few hours ago, while she was in the smoking area. She gripped it firmly.

He's lying, she thought to herself. *All lies.*

You know the truth.

Chapter 10

'Ms Hansen? Time to wake up.' The words penetrated the depths of her sleep.

Jasmin blinked. 'What?' she heard herself say in a voice that sounded nothing like her own; it was hoarse, as if she'd barely slept. *That dream*, she thought, *that strange* . . . Had she really been dreaming about Johann Larsen, or was it a memory? Had she met him once before? The room where she'd been playing chess with him – where was it? Was any of this even possible?

'It's nine o'clock.' Only now did she recognise the man who was trying insistently to rouse her. It was Henriksen.

'Nine?' Jasmin blinked, amazed at the bright light dazzling her eyes.

'Nine o'clock in the *morning*, Ms Hansen.' Henriksen sounded amused. 'You slept all evening and through the night.'

'What?!' Jasmin shot upright. Everything came flooding back: Paul's disappearance, the threatening letter, the attack on Henriksen after their visit to the secret cemetery – and the letters on the gravestones.

Hanna Jansen.

The duvet slid noiselessly to the floor and she realised she was still wearing the same jeans and grey woollen jumper as the day before. Then she looked over at the window. The sun had emerged from the grey clouds; the rain was in retreat and slants of sunlight poured through the thin blue fabric of the curtains. Henriksen pushed them aside.

'Nine o'clock in the morning,' he repeated. 'You really needed the sleep.'

'Is there any news?' She scarcely dared to ask for fear of the awful truths that might be waiting for her – yet at the same time, she knew she'd have to face up to them sooner or later.

We've found him, she could already hear him say in her mind. *We've found his lifeless body—*

'We haven't managed to find any useful evidence. I'm sorry. We examined the letter, but the kidnapper knew what he was doing. He must have been wearing gloves. There wasn't any saliva either; he moistened the glue strips with water. That said, we did find something in Paul's room.'

She cleared her throat. 'And what was that?'

'Hairs. Long, blonde ones.'

'Mine?'

'Maybe,' Henriksen replied. 'But they might . . .' He shook his head. 'They might belong to someone else.'

Hanna Jansen. Had she really been here?

'But it was almost certainly a man who broke into the room.'

'Yes. A man who might have carried these hairs in on his clothes. But this is just vague conjecture. It'll take a couple of weeks to get a DNA comparison.'

Jasmin lowered her head. 'So it was a man who knows how these things work? How to kidnap children without getting caught by the police? How to write threatening letters, cover up evidence and make himself invisible, like a ghost?'

'That about sums it up,' Henriksen confirmed, nodding gloomily.

'But you haven't told me everything, have you?' There was something in Henriksen's eyes that she couldn't quite place. Disappointment, and deep concern.

What was he disappointed at? That they hadn't managed to make any progress? Or was there more to it?

'There was a fire last night. A serious fire that claimed a man's life. A horrendous incident.' He gave a sigh. 'Right now, we have to assume there's a connection with the kidnapping.'

'Was Paul there?' *Please, don't let it be true*, a voice pleaded in her mind. *Please.*

'No. Paul is still missing. But I now have to assume that the problems we face here are significantly more serious than we previously thought.'

'Who was the victim?' asked Jasmin, throwing her legs over the side of the bed. She felt exhausted, despite her long sleep. The muscles in her arms were burning and her neck felt like it was filled with lead. 'Who?'

'I shouldn't really tell you this, but . . .' Henriksen glanced at the open door. The corridor behind it was empty. There was something oddly conspiratorial about his gesture, Jasmin thought. 'It was Johann Larsen. The historian. Somebody started a fire and everything went up in flames. His whole house burned down. His house, his books, his notes, his computer – everything. I can only hope the culprit – or culprits – killed him before they started the fire. It'll be at least a day before the arson specialists get here from the mainland.'

'Oh God.' Jasmin didn't know what to say. She thought of Larsen, how he'd led her into that small, overheated room with all those strange Nazi medals on the wall. She thought of the origami sculpture of the triangle that the kidnapper had left behind. The same symbol Larsen had shown her in an old photo of the sanatorium.

Did the kidnapper know about that? What if Larsen had to die because he'd spoken to her? If so, didn't that mean she had to do all she could to keep following the trail?

If he's got Paul, you need to find him. Whatever it costs. And you shouldn't put any more people in danger either.

'Ms Hansen?' Henriksen asked. 'Jasmin, do you know who might have done this? You were at his house yesterday. Did he say anything or drop any hints that could be perceived as a threat? Anything the kidnapper would be forced to respond to?'

Jasmin shook her head. 'He only mentioned the graveyard. That was all – he didn't tell me anything else. You know that already.'

'The graveyard,' Henriksen repeated. 'Yes. That could be it, of course. Maybe that was the trigger. But I still don't understand. Why all this? What did we find there that provoked the kidnapper to go to such extremes? Was it the letters on the gravestones? Or are we missing something?'

'Maybe.' Jasmin shook her head. 'But the question should really be: how does he know what we found, or what we failed to find?'

'You mean . . . ?' A shocked expression passed over Henriksen's face. 'You mean he's watching us? And he saw something he thought was dangerous? Something that prompted him to get Larsen out of the way because he'd said too much, and we were too blind to see it? Maybe we were looking for the wrong thing.'

Jasmin nodded. 'I think so.' She walked towards the door. 'Are you coming? We need to go and take another look.'

The cemetery lay before them, just as they had left it – the mossy paving slabs, the rusty iron gate, the weathered headstones beneath the endless whisper and rustle of the birch trees. The wind picked up yellow and orange leaves from the ground and whirled them in circles past their shoes as they wandered among the graves – and although Jasmin had already visited this place and photographed all these names before, it felt to her now like something had changed.

The rain had stopped, but that wasn't it.

The air was colder. An earthy, mouldy odour drifted up from between the graves. Winter was on its way, or at least its earliest harbingers.

And on the radio, on the way here . . .

'What was that?' she'd asked Henriksen. 'I didn't quite catch it – my mind was elsewhere. What did the presenter say?'

'That the first big autumn storm will be hitting the island tonight,' Henriksen replied, his voice filled with concern. 'Tonight, maybe tomorrow. It won't be long now before it arrives.'

'And what does that mean?'

'I can tell you're from the mainland,' Henriksen laughed.

'So are you,' Jasmin retorted. 'And that doesn't answer my question.'

'It means the little bit of rain and wind we had yesterday will feel like a mild summer day in comparison. It means you should lock all your windows and hope the wind doesn't shatter the glass, and that the trees don't snap and fall on the roof.'

'That doesn't sound good at all.' The word 'roof' reminded Jasmin of her trip to the attic and how she'd found the picture of the burning building – the sanatorium – that Yrsen had painted. It felt like an eternity ago, as if Paul's disappearance had cast a veil over everything that had gone before. A veil that submerged her memory in a grey murk.

The painting Yrsen had promised her – if she could believe what the artist told her – would be ready in two days' time. She couldn't wait that long. If Yrsen really did have the gift of second sight, maybe she'd foreseen what would happen to Paul.

Maybe you should go back and see her again.

Ideally before the storm breaks.

'We're missing something,' Jasmin said out loud, pacing up and down between the crooked gravestones. A mouse rustled through the foliage on the ground and disappeared into a pile of leaves that had gathered against the back of an eroded gravestone. It was a tall block of granite, almost the height of a man, with the initials JH engraved into it.

Jasmin froze. *JH. Short for Jasmin Hansen.*

She blinked. Now, as she looked a second time, she saw the letters JN – not her own initials.

Something is very wrong here. You can feel it with every fibre of your being. You're getting stranger with every day you spend here. As if the island itself is getting under your skin.

She couldn't stop thinking about the sanatorium. About the way Larsen had stared at her, as if he'd been expecting her to recognise the photo of the old institution.

But that was absurd. Larsen had been half-crazy, and now he was dead. *Murdered,* Jasmin thought, and the idea alone sent a cold shiver up her spine.

Somebody on the island will stop at nothing – not even murder. They started a fire, a dreadful way to kill a man. Somebody out there has abandoned all scruples and restraint.

A flash appeared before her eyes like the headlights of a Jeep hurtling towards her in the night.

You're losing your mind. Find Paul and get out of here – it's the only way. Flee, as far as you can. Flee from this place.

'Ms Hansen?' Henriksen asked. She turned to face him. 'There's just one thing I don't understand.'

There's more than one thing I don't understand, she thought, but she gave him a weak smile. 'What's that?'

'"I know what you are", it said on the letter.' Henriksen examined another gravestone and shook his head. 'This is pointless. No, I'm much more interested in what the kidnapper might have meant by that. "I know what you are." He seems to know you, or at least he thinks he does.'

Jasmin nodded and took a step to one side. *If Henriksen tries to accuse you of anything or arrest you*, she thought, *you'll take off. You're quick on your feet – he'll have trouble following you through the undergrowth.*

And later today you're going to go and see Jan Berger to learn how to shoot, if you have time.

You need to be able to defend yourself.

But what if Berger is involved too?

If he is, you don't stand a chance. But you need to try, for Paul's sake. You need to keep going, keep trying. You have to find him. The kidnapper has to be stopped.

And when you have Paul back again, you should take him by the hand and run away, run far, far away. Because whatever's going on here, it looks like someone is doing all this to drive you insane.

Jasmin felt a merciless rage hovering quietly at the edge of her soul, and she gave a start as she realised she didn't quite know what she would do if she found herself face to face with Paul's kidnapper.

If you were alone with him – even if he hadn't done anything to Paul, though that seems less likely with every passing minute – then

you'd want to hurt him. You'd try to make him feel the same pain you're
enduring right now. You'd hurt him without batting an eye.

What does that say about you?

'But I don't know him,' she replied. 'Whatever he thinks.'

'He's claiming to know something,' Henriksen went on. 'He "knows what you are",' he quoted. 'And from the way he phrased it, I assume he's not referring to anything positive.'

Jasmin looked at Henriksen. His eyes were searching, questioning, as if he were trying to look into her soul. The wind rustled though the birch trees. A lot of them were old, and many others far too young to survive a violent storm of the kind that was predicted.

The oldest and the youngest perish.

Like in war.

'I don't know what he's referring to.' Jasmin put her hands in the pockets of her raincoat. 'I don't even know why he would send such a vaguely worded threat to me, of all people – the mother of his victim. Why hasn't he made any demands? Why won't he give me a chance to get Paul back?'

'You know the answer to that, Jasmin.' Henriksen's expression was serious. 'It's possible he isn't after a ransom; it's possible he never intended to let Paul go.'

Jasmin nodded sadly. 'That's getting clearer to me with every passing second.' The fingers of her right hand brushed against an object she hadn't expected to find there. It was a piece of fabric – it felt like a handkerchief – wrapped around something more solid. She couldn't remember putting it in her pocket. When Henriksen wandered a little further away among the gravestones, she turned her back on him and pulled out both items.

The scrap of cloth was checked – maybe a piece of a shirt, though the pattern didn't look familiar to Jasmin. It was wrapped around a shard of glass, the jagged edge of which was smeared with blood. *How did it get into your pocket?* She looked up at Henriksen and caught him casting a covert glance in her direction, but she quickly turned away when she noticed him.

This cloth and piece of glass are covered with your fingerprints now, she thought. *What if someone planted them on you? What if they're trying . . . ?*

Then she noticed the small cut on her palm. *Your hand was bleeding yesterday too, when Henriksen got out of the car. Did you cut yourself on this glass?* Jasmin gave a start at the thought.

What are they planning, if you're right about this? What are they trying to pin on you? Is it to do with Paul? Or Larsen? That would be a nightmare. But what can you do about it? Jasmin clenched her fists. She was shaking, and not because of the cold.

You need to think. Think carefully and look for a way out. A way to find out if your suspicions are really true, or if you're just seeing phantoms.

Then her mind went back to the numbers on Henriksen's phone – Larsen and Yrsen – and she felt all her doubts fall away, scattered like a bank of fog that had clouded her mind and obscured her vision but had suddenly been dispersed by the north wind. *However hard he tries to pretend he's on your side, something about him doesn't add up.*

Jasmin stuffed the cloth back in her pocket as Henriksen walked towards her. 'Did you find anything?' she asked him, watching his reactions carefully. *You've been so blind. But if Henriksen thinks you're a suspect, it doesn't mean he'd try to plant anything on you, does it? He isn't a local, he's an outsider, and he's as shocked by all this as you are. He can't be the one who's trying to set you up.*

Can he?

Jasmin didn't know. She felt helpless, alone on the island, surrounded by strangers whose motives she didn't understand.

'Nothing,' Henriksen replied. 'I don't understand what might have prompted such a brutal killing. What did Larsen know that had to be kept secret at all costs? That justified even murder?'

Jasmin cast her eyes one last time over the grey gravestones and the moss-covered rocks that protruded from the forest floor like crooked teeth. 'I don't get it either.' She sighed and yawned extravagantly in the hope that Henriksen would notice her exhaustion. 'I feel like I need to get some more sleep soon. All I want to do is lie down and give up.'

'You can't, Jasmin.' Henriksen put his hand on her shoulder. 'You can't give up yet.'

'Not yet?' she answered. The pang of grief in her voice was unfeigned. 'Does that mean I can only give up when we find Paul's body? Does it?' She wanted to scream all her frustration and fury into the woods, to punch and kick Henriksen, who was standing so apathetically in front of her. 'I can finally give up once Paul is dead?'

'You can never give up. You know that, Jasmin. We've talked about this so often already.'

Jasmin stared at him. Henriksen's face suddenly seemed so familiar to her. Once again, those blinding lights appeared before her eyes; once again her thoughts turned to the symbol on his phone, the upside-down triangle with the open top-right corner.

You've seen all this before.

The thought scared her because she couldn't quite place it. It scared her because she realised it was the truth – that her subconscious had recognised something her rational mind couldn't quite piece together.

'I want to go home,' she said quietly. 'I need to think.'

'Sure.' Henriksen reached out his hand to take Jasmin's arm, but she pulled away from him. They made their way through the woods in silence, back to the car. By now, the sun had disappeared once more behind heavy, low-hanging cloud.

The storm.

It was getting closer.

Chapter 11

'This is Jan Berger,' said the voice on the answering machine. 'I'm not here right now, but you know what? Leave me a message.' *He isn't picking up*, Jasmin thought. *And at a time like this when you really need him.* For a moment, she debated driving out to the lighthouse to look for him. *No. You can't trust him either.*

A damp nose nudged her hand. *Don't forget about me*, Bonnie seemed to be saying. 'Of course I haven't forgotten you,' said Jasmin. And so, instead of driving to the lighthouse, she decided to take her Labrador for a walk on the beach. The cold wind blowing in from the sea made her shiver, but it also brought clarity to her thoughts.

It's time you finally visited the place where all the evidence seems to be pointing. The old sanatorium – or what's left of it.

They were alone down here, aside from a man in the distance standing close to the water and looking out to sea. Bonnie caught his scent and growled quietly.

At first, Jasmin thought the stranger on the beach was Karl Sandvik, going by his height and his slight stoop – like he was carrying a weight on his shoulders. But then she realised it was Veikko Mattila, the odd bookseller from the village.

'Ms Hansen,' he said as she passed him. Jasmin was in no mood for making conversation and was about to walk on without saying anything when he added, 'You ought to know that people have been asking about you.'

Jasmin stopped, with one hand clenched into a fist in her pocket and the other gripping Bonnie's lead. The Labrador wagged her tail as she looked up at Mattila. *You aren't much help*, Jasmin thought.

'Who's been asking about me?'

'The police. I told them that I mentioned Mr Larsen to you and that I sold you a copy of his book. They were very interested to hear it.' Mattila took a step backwards as Bonnie moved towards him. 'Please control your dog. I'm allergic.'

Jasmin pulled Bonnie back on the lead. 'And? What are you trying to tell me?'

'Larsen is dead, in case you haven't heard already. There are rumours in the village that all the bad things happening on the island are connected to your arrival. You've brought something back to life that's lain dormant for a long time. You've been sniffing around too much. We don't like that sort of thing around here.' Mattila put his hands in his pockets. 'I heard your son disappeared because he couldn't stand living with you anymore.'

'That's . . .' Jasmin swallowed. A chill seeped through her body, as if she'd been drinking ice-cold seawater. The lights reappeared, harsh and dazzling to her mind's eye, and Mattila's blurred face danced back and forth behind them. 'That's a lie. Somebody is trying to cover up a mass murder, and they'll stop at nothing in the process. But they won't manage it. I'm going to uncover the truth.'

'A mass murder?' Mattila sounded amused. 'There are no murderers here. It was *you* who killed him. And now you should leave, before I call the police.'

'You're insane,' Jasmin blurted. Bonnie sensed her mood and started up with a deep growl, but Mattila seemed unmoved by it.

He looked west, down the beach, and Jasmin followed his gaze. There were people out there in the distance standing and watching her. Sunlight glittered from their binoculars. Then she noticed Mattila was wearing a small earpiece tucked deep inside his ear, one that was flesh-coloured to avoid detection.

'Who are you communicating with? Who are those people?'

'You know exactly who they are.' When Mattila's hand re-emerged from his pocket, it was holding a dangerous-looking syringe with a long needle.

Jasmin staggered back a few steps. 'What on earth?'

'Stay calm, Ms Hansen. Stay calm and keep still.' Mattila's voice suddenly sounded different; it was cold and professional.

'I most certainly won't – I'm going to tell Henriksen about this and he—'

'Henriksen?' Mattila echoed scornfully. An expression of disbelief briefly passed over his narrow face. 'That would be foolish, and you know it. Forget it, Jasmin. Now, keep still.'

But Jasmin had no intention of complying. She turned and broke into a run, her shoes kicking up sand in all directions. At one point she stumbled and fell, but she scrambled back to her feet, her knees stinging and her hands burning. Bonnie's lead slipped through her fingers and she saw her dog running ahead of her, barking loudly, back to the narrow path through the woods, back to the house.

There's more than one of them. Mattila, the drifter, the others down on the beach. You need to warn Henriksen.

But when she reached the house, she saw the tail lights of the inspector's car disappearing into the encroaching darkness like a pair of red-hot coals. She was too late, maybe by only a minute, and he didn't pick up when she called him. His phone was switched off. Jasmin's heart was pounding. She grabbed her keys and leapt into the car with Bonnie.

Go, get out of here, she thought. *But where to? The ferry is a dead end. They'll find you there. You can't stay in the house either.*

The old sanatorium. Although she'd told people about it, nobody knew what Larsen had shown her and what she'd found out.

Jasmin put the car into gear and sped off with screeching tyres.

Chapter 12

The ruins rose up from the landscape like the skeleton of a slain giant from a Nordic folk tale who had lain here until the sea air had weathered away his remains and vegetation had grown over his bones.

A construction hoarding blocked the way, but Jasmin decided not to let it stop her. She couldn't get hold of Yrsen or Henriksen, and although she'd been constantly scanning her rear-view mirror to check if anyone was following her, she hadn't seen anybody. Though that didn't mean they weren't looking for her, of course.

Whoever they were.

Mattila had tried to sedate her, or possibly even kill her. She still felt shocked to the core, but she tried to suppress all thoughts of it as far as she could. The drifter must be working with the others – and if she'd interpreted the message *I know what you are* correctly, there could only be one reason for that. They were trying to set her up. Because for these people – for Hanna Jansen, if she really was involved – the phrase *I know what you are* could mean only one thing. I know what you are: a murderer.

First off, there was the homeless man she'd killed. Maybe they would try to pin Johann Larsen's murder on her too, along with the arson attack on his house. But any attempt they made to frame her for that would be complicated. They would have needed to plan too much in advance, too much could have gone wrong, too many conspirators would have had to be involved . . .

You're missing something.

If they're trying to frame you for murder, there are much easier ways of doing it.

They didn't need to lure you to the island.

Even if Hanna Jansen is behind all this – and you know how badly she wanted Jørgen, how much she wanted to get you out of the way.

The thought gnawed away at her as she pushed aside the hoarding that blocked the drive leading up to the sanatorium, climbed back into the car and drove through the gap. The main building was still largely intact, though the flames that had licked at the red facade had left brown patches of soot. The windows had been destroyed or removed altogether and the doorways were nailed up with thick boards. Weeds and tall grass sprang up between the paving stones and a *Keep Out* sign squeaked in the wind, the metal covered in patches of rust.

Jasmin took the key out of the ignition, put Bonnie on a lead and got out of the car. A powerful gust buffeted against her, as if trying to stop her from approaching the crumbling building, but she leaned into the gale and pressed on.

The wind made a hollow, whining noise as it whirled over the buckled roof and through the empty window frames, which seemed to watch her like countless eyes while she circled the old sanatorium through the knee-high grass.

You're insane if you really go through with this. God knows what might happen if you go in there – assuming you even manage to find a way in. The walls are all on the point of collapse, the roof beams are rotten and there'll be rusty nails everywhere.

You can't do this.

And yet she kept going. The symbol, the inverted triangle she'd seen in Larsen's photo – it must be here somewhere. Jasmin instinctively sensed that she was on the right track; that she was on the cusp of making a significant step forward; that she was about to uncover a secret that had long been hidden.

A terrible crime was committed here. The historian's words echoed in her ears, her memory. *A sin against human nature.*

Bonnie sniffed at the tall grass, but after a few yards she sat down and refused to go any further. She fixed her eyes fearfully on the edifice looming in front of her and whimpered quietly.

'What's the matter? It's just an empty old—' Jasmin fell silent as a fresh gust of wind brought forth an unsettling howl from the depths of the sanatorium. Bonnie gave a loud bark, but it didn't sound as boisterous as usual. This time, her dog sounded small and scared.

'OK. You're right. The floors in there are too dangerous. I don't want you stepping on any broken glass,' Jasmin told her. 'You can stay behind.' She led the dog back to the car, took the checked picnic blanket out of the boot and laid it on the grass. 'Wait here for me. And look after yourself, all right?'

Bonnie nuzzled her hand with her damp nose, as if to say there was no need to worry about her. Jasmin held her torch out in front of her like a gun and headed back towards the sanatorium.

Though the doors and most of the ground-floor windows were boarded up, an opening at the rear of the building looked more promising. A number of leftover planks were piled up beneath a window where one of the boards was dangling loose and beating with the wind against the facade. Large patches of render had crumbled away underneath it.

Jasmin climbed onto the stack of wood, teetering slightly, and reached for the windowsill. Bracing herself against it, she gripped the loose board and tried to pull it out of the wall. It put up some resistance, but eventually gave way.

Cold, damp, stagnant air rose to meet her through the opening. Jasmin pulled herself up onto the windowsill. Just as she switched on her torch and set about climbing through the gap, the pile of boards gave way beneath her and clattered to the ground.

The beam of light from her torch fell onto a fragment of brown, patterned wallpaper that hung in ragged strips from a damp wall. Jasmin shone it at the floor, which lay around eight feet below her.

Shit, she thought.

You can still turn back.

There's still time to call Jørgen.

Jørgen. There it was again – that nagging thought, haunting her mind. *What are you missing?*

You thought it would be far too complicated for anyone to stage all this. You thought it'd be impossible.

But you forgot about one thing.

The person who sent you out here to the island. The person who knew about your plans the whole time.

Jørgen knew.

And if his ex-lover Hanna Jansen knew too, it would have been easy for them both to prepare everything together.

Wouldn't it?

A sudden gust of wind hit her from behind and knocked her off balance. Jasmin shrieked and wheeled her arms, but then she fell.

She landed feet-first on the floor inside the old sanatorium and felt a sharp stab of pain shoot through her left foot as far as the ankle.

'Fuck!' she cried, grabbing her foot. Her torch had slipped out of her fingers when she hit the floor and it rolled a few yards before going out. Jasmin was now submerged in pitch darkness. She sat up with a groan of pain and groped around her, her hand splashing into a puddle on the floor and fumbling across the swollen floor-boards. The inky darkness whispered and rustled, as if multi-legged creatures were crawling back and forth.

Jasmin took her phone out of her coat pocket and activated the torch function, casting a bright patch of light in front of her.

Two glowing eyes stared back at her from the darkness.

Chapter 13

Jasmin screamed and the animal scurried away. She could hear the rat dragging its tail along the floor before it vanished through a gap in the floorboards.

It was enormous, almost like a small dog.

Jasmin struggled for breath. Using the light from her mobile phone, she spotted the torch that had fallen from her hand and hobbled over to it. The metal was ice-cold beneath her fingers.

Please work, she thought imploringly as she pressed the button.

A bright circle of light appeared.

Thank God. Jasmin put her phone back in her pocket and cast her torch over the room. The hallway she'd landed in resembled the interior of a Victorian manor house: dark wooden floors, oil paintings in huge, ornate frames, and floor-to-ceiling curtains that hung damp and heavy from their rails. The walls were covered in wet patches, the wallpaper sagging like wrinkled skin. Beetles danced in front of her torch and mould proliferated in the corners. It stank of rot and mildew, and for a second Jasmin thought she heard a scream from the depths of the building – as if one of the former inmates was still locked inside, ceaselessly pacing the corridors for all time.

'Warm and welcoming,' Jasmin said to herself, purely to break the oppressive silence.

Hopefully no one heard you, was her next thought. *That would be unfortunate. And in future you should think twice before you embark on a crazy plan like this.*

Just think twice.

Next, Jasmin turned her attention to her ankle, feeling it carefully. The water clinging to the tall grass outside had soaked her jeans up to the knees. She rolled up her trouser leg. Nothing seemed to be broken but she could already feel it swelling.

No going back. She looked up at the window, at the narrow grey strip where the afternoon light was barely peeping through. It was far too high to climb out again.

No, you need to find another way out of here.

But before that – Jasmin took a deep breath and gathered all the courage she could muster – *you're going to take a look around. You're going to find out what's hidden inside this place. That symbol – it has to be here somewhere.*

She wandered cautiously down the hallway, shining her torch over the peeling wallpaper and the puddles on the floor. Dark, dirty water gleamed like an oily film.

Soon, the corridor emerged into a large hall with a smooth, polished stone floor laid out in a black-and-white chessboard pattern. To her right, Jasmin saw a wide staircase leading to the upper floors, while on her left stood a cluster of sofas and chairs, their beige fabric now covered in black mould. Loose sheets of paper lay on the floor, scattered there by the wind. The southern end of the hall was lined with tall bookshelves. Jasmin put her hand on the ladder leaning against them and heard the wheels squeak softly. She couldn't shake the feeling that something was watching her from the darkness, and when she turned around, she expected to see animal eyes peering at her from the shadows – but no, there was nothing but the wind blowing through a narrow gap in a boarded-up window, producing an eerie whine.

Above Jasmin's head hung two enormous chandeliers covered in cobwebs. The glass crystals glittered dully in the light from her torch.

You need to find the place you saw in Larsen's photo. The place with the symbol. The place the kidnapper was hinting at with his origami sculpture – the triangle he left for you.

But what if he's waiting for you there? What if this is a trap?

Jasmin pushed the thought aside. *You have no other choice. If you ever want to see Paul again then you have to face up to him. To his kidnapper. Whatever it costs. Otherwise you'll lose him for good.*

She picked her way past the armchairs and sofas. An abandoned serving trolley stood in her path, its metal frame now rusty. There was still a plate on top of it, along with a set of cutlery – a plastic knife and fork with rounded tips and a dull blade – and a folded-up newspaper.

It must be upstairs. Jasmin approached the staircase. The wooden treads were sodden from all the rainwater, cracked and broken in many places. Leaves had collected on them and decomposed into a dangerously slippery sludge, making climbing the stairs a hazardous prospect.

Jasmin clung firmly to the banister and headed upwards, carefully planting one foot at a time and listening for any sounds.

Was that the echo of footsteps following her? Footsteps that stopped whenever she herself stood still? Could she hear breathing in the darkness? Ragged, laboured gasps?

She pointed her torch down the stairs. Nothing. Just the steps she'd already climbed, and beyond them the hall.

The serving trolley was standing a few yards further to the left than before.

Someone had moved it. Someone had passed through the hall after her.

Jasmin started to shake. Her hand on the banister suddenly felt slick with sweat. She rushed onwards, hurrying up the stairs, the treads squeaking and groaning beneath her hasty footsteps.

Water was dripping from the ceiling. The corridor she arrived on was laid with a mouldy carpet that had a dark trail leading over it – dark like dried blood.

The staircase behind her creaked. Heavy, lumbering footsteps were following her upstairs.

Jasmin splashed through a puddle, opened the nearest door on her left and dashed through it, slamming it behind her. Looking around frantically, she realised she was standing in one of the patients' rooms. There was a bed in front of a window overlooking the grounds, a bedside table, a wardrobe, a modest painting on the wall, and not much else. Jasmin grabbed the bedside cabinet and dragged it over to the door, where she managed to wedge it underneath the handle. She took a step back, breathing heavily, her heart hammering in her chest, and listened in terror for any sounds from the corridor – for any approaching footsteps.

Nothing. Silence reigned. For a moment, even the wind seemed to hold its breath.

Has he gone?

I hope he's gone.

Jasmin took another look around. Here too, there was a gaping hole in the ceiling where the roof had leaked. Brown water was trickling through it, running down the wall and collecting in a slimy pool on the floor.

She turned her attention to the bed. The blanket was oddly rumpled, and in the last rays of daylight filtering through the boards over the window, Jasmin's eyes were drawn to an object lying on the mattress.

The blanket moved.

Jasmin shrieked as it fell to one side and a creature leapt out with a hiss from beneath it – and then she dissolved into hysterical laughter.

It was a cat.

Only a cat.

'You scared me half to death there,' she whispered reproachfully.

The cat slunk past her and slipped through a gap into the wardrobe. Jasmin opened the door and was met with a chorus of faint mewing – the cat had five kittens, which were huddled together on an old blanket. The mother looked up at her and hissed again, but soon seemed to stop viewing Jasmin as a threat and lay down beside her offspring instead.

'Look after your babies,' said Jasmin quietly. 'I'm not sure this is the best place for them.'

The door at the other end of the room led into a small bathroom. She tugged at the light switch but nothing happened. Water had gathered on the tiles here too, and the mirror was cracked. Jasmin stopped and briefly examined her pale, frightened face.

You look horribly tired. You slept for ages – all yesterday evening and last night, like Henriksen told you – but you look like you just tossed and turned for hours on end.

And you can't remember any of it.

Behind her, something creaked. Jasmin whirled around. The door to the shower cubicle was closed, but behind it . . . When she shone her torch on it, she thought she saw a figure moving behind the frosted glass, a shape rising up from the floor. Jasmin staggered backwards, colliding with the sink. The bathroom door slammed shut.

'What the . . . ?!' she cried. The shower cubicle groaned; the hinges creaked like bones being crushed in a grinder. Jasmin wanted to run, to tear her eyes away. She fumbled blindly at the doorknob.

A hand reached out and slammed against the door of the shower. It was caked in blood and long-fingered, like a huge, pale spider.

This isn't real. The thought was like a lifeline that she tried desperately to cling to. *It isn't real, none of it is. Why can't you realise that?* Jasmin forced herself to close her eyes.

It's not real.

When she opened her eyes again, the dark silhouette behind the shower door was gone. Jasmin turned and dashed out of the room. The cats had disappeared from the wardrobe, but once again there was movement beneath the blanket on the bed. Jasmin reached out and flung the cover aside, revealing pale, slippery maggots that made smacking noises as they ate their way through the mattress.

Get out of here, she thought. *Now.*

Jasmin was about to grab the cabinet and push it aside when she heard a faint noise from behind the door. Footsteps. So quiet that she could easily have missed them. There was a person out there, creeping around on tiptoes.

She held her breath. Her heart was pounding so quickly and heavily that she felt sure it would give her away. *He can't hear you. He's trying to sneak up on you, but he won't manage it.*

Just then, a heavy blow struck the door with such force that the entire frame trembled in the wall. Dust and plaster fell from the ceiling.

Jasmin sprang backwards, colliding with the bed. Another blow. The door shook again. A crack appeared in the door leaf; the bedside table she'd shoved under the handle began to move to one side. Then came a third, even more powerful blow.

'No,' she screamed, bracing herself against the door, 'I won't let you!'

Jasmin felt the door shake under a fourth blow as the wood splintered. An axe drove its way through before being pulled back out, ripping huge chunks of particle board with it and leaving a gaping hole. The light from her torch shone through it.

On the other side, she saw the drifter.

He grinned.

She saw his long, grey coat hanging limply from his body like a shroud. Almost mechanically, her torch wandered up to his face.

She recognised him.

This was impossible.

It couldn't be true.

It was Jørgen.

Chapter 14

Jasmin heard a tormented shriek of terror escape her lips. Jørgen was standing in front of her, the axe in his hand gleaming threateningly in the light, its blade as sharp as a carving knife.

He smiled malevolently.

'It can't be you!' she cried. 'This can't be real!'

'And yet,' he said, sounding nothing like the Jørgen she remembered, 'here I am.'

He hefted the axe once more and drove the blade into the door, again and again, until his path was clear. Jasmin had retreated to the far wall, shaking from head to foot. Her instincts screamed at her to push past Jørgen and run, and yet a small, lingering part of herself – one that trembled with fury – urged her to attack him.

'I don't understand,' she croaked. 'What – what are you doing here?'

'You still don't get it?'

Jørgen drew nearer. He lifted the axe. 'Come here, let me explain it to you.'

And then he screamed. Jørgen dropped the axe and cried out as his hands flew up to his face, which had disappeared under a wild, hissing, furry bundle that latched on to him with her claws. It was the cat – she had leapt up at him, ready to defend herself and her young from this dangerous intruder.

Jasmin sprang forward, barging past Jørgen and dashing through the door. He continued to scream as she ran on blindly down the stairs. Dazzling flashes of light appeared before her eyes. She slipped on the leaf litter that had gathered on the staircase, lost her footing and tumbled down the last eight or so steps. The edges of the treads jabbed painfully into her side, into her ribs. At the bottom, she landed feet-first and shrieked as her ankle gave way. Her foot felt like it was filled with red-hot splinters. Panicking, Jasmin reached for the banister and hauled herself up, struggling to get back on her feet.

You need to find a way out of here. Get out, just get out. She heard Jørgen's footsteps from upstairs and the sound of an axe being dragged along the floor.

Jasmin hobbled on.

Once again, she crossed the large hall with the chessboard tiles. The light from her torch fell on the loose sheets of paper scattered on the floor, and this time she took in what was written on them.

> Dangerous criminal duo break out of high-security hospital!
>
> Criminals on the run!
>
> Extreme danger to the public!

Beneath those words, she saw a picture of Hanna Jansen, just as she remembered her, looking completely deranged.

The newspaper had fallen off the serving trolley and a gust of wind blew the front page past her feet.

There was a picture of Jørgen on it.

He was grinning at the camera, looking no less insane than Jansen.

No, this can't be. He isn't what these people think he is.

Jasmin searched for a way out, but all she found was a door with a narrow staircase behind it that led deeper into the building. The key was still inside, so she stepped through the doorway, slammed the door and locked it.

The solid metal of the red security door reassured her. It was cold and hard, and Jørgen wouldn't be able to break through it so easily.

Slowly, she began to descend the staircase into the darkness.

Think, she urged herself. *It can't be Jørgen. You must be imagining things.*

And yet you saw him.

It was a hallucination. The light, the strain you're under. Your panic. This place.

It was the drifter. It can't have been Jørgen.

But what about the newspaper? All those flyers upstairs?

None of it makes any sense.

But there has to be an explanation. There has to be!

At the bottom of the stairs, Jasmin found herself standing in a brick-walled corridor lined with steel doors on the left and right – doors with small hatches to let you look inside.

Cell doors.

Who did they keep locked away down here?

The most dangerous inmates?

Then she heard the banging. Somebody was beating at the inside of their cell door in a slow, even rhythm.

Clang. Clang. Clang.

It was coming from close by. And there was also a strange substance gleaming on the walls, on the doors.

At long last, Jasmin had found the symbol she was looking for – the symbol from Larsen's photo. There it was: the upside-down triangle with the open top-right corner. Gooseflesh crept over her entire body. The symbol had been daubed onto the bare brick wall in black paint, which had run down to the floor in thick rivulets before it had set.

Jasmin's heart was in her mouth.

Clang, came the noise. *Clang*. Again and again, like an iron bar being beaten against the wall. The echoes built up into a wall of sound that reverberated down the entire corridor.

He's here, a voice seemed to say – or to whisper. A voice that came from inside herself. *He's here. The man you're looking for, the cause of all your suffering. He's right here, and he has Paul with him!*

Jasmin glanced over her shoulder, half-expecting to see the drifter emerging from the shadows in his long grey coat – and yet her encounter with him upstairs already felt unimportant, half-forgotten, like a dream. The only thing that still mattered lay in front of her, drawing nearer with every step she took over the stained concrete floor.

The noise was coming from a cell on her left. Somebody was inside it, pounding on the door. With trembling fingers, Jasmin reached for the hatch and opened it before shining her torch inside.

'Ha!' A face pressed itself against the aperture, which was wide enough to reach through. Jasmin instinctively took a step backwards. There was a man inside, his face encrusted with blood and filth, as if he hadn't washed in weeks. Maybe even months. He stuck out his tongue and stared at her with ice-blue eyes that reminded Jasmin of somebody. His face was like a piece of wood that had been shaped by a clumsy carver; his cheeks and lips were swollen as if he'd taken a severe beating.

Who do those eyes remind you of? Think, for Christ's sake!

Then it hit her.

No, Jasmin thought, *it can't be.*

226

His eyes reminded her of Sven Birkeland. Her colleague from the hospital – the specialist registrar at whose side she had saved so many lives.

And there was another memory too. Something lurking at the edge of her consciousness that felt like a trap, ready to spring shut if she approached it carelessly. *You and Sven – what have you forgotten?*

Once again, she saw flashes of light before her eyes – once again, she felt a piercing pain behind her temples, as if a drill was boring into her head. For a moment she was back there, on that terrible night, on the wet road, watching the Jeep race towards her. She swerved to one side. There was the homeless man, raising his arms – and she hit him.

There was something about that night – something she still hadn't fully understood.

'You don't remember,' said the stranger in the cell. His voice was rough, and as he spoke, Jasmin could see in the torchlight that he had no teeth left; they'd been knocked out of his jaw. 'You don't remember anything at all.'

'Who are you?' Jasmin asked, and the man gave a start as she addressed him. 'Why are you here?'

'I can't tell you, you wouldn't believe me anyway.' It sounded like the plaintive sing-song of a child.

'This place was abandoned a long time ago,' said Jasmin. She gathered all her courage and took a few steps forward. A sour odour emanated from the hatch. Dear God, how long had this man been locked up in there? 'How can you still be here?'

'I'm here because you are,' he replied. 'Don't you get it? I'm everywhere you go.'

'But—'

'No buts!' His hand shot out and tried to grab her, but Jasmin managed to avoid him and lashed out with the handle of her torch. The man yowled in pain and pulled back his arm.

'Stop it,' she said coldly. 'I want answers. The symbol led me here.'

'Yes, it did. You've seen it over and over again, haven't you? You see it everywhere, but you don't understand what it means. Because you're suppressing it. Oh, you've always been very good at that.'

'Enough. Tell me what's going on. In here, and elsewhere on the island.'

'Do you really think I know? What are you expecting from me? Answers? You have all the answers already. You just need to remember.'

'Bullshit!' Jasmin yelled. She could feel herself growing more anxious with every word the man said to her. And angry – she was getting angry too. *You're losing control of the situation.* 'You need to start talking. Everything is so – so horribly confusing.'

'Confusing? Oh, but it isn't. This is a reflection of a reality, a truth you've been suppressing. *Jasmin.*'

She froze. A smile passed over the stranger's bloody mouth. 'How do you know my name?'

'I know everything about you.'

Jasmin's hand clenched around her torch. 'My son has been kidnapped. If you know so much, maybe you can tell me who did it and where they're keeping him? I was nearly attacked by a man with a syringe earlier today. I – I don't know what's going on anymore. I feel like I'm living a nightmare.'

'They're worried. You're in danger of veering off track.'

'Off track? What's that supposed to mean?'

'You say your son has been kidnapped. Are you really sure that's what happened?' The stranger's eyes narrowed to slits as he gave her a thoughtful, penetrating look. 'Are you really sure you can trust your own eyes, your own mind?'

No, said a quiet voice in her head that sounded like Jørgen's. *You can't. You imagined I was here with you in this old sanatorium, that I even tried to attack you,* the voice said reproachfully. *Would I ever do that?*

Jasmin gulped. She felt a tear well up in her eye and trickle down her cheek.

Then again, another, more energetic voice warned her, *other people have been trying to attack you too.* Mattila with his syringe; the drifter at her house; the threatening letter. Henriksen was keeping secrets from her, and there was also Yrsen with her insinuations. Paul had been kidnapped; Larsen the historian had been burned to death in his own home. The scrap of cloth in her coat pocket. Was all this an attempt to frame her for something? For murder? Were they trying to take her son away from her?

And the question behind it all . . .

Why?

When she looked up again, the wounds on the stranger's face seemed to have worsened. He was bleeding from his nose and his mouth and barely seemed able to hold himself upright.

'You really want to see this through to the end,' he said in a disappointed tone. 'That's a pity.'

'Talk!' Jasmin hammered her torch against the steel door, producing a metallic din that echoed down the whole corridor. 'Talk, and then I'll let you out of here.'

'No, you won't. We both know that. You're afraid of me. You know what I am.'

Jasmin simply stared at him. For a moment, it seemed like the stranger had spoken with a completely different voice. Her own voice.

'Paul has been kidnapped,' said the stranger, although it sounded like it caused him great pain to speak these words, 'and is being held in a place you know very well. Think. Who stands to gain most from all this? Who would benefit if you were certified insane and locked in an institution because you risked your son's life, over and over again? Because you're a *murderer*, Jasmin?'

She stared at him. Her thoughts whirred in her mind like the slow, interlocking gears of a clock. 'It would benefit . . . Dear God.'

'God has nothing to do with this! Think!'

'Jørgen would benefit. My husband. He would get everything.'

'Well? Isn't it likely that he *wants* to get everything? You're wealthy, Jasmin, your family is wealthy, and as for him – hasn't he always felt like a failure, like he wasn't enough for you? Doesn't he feel angry – frustrated – at always being the little man? And doesn't he want to get back at you for that? Have you forgotten about *her*? About Hanna Jansen? What if the two of them have plotted all this behind your back? Hmm? What about that?'

Her. Jasmin had to reach out and steady herself against the brick wall as she realised what the stranger was hinting at. 'It's true,' she replied in a hoarse voice. 'Jørgen had an affair. But that's all over now. Water under the bridge. He would never – *never* do that to me. He loves me, he's worried about me, and he hasn't stopped calling me. He even wanted to join us out here—'

'Bullshit,' replied the stranger. 'And you know it.' Blood was now pouring from his ears. He was going to die, Jasmin realised, and she knew she couldn't help him because this stranger wasn't really here. He was a projection of her subconscious, a reproachful voice, urging her to – what, exactly?

To remember?

And why did you think he looked like Sven Birkeland?

'Jørgen planned everything with *her*. He's been pulling the wool over your eyes the whole time. And you have to admit that you tend to obsess about things. When you lost your second child—'

'Jørgen was always by my side.'

'You started to create a fictional world, which grew out of all proportion. Don't you understand? Jørgen hated it. He wanted you to find your way back to reality. And then the accident happened. You maintain that you killed a man, even though no one ever found any evidence for it. So he came up with a plan to get rid of you once and for all. And it had to be a good plan, as he wouldn't get anything from you otherwise. The two of you signed a prenuptial agreement, didn't you?'

Jasmin felt a steady stream of tears falling down her cheeks. 'I thought he was here just now. He tried to attack me. I thought he was the drifter in the grey coat—'

'Because your subconscious has already worked out what's really going on here. Because you've secretly realised Jørgen wants to hurt you.'

'But he isn't here!' she cried in panic. 'You must be lying!'

'Of course he isn't here, but there are people working for him to carry out his plan. And of course I'm not lying. I don't even exist!' The stranger reached his hand out once more, grabbed the hatch in the cell door and slammed it shut. It fell closed with a loud, metallic bang, leaving Jasmin alone in the darkened corridor.

'You – you liar!' Jasmin sobbed. She pulled the hatch open again, but when she shone her torch inside, the cell was empty. The floor was stained, the walls were covered in a chaos of scratches, but there was nobody inside, least of all a stranger with ice-blue eyes.

You were talking to yourself, she thought. *What does that say about your mental state?*

And yet her thoughts all made perfect sense. Jørgen. She had to follow this new lead. He could hardly have been acting alone. He must have helpers.

'And you know exactly who's helping him,' said a voice. When she turned around, the stranger was back again – only this time, he was leaning against the wall, as if he'd walked through the locked cell door like it was nothing more than thin air. Jasmin realised he was wearing a long, white doctor's coat with a name badge that said *S. Birkeland*. The coat was tattered and covered in blood. 'You know Hanna Jansen is here. She's changed. You've met her already.'

'What's happened to you?'

'You did this to me, Jasmin. You and no one else.'

'I – I don't understand.'

'It doesn't matter right now. What matters is that you need to find Paul. You need to stop them before they can bring their plan to fruition. Before they manage to spring a trap that you'll never be able to escape from. If Jørgen wins, you'll lose everything, and he'll be able to live happily ever after with his new lover. Is that what you want?'

'No,' Jasmin replied. 'He'll pay for this.'

'And where can you start?' Birkeland drew nearer. Jasmin realised he was limping, as if he'd broken his leg. Then she saw a piece of bare bone sticking out from below his knee. She closed her eyes. *It's just your imagination. He isn't here.*

'That's not how this works,' Birkeland declared. 'I'm always with you. I'm a part of you.'

'Go away!' Jasmin cried. 'What's happening? Am I going crazy?'

'You're showing all the signs, aren't you?' Birkeland folded his arms. 'Have you really forgotten about me? About that night when we—'

'Shut your mouth!'

Birkeland smiled and shook his head. 'As you wish. Now you need to think carefully about what you're going to do next.'

'I don't know.' Jasmin wiped the tears from her cheeks. 'I really don't know. There's no trail to follow, nothing that will take me closer to Paul. The kidnapper hasn't tried to get in touch with me.'

'Haven't you been listening to anything I've said?'

'You aren't real,' she retorted and turned away. 'Why should I listen to you? I'm going to look for a way out of here and then

I'm going to tell Henriksen everything. How I saw the body in the freezer and that it was the man from the night of the accident.'

'Oh, very smart. And then they'll accuse you of stealing the corpse. More than that, in fact. They'll accuse you of starting the fire that killed Larsen. After all, they know how much you love fire.'

'Excuse me?' Jasmin froze. 'What did you say?'

'The exit is at the end of the corridor.' Birkeland pointed into the darkness with his bloodied arm. 'Go, if you have to. Run to your destruction.'

'What other choice do I have?'

'You could look at a painting instead.' Birkeland cocked his head and a cynical smile played over his lips. 'You know what I'm talking about.'

Gabriela Yrsen, Jasmin thought. The woman with the second sight; the artist who'd promised to paint her a picture that would answer her questions.

Had she finished it already?

'You could ask her what she's hiding from you. What Henriksen doesn't want to tell you. And you could stop to consider who this woman really is.'

The contact list. Yrsen, Larsen – both their numbers had been saved on Henriksen's phone. Maybe it was worth a try.

Jasmin shone her torch down the corridor. Dirty, stained concrete. Bare masonry with bricks protruding here and there, as if subsidence over the years had caused the walls to gradually shift. A rat scuttling along the floor, away from the light. That was all she could see. She was alone and everything was silent.

Birkeland had vanished. Jasmin followed the corridor until she encountered a second metal door that was bolted shut. The iron was rusty, but after a few tugs, she managed to pull back the bolt and cool, fresh air blew into her face. Jasmin was standing at the

233

foot of a covered staircase that led up to the rear of the sanatorium. She was outside – she was free.

Everything you saw in there was an illusion. She did her best to cling to the thought. *Maybe it was more than that. After all, people don't normally have conversations with figments of their imagination. Whatever it was, you could try to forget it – or you could view it as a message from your subconscious and learn from it.*

Jasmin made her way back to the car. The clouds had thinned and the sun had wandered a considerable distance along the horizon and was starting to sink beneath the treetops. *You must have spent a few hours in there, though it felt shorter.*

Bonnie was lying asleep on the grass, but woke as soon as she heard Jasmin approaching and wagged her tail joyfully. Jasmin clasped her arms around her and stroked her, and they both got into the car.

She took out her phone and looked up Jørgen on her contact list. For a long while, she sat and stared at his number, her finger hovering over the call button.

There's a chance he really is lying, that he never ended his affair. There's a chance he really does want to get rid of you. But would he risk Paul's life? No, she realised, *he would never do that. So if Jørgen and Hanna Jansen really are working together, the kidnapping must have been staged. Paul is alive – Paul is OK.*

This was all about her. This was all an attempt to set her up.

Her hand reached mechanically into her coat pocket and wrapped itself around the scrap of cloth she'd found earlier. Jasmin held it up to her nose and sniffed. There was a distinct odour of petrol.

Petrol that had been used to set a house on fire.

Larsen's house.

Her heart started to beat faster. Could it be true? Were these people really devious enough to try to frame her for murder?

It was possible. People weren't always what she thought they were. They weren't always as good as she wanted them to be. 'You're naive,' Jørgen had once said to her. 'You always misjudge everyone. Your life is far too sheltered.'

Jasmin scrolled down her contact list until she found Birkeland's number, followed by her mother, Marit. She called both of them, but each time all she heard at the other end was an answering machine.

It was like she was jinxed.

Last of all, she dialled Henriksen's number, which she'd noted down from his business card and saved to her phone. *You can tell him the truth. You can try to ask him to meet you, in private. You can try one last time to persuade him that you're trustworthy.*

She tapped the green button and Henriksen picked up after the first ring.

'We've been worried about you,' he said. 'You've been missing for hours. Where on earth are you?'

'I was investigating something,' Jasmin replied, her voice raw. 'A matter I had to look into on my own.'

'We've heard you were down on the beach. When I got back to the house, I ran into Boeckermann. He'd met a man named Veikko Mattila on the shore who told him you were trying to dispose of something in the sea.'

Jasmin couldn't believe her ears. 'He says I did what?'

'Papers, Ms Hansen. You were scattering burned-up papers into the wind. Documents from the historian's house.'

'That isn't true. That's a lie!'

'So you weren't on the beach?' Henriksen sounded completely unmoved; she couldn't tell if he believed her or not. She paused, and during the moment of silence, she heard a faint noise in the background from his end of the line.

You know that sound. Dear God – you know where he is right now. Where he's calling from.

'I was on the beach,' she replied, 'and I met Mattila, but I definitely didn't scatter anything into the wind.' *He tried to attack me*, she almost added, but she bit her tongue. 'Are you back at my house? Is there any new evidence?'

'I'm in the village. At the police station.' Henriksen hesitated. 'You should come here. We need to meet up in person and talk.'

'All right,' Jasmin replied quickly. 'Let's do that. But I can't right now. Let's say tonight. Eight o'clock at my house.'

'Eight o'clock?' Henriksen said again. Jasmin had the impression he was repeating her words for the benefit of somebody standing beside him who was trying to listen in. 'Perfect. I'll see you then.'

Jasmin hung up. Her hand was shaking. *Oh no you won't*, she thought.

You recognised that strange noise from his end of the line. You know where he is right now.

The noise had come from the wind blowing through a cleverly designed pipe, and it was a noise she'd heard before. It was the sculpture in Yrsen's garden. The one of the sailor with the telescope.

Henriksen was there. He was at Yrsen's house.

Chapter 15

Dusk was starting to fall by the time Jasmin parked her Volvo. She'd turned off her headlights a couple of hundred yards down the road to avoid anyone spotting her as she approached, and she pulled up some distance away from Gabriela Yrsen's property in a spot where her car was screened by a cluster of bushes. The wind was rushing through the trees, making the branches and leaves that hadn't yet fallen to the ground dance back and forth above her head. *You're acting like a criminal,* she thought – and to her own mounting unease, she was finding it all so easy. Bonnie looked up at her attentively, with alert eyes, but Jasmin shook her head.

'I can't take you with me here. That's not an option. You're clever – probably clever enough not to give me away – but I still can't risk it.' She stroked the dog's head and Bonnie licked her hand. 'I'm sorry. I'll be back soon, I promise.'

Jasmin got out of the car, and as she crouched down and crept towards the house, she felt as though she'd lied to Bonnie. *Maybe you'll never see her again,* it dawned on her painfully. *Maybe that was the last time.*

If they catch you . . .

But what if you manage to stop them first?

Uncover their plot?

Jasmin came to the garden gate set into the fence and hopped over it. The darkness that had now fallen formed a protective cloak that hid her movements from view.

Hopefully.

She peered at the ground-floor windows. They were dimly lit, while the ones upstairs were all dark. If anyone was looking out from up there, they'd be able to see her and she would have no way of knowing. It was like when the drifter had appeared at the bottom of her garden, though this time the roles were reversed.

She looked back to the road and saw Henriksen's car. It was hidden among the trees at the top of a narrow path, but the paint-work gave a tell-tale gleam from the glow of a nearby streetlight. Had he deliberately parked there to avoid being immediately spotted by anyone approaching the house from the south?

Of course he has.

The air was filled with the salty odour of the nearby Norwegian Sea, along with the low moan produced by the wind blowing through the pipe on the strange metal sculpture beside the house.

The gale had gathered force. She'd listened to the radio on the way here to calm her nerves and the presenter of the local station had issued a warning: the storm was getting closer. All ferries to the mainland had been cancelled, so nobody would be able to leave the island for the next few hours.

That meant they were all stuck here together. Everything would come to a head tonight – and now they had her up against the wall, she didn't have many options.

Now or never, Jasmin thought. *You don't have much time.*

Jasmin pressed herself against the wall of the house. The howling grew much louder as she crept around the side of the building. She raised a hand to wipe the sweat from her forehead. Despite the chill, she felt hot, and her hands were trembling. She swept her eyes over the building. There – a small window on the north end had been left open.

Coincidence?

Maybe not. But you're here now.

There's no turning back.

Jasmin hadn't driven here directly from the sanatorium. She'd gone back to her house on the coast first, and although she was worried they'd be waiting there to arrest her, the house and garden had been empty when she arrived. She'd checked the cameras and the motion sensors. Henriksen had been telling the truth, at least. He'd left the house and hadn't returned.

Everything had been silent and deserted, and as Jasmin looked at the pictures Paul had painted, which she'd hung up on the walls – as she stared at the green sofa in the living room and the long wooden boards of the veranda, which Jørgen had built himself – she'd been overwhelmed by such an intense sadness that she'd wanted nothing more than to sit down in a corner on the floor and bury her face in her hands.

Things will never go back to how they were.

However much you try, you can't turn back the clock. Nobody can.

Jasmin had climbed the stairs to her bedroom, pulled out the bottom drawer of the bedside cabinet and emptied it onto the floor. A few boxes of medication, a handful of hairbands, shards of a broken mirror and a lipstick all fell out, scattering noisily across the floor. It was so quiet inside the house; all she could hear was the quiet click of Bonnie's claws on the floorboards as the Labrador trotted into Paul's room, snuffling around in search of her little friend.

When her search proved fruitless, she gave a brief, mournful howl.

Jasmin dug her fingers into the corners of the drawer and levered out the base. Beneath it was a hidden compartment containing a silver snub-nosed revolver, like a foreign body that didn't belong there.

It was *her* secret – one of the dark secrets she'd been keeping – and it had sprung up in her memory like a hidden plant that had blossomed as she'd lain awake over the last few nights, listening to the noises made by the old house, by these old walls.

It had dawned on her that the shotgun in the cellar wasn't the only firearm she owned.

This special pistol didn't belong to Jørgen. It was hers, and hers alone.

Jørgen didn't know about it. She'd acquired it and hidden it here years ago, back when she'd had to spend nights on the island on her own. It had lain here ever since, forgotten by her until now. Jasmin had taken out the revolver and the small box of ammunition – the nine-millimetre rounds rattling around inside it like tiny silver coins in a treasure chest – and she'd loaded it and tucked it into her coat pocket.

Then she'd noticed the tiny scratches on the bottom of the drawer. The fingerprints on the gun. The patches of blood.

Someone has been here recently, she'd thought. *Someone who knew about the weapon.*

And now that she was standing outside Yrsen's house, her back pressed against the wall, feeling every bump in the brickwork through the fabric of her raincoat, the weight of the gun in her pocket reassured her.

Just in case, she thought. *Just in case.*

Jasmin reached up to the window, opened the casement a little further, and put her hand into her coat pocket to grab a pair of gloves. Not because of the cold; she couldn't care less about that right now. She was thinking about fingerprints. Once she'd put them on, she climbed inside.

Chapter 16

Entering the artist's house felt like venturing into a cave – the lair of a big cat, or the last refuge of a wanted criminal. Jasmin almost thought the walls were breathing. The long oak floorboards creaked beneath her feet.

Be brave. You've made it this far.

She followed the corridor, feeling like all the paintings and drawings hanging on the walls were watching her. To her left was a row of doors, all closed. She could hear quiet voices from elsewhere in the house – two of them, if Jasmin wasn't mistaken.

Henriksen and Yrsen, she was sure of it.

For a moment she stopped on a thick, cream-coloured rug, her heart pounding, and considered how insane this nocturnal escapade was. *You're trying to spy on people who've resolved to hurt you. Instead of running away, you're letting yourself get drawn further and further in.*

But deep down, Jasmin felt tired of always running away. She wanted to *fight*.

The first door on her right led into a small studio with a desk on which a number of letters and half-finished sketches had been arranged in a rough pile. They were enquiries from people asking Yrsen for an appointment.

People who knew what she'd done for others in the past.

Jasmin leafed through the letters. None of them were older than five months. That was strange, wasn't it?

Beside the PC, which occupied most of the desk, Jasmin found a few opened envelopes that looked like bills. Underneath those was a stack of books. She picked one of them up. *The Beginners' Guide to Painting and Drawing*, it said on the cover. *An Introduction to the Art of Oil Painting* was the next title.

Jasmin realised her hands were shaking.

Landscape Painting for Dummies.

The Big Book of Art History.

Jasmin couldn't believe her eyes. It was hard to process.

So you were right. She lied. She's a – well, what exactly? What on earth is going on here?

Jasmin pulled open the drawers of the desk, listening all the while for noises, for footsteps coming from the corridor, but everything was quiet. All she could hear were the subdued voices of Yrsen and Henriksen, who must be in the living room at the other end of the house.

If they catch you here, you're done for. And yet she was finding clear evidence: an electricity bill dated four months ago that included a reconnection fee.

As if Yrsen had only just moved in.

Or – Jasmin realised with a shudder – as if the Yrsen she'd met wasn't the woman she claimed to be. She'd been playing a role. Inhabiting a false identity. What had happened? What had become of the real artist?

In the bottom drawer, she stumbled across a small, barely used notebook and began to leaf through it, her fingers trembling. Inside Jasmin found a photo of herself that looked like it had been taken while she was in hospital. Underneath the photo, Yrsen – or whoever she was – had written the name Jasmin Hansen, along with an abbreviation of some kind: MPS. F44.81.

What did it mean?

How had this woman got hold of a photo of her? Jasmin felt an urge to pocket the notebook or to rip out the page, but she managed to resist the temptation.

She flicked on through the book and came across a second picture of a gaunt man smiling at the camera. It was a passport photo, of the kind you might tuck inside your wallet so you could carry your loved one with you wherever you went.

She didn't recognise the man's face, but she couldn't shake the feeling she'd seen him before.

That's strange, isn't it? Like everything in this place.

She kept turning the pages and suddenly saw a third entry that made her gasp. *Hanna Jansen*, it said on the page. The woman Jørgen had had an affair with. Yrsen hadn't included a photo, but she'd drawn a large question mark next to the name.

A horrible suspicion crept into Jasmin's mind. *Gabriela Yrsen isn't real*, she thought. Maybe it was only a name, a pretence, an attempt to deceive her. Maybe Gabriela Yrsen was none other than Hanna Jansen herself. *They're one and the same person.* Her old enemy was here, right under her nose, and was mocking her.

Is that possible?

Of course it is.

Hanna Jansen has always been dangerous, cunning and malicious.

And then she saw it, looming in the darkness at the back of the room, still resting on its easel and hidden under a cloth that hung over the frame. The picture. *Her* picture – the one Yrsen had said she'd paint for her.

Jasmin reached for the cloth and cautiously tugged it onto the floor.

She saw herself – albeit blurred and not a particularly good likeness – holding a burning lighter in her hand. A building behind her was on fire – it looked like a modern version of the old sanatorium, one built in the twenty-first century.

'You piece of shit,' said Jasmin hoarsely. 'You really are trying to frame me for things I never did.'

She spotted a pair of scissors on the desk. Snatching them up, she attacked the picture, stabbing it furiously until it lay in tatters. After that she left the office, closing the door behind her, and crept back down the corridor to the still-open window. The wind had blown colourful leaves inside that lay on the rug like splashes of paint.

Yrsen isn't really Yrsen. You know that now, and that's why you need to get out of here. MPS F44.81, she thought. *You need to find out what it means.*

She climbed up onto the windowsill, which wobbled alarmingly beneath her weight, before swinging a leg through the opening and hopping down on the other side.

Jasmin landed on the tall grass with a quiet thud.

She'd made it out.

Then she froze.

The voices from inside were suddenly clearly audible – so close that it made her jump, as if they were coming from right next to her. One of them was Yrsen's, the other belonged to Henriksen.

Jasmin held her breath and cocked an ear. The two of them seemed to be arguing; Henriksen was speaking in a soothing tone, and Yrsen was upset – beside herself – in a way that Jasmin hadn't heard before. A light went on and a dull, buttery-yellow glow fell through the window onto the lawn, painting a bright strip on the grass and the hedges. Jasmin could feel the hard brickwork digging into her back as she strained to listen.

'It's too dangerous, as you very well know,' Yrsen was saying. 'It has to end. We can't wait any longer. Tonight is the finale – tonight we finish with all this, with her. I'm tired of watching this drag on. It's too dangerous.'

'I know it's dangerous,' she heard Henriksen reply. His sonorous voice still had its usual soothing, ingratiating tone, but Jasmin felt sure she could hear something else underneath: doubt, unease and worry.

'It's more than dangerous. Your *head*, Hendrik. You got hurt.' By now, Yrsen sounded almost affectionate. Jasmin could hardly believe her ears. Yrsen's voice was husky, almost honeyed, as if she and Henriksen were more than just acquaintances.

My God, what's going on here? If these two know each other . . .

'It was nothing,' Henriksen answered calmly. 'An accident. We're dealing with an extremely unusual case. There's no textbook we can follow; we don't have any experience to draw on.'

'She needs to come here.'

'I'm meeting her tonight, as you already know. She called me and we arranged to meet at her house. I've spoken to her husband and he agreed. She gets one last chance, and after that—'

'We end it. And I couldn't care less if Jørgen agrees or not. The situation is getting out of hand. We never should have got ourselves into all this. There are easier ways – methods that are much less complicated and intrusive.' Yrsen's voice was now so cold and emotionless that it could have belonged to the sculpture in the garden.

They just mentioned Jørgen. Jasmin clenched her fists and her fingernails dug painfully into her palms. *So I was right. They want to end it. And Jørgen really is involved. Dear God, I was right about everything.*

Jasmin wanted to break down in tears – could have sat down right there and then and blocked out the world – but something deep inside her wouldn't let her.

Something else had risen up within her.

Something more powerful.

A voice that didn't sound quite like her own.

'What about the picture?'

'How should I know?' Yrsen retorted sharply. 'I'm playing a character. How am I supposed to suddenly become an artist?'

Jasmin felt her heart hammering against her ribs. *It was all a lie. Yrsen, Henriksen, Jørgen and who knew who else was involved.*

You need to run. You won't be able to find Paul, not like this. They've lured you into a trap and you've figured it out far too late.

'What if she's still interested?' Henriksen asked. 'What if she wants to talk to you about it?'

'I'll avoid her. Nothing could be simpler.' For a moment, neither of them spoke. Then, in a quiet voice, Yrsen added, 'It'd make things a lot easier if we could bring her here. Those cameras she's installed at her house make it impossible to plan anything. We're going in completely unprepared and you don't know how she might react.'

'That's true. But it was her suggestion. She'll get suspicious if I ask her to meet anywhere else.'

I already am suspicious, you fucking bastards, Jasmin thought. *If only you knew who was standing outside your window, listening to every word you say. If only you knew.*

'In that case, maybe we should take a different approach. You've given me an idea.' Jasmin heard footsteps as Yrsen walked across the room. 'I'll call her and tell her the painting is ready. I'll ask her to meet me here. And then we'll end it.'

'Hmm.' Henriksen sounded unconvinced. 'I suppose it might work.'

'Hold on, I'll do it right now.'

Jasmin gave a start and fumbled for the phone in the pocket of her jeans. *If she calls you, it'll ring. They'll hear it. And if she finds what's left of the painting . . .*

Fuck – they'll know you're here, that you're standing outside the window and listening in. They'll know you heard everything. You'll be done for.

The phone slipped out of her trembling hands and fell into the wet grass.

'Now where did I note down her number?' she heard Yrsen say from inside the house.

Shit. Fucking shit. Jasmin knelt down and groped in the dark for her phone. The tall grass was sharp and the frost felt chill beneath her fingers.

'There it is,' said Yrsen.

Just then, the screen of her phone lit up in the grass. Jasmin lunged forwards, grabbed hold of it and tapped the *Decline* button as the ringtone began to sound.

Shit, shit, shit.

'She's not picking up,' she heard Yrsen say. 'That's less than ideal.'

'Did you hear that?' Henriksen asked.

'What?'

'A noise, from out back. Like there's—'

She heard footsteps coming closer and closer. Jasmin shoved her phone back in her pocket and leapt to her feet, sprinting away from the house and diving into the hedge at the end of the garden. Sharp twigs poked through the fabric of her coat and jabbed into her back. The front door swung open and a broad shaft of light poured out. Yrsen and Henriksen appeared in the doorway, two dark silhouettes in the yellow light. When Yrsen turned to face Henriksen, Jasmin caught a glimpse of her face in profile. Her cheeks were smooth. Her burn scars had vanished.

'Nobody,' said Henriksen. 'Let's go back inside.'

'Yes,' Yrsen replied, 'we should.'

No sooner had they shut the door behind them than Jasmin hopped over the low gate in the fence and ran back to her car.

Yrsen isn't who you thought she was. She wasn't even hurt in the fire. Who is she?

Jasmin started the car. Her dipped headlights bored dazzling tunnels of light into the mounting fog before a powerful gust of wind swept the mist aside. Jasmin was crying, but she kept wiping the tears from her cheeks.

You can't let them win. You can't.

Almost blinded by tears, Jasmin drove on through the darkness. The tops of the pine trees along the side of the road were bending under the merciless power of the storm. Leaves and twigs swept across the asphalt and Jasmin felt the wind pushing against the side of the car, trying to force her off the road.

Why weren't there any burns on her face?

Why?

You know why. Because she isn't Yrsen. Because she . . .

The headlights of her car swept over the sign welcoming her to Skårsteinen but the village was deserted, as if the residents were all holed up in their homes already, taking refuge and waiting for the storm to hit. The streetlights hanging from cables strung along the road swung back and forth wildly, a few sparks spraying down from the wires. A fist-sized rock slammed into the windscreen. Jasmin gave a start and her car weaved across the road before she managed to get it back under control. Her wheels bumped over a pothole and her shock absorbers screeched. The rain set in once more, at first barely more than drizzle sprinkling against the windscreen, but it grew heavier and heavier.

There was an object on the passenger seat. When Jasmin slowed down to take a closer look at the object, she realised part of the panelling over the door had fallen off. She saw wiring connected to a minuscule camera that had evidently been fitted underneath. The panel had a barely visible hole in it for the lens.

A camera they'd been watching her with.

A camera that had recorded everything she'd done inside her car.

Jasmin's fingers gripped the steering wheel like she was trying to strangle it.

If they were watching you here, maybe they were watching you in the house too.

Maybe you even helped them. Maybe Sandvik's cameras were a trick.

Bonnie barked at the window, pulling her out of her thoughts. Jasmin reached for the camera, but then, in the beam of her headlights, she saw a figure in a grey coat cross the road and disappear into an overgrown garden. A handful of empty houses stood out here on the edge of the village. Some of them were uninhabitable, crooked and weather-beaten.

Was it him?

Had she just seen the drifter?

Jasmin braked. With a sharp tug, she managed to rip the camera from the wiring. She grabbed Bonnie's lead and leapt out of the car, then hurled the tiny camera into the undergrowth and took the gun out of her pocket. She was burning with rage; her finger was poised on the trigger.

They've been watching you. They've been following your movements the whole time.

A rusted wrought-iron fence blocked her path but the gate gave way with a single kick. Weeds proliferated between the paving stones. The crooked house looked deserted; its roof had caved in at the eastern end, the thatch collapsing in on itself. Jasmin switched on her torch and braced herself against the wind.

Then she entered the house. It stank of rotting wood and a smouldering fire.

Goosebumps spread over her neck and down her back. Her instincts screamed. *You aren't alone*, they seemed to be warning her.

The beam from her torch swept across the wall and fell on the symbol – the inverted triangle with the open top-right corner.

A flash of light appeared before her eyes. A bare white wall. A window with iron bars. A corridor she was walking down. The symbol was here too.

Fire. Flames. The smell of petrol.

'So,' said a voice from her memory, which sounded like Henriksen's. 'Who are you today? Am I talking to Jasmin Hansen? Or to Hanna Jansen?'

Jasmin blinked, suppressing these images, forcing herself to breathe.

The drifter was here. She could sense it.

'I know you're close,' she said quietly. 'And I'm warning you: this time I'm armed. It's time you showed yourself.'

Jasmin cocked her revolver. The cylinder clicked quietly as it rotated. 'I'm only going to warn you once.'

'I thought you didn't know how to shoot, Ms Hansen.' The voice that emerged from the darkness, so close at hand, made her jump. Jasmin whirled around. There he was, standing in the doorway behind her and looking right at her. She lifted her torch.

He blinked as the light shone directly into his eyes.

The drifter wasn't Jørgen. Nor was he Sven Birkeland, or the body from the beach somehow resurrected before her, or Jan Berger from the lighthouse. She didn't know him; he was just a man, tall and thin, with a long beard and a scar on his face. His coat had been patched up in several places and his jeans were dirty and torn at the seams.

He coughed.

'You were there. In the garden. You were watching me and Paul.'

'I've been watching you the whole time. It was a shitty job, but someone had to do it.'

Jasmin stared at him. His face – strange, and yet so familiar. She felt like she'd seen it before. After a few moments, it clicked. 'You're the man I saw in the notebook at Yrsen's house. My God. That woman – she has a photo of you too. A *photo*. What is this? What's going on here?' Jasmin was still pointing her gun at him, but now she lowered the barrel slightly. 'Who exactly is she?'

'You tell me.' He lifted his hands, which were empty, and held them out to her in a placatory way, as if to say, *What do you need a revolver for? I'm only a simple drifter, a stalker who's been sneaking around outside your house at night.* 'I need to know if I can trust you.'

'Either you're all working together – or *you're* on my side. And if she's trying to get rid of *me* . . .' Jasmin replied.

'You mean, your enemy's enemy is your friend?'

'I don't know,' Jasmin admitted. 'I don't know what to believe anymore.'

The stranger raised his arm and rolled up the sleeve of his coat. There, on his left forearm, Jasmin saw a scar. It was a burn, and it looked relatively recent.

'Was that her? Did she try to take you out? Like she wants to do to me? Only you managed to give her the slip?'

'Is that who you think I am? Another victim?'

Jasmin didn't reply; instead, she whirled around as she heard the door behind her opening. A man appeared in the doorway, shining a torch at both of them. It was Arne Boeckermann. Rainwater dripped from his coat.

'Ms Hansen, we've all been looking for you. I spotted your car as I drove past and . . .'

Jasmin noticed him exchange glances with the stranger, who gently shook his head. As if they knew each other.

'Move away from him, Ms Hansen. Right now.' Boeckermann reached for his belt to draw his gun, but Jasmin was quicker. She aimed her revolver at him. The metal felt cold as a block of ice in her hand, but she knew it could spit deadly fire.

'Oh no you don't,' she cried. 'You're in cahoots with the others, aren't you? This man has shown me what Yrsen did to him.'

'Yrsen? The artist? What's she got to do with this?' Boeckermann sounded genuinely perplexed.

'Don't play the innocent. Get back!'

Boeckermann held up his hands. 'Ms Hansen, please calm down. There's no need for violence.'

'I said get back!' She took a step forwards and Boeckermann obeyed her command. He looked confused; his eyes went not to her, but to the stranger behind her.

'You too,' Jasmin ordered the drifter. 'Move over there.'

The stranger whose photo she'd found at Yrsen's house did as he was told – but when he arrived next to Boeckermann, his coat parted slightly, revealing a pistol in a holster on his belt. He was armed and he could tell she'd noticed.

'Stay calm, Ms Hansen,' he said. His voice sounded composed and professional. 'You aren't in any danger.'

Jasmin felt tears welling up in her eyes. The barrel of her revolver started to shake in her hand, her finger resting on the trigger. Boeckermann's radio burst into life with a crackle. 'We can't find her,' said a male voice that Jasmin didn't recognise. 'She must be out in her car. And the storm is getting worse.'

'Who was that? What are you planning?'

'Nothing, Ms Hansen. Now please, put your gun down.'

'No way. And if either of you try to stop me . . .' She glanced again at the burn on the stranger's arm. Something about the sight of it sent a shiver up her spine; something about it was so horrifying that she had to avert her eyes. 'I don't understand why you aren't helping me if Yrsen did that to you. We could bring her down, uncover this whole plot.'

Boeckermann snorted, as if he wasn't sure whether to laugh or look incredulous. 'You're concocting a story. Do you really think he's here because of Yrsen?'

'The people in the village told me he only started appearing around here over the last few months. And Yrsen only moved here four months ago too; the electricity bill in her house proves that! I can prove everything!'

'I admit it,' said the stranger abruptly, as if he'd just come to a decision. Jasmin noticed Boeckermann staring at him in disbelief. 'By rights, I should be dead. Yrsen tried to kill me. But she failed.'

'Who is this woman?' Jasmin gripped the revolver with both hands. 'Is she a – I don't know, a hitwoman?'

Or is she an old enemy who you know very well? Is she Hanna Jansen?

'I survived the attack. I escaped with my life and I followed her. I'm going to have my revenge, I've sworn it to myself.'

Boeckermann looked aghast. 'What are you talking about, man? We aren't supposed to—'

'Shut up,' the drifter cut him off. 'Now you know the truth, Ms Hansen. You can put your gun down.'

'Not yet,' Jasmin replied. She pivoted, aiming the revolver at Boeckermann. 'We can't trust him. Take his gun and his handcuffs. Put them on him and . . .' Jasmin looked around the room. 'Cuff him to that old heating pipe over there.'

'But that's—'

'Silence!' Jasmin screamed at Boeckermann. She heard her phone ringing in the pocket of her jeans. *Not now.*

She watched as the stranger took Boeckermann's gun from his holster and grabbed his handcuffs. Then he marched him across the room towards the rusty pipe and cuffed his left wrist to it. The two men exchanged a glance, as if they already knew each other and were striking a wordless pact.

'Now come here. We're going outside. You first, and no sudden moves.'

The stranger obeyed. Outdoors, the rain had swelled into an ice-cold deluge that sprayed into her face. Visibility had fallen to around six feet, and the wind tugged at them as if they were little more than toy figurines that the storm was trying to sweep away.

Jasmin gestured towards the car. 'Get in. You're driving.'

Again, the stranger complied. Jasmin sat down beside him on the passenger seat. With the doors closed, the howling of the wind subsided into a low moan in the background, but the rain continued to hammer on the roof of the car.

'Why are you carrying a gun?' she asked him.

'Because I assume Yrsen isn't done with me yet.'

'So why didn't you act straight away? If you knew about her – her *true* identity – why didn't you go to the police?' Jasmin stared at him. 'Because they're all in on it, right? Because it would have been no use?'

The stranger merely gave her a pitying look, as if he was disappointed in her reasoning. 'What next, Jasmin? What are you going to do with me?'

Jasmin's phone rang once more and she pulled it from her pocket, keeping the revolver trained on the drifter. The number was unknown but the area code was a local one, from the island.

'Yes?'

'Ms Hansen,' said Gabriela Yrsen's quiet voice. 'It's me.' Down the line, Jasmin could hear the rush of the wind and the drumming of the rain on an attic window, much like the one in her own house by the coast. And now that she stopped to listen, she realised she could hear the branch of the overgrown pine tree scraping over the outside wall too.

Jasmin clenched her fist. 'What do you want?'

'The picture is ready. I finished it much sooner than I'd expected. I wanted to let you know before this storm brings its full strength to bear. In fact, I've already driven down to your house.'

'I'm sorry?' Jasmin feigned surprise. 'You've already . . . ?'

'It wasn't hard to find.'

She's lying, Jasmin thought. It was so obvious and Yrsen was such a bad actor that she almost felt sorry for her. Jasmin covered the phone with her hand. 'Start driving,' she ordered the stranger beside her. 'We're taking the old country road. Head south, back to my house on the beach.'

'But the storm—'

'Just drive.'

He did as he was told, starting the engine and manoeuvring the Volvo onto the road.

'And now?' Jasmin asked Yrsen over the phone. 'You're standing outside my front door in the wind and the rain?'

'No, I'm inside the house. The door was unlocked. I hope you don't mind, but I wanted to keep the painting dry.'

You miserable liar. I locked the door when I left earlier. I'm certain of it.

'Then I'll meet you there,' Jasmin replied, doing her best to sound indifferent.

'I'm looking forward to it already.' With that, Yrsen hung up. Jasmin's hand shook violently as she put her phone away.

'I'm looking forward to it too,' she said softly into the car. 'I can't wait, you piece of shit.'

Chapter 17

'We're here,' said Jasmin, though the rain beating against the windscreen nearly smothered her words. The stranger beside her gave her a piercing look, sizing her up.

'You don't have to do this.'

'What don't I have to do?'

'Go in there with your gun. Threaten people. You could stop and think instead.'

'I've done enough thinking. I know everything I need to know. Yrsen is dangerous. She must know about Paul's disappearance.'

'Maybe she does. Maybe we all do.'

The barrel of her gun quivered, but she kept it trained on the man, whose name she didn't even know. 'Get out.'

He obeyed. By now, the rain was coming down in such torrents that Jasmin was soaked to the skin in a fraction of a second, despite her raincoat. The rainwater was ice-cold and felt like the touch of death itself.

The nearby sea was high, and it rushed and roared in the night.

'Inside the house!' she screamed as the wind buffeted against her. Through the dense grey shroud that had fallen over the world, Jasmin could just make out a car parked a little way down the road.

It might be Yrsen's. Or Henriksen's. Or maybe it belonged to somebody else. Maybe they were all here.

The stranger put his hand on the front door and it swung open. He disappeared into the darkness inside, which swallowed him up.

Jasmin followed him, holding her six-shooter out in front of her, her hand trembling. She fumbled for the light switch, but when she flicked it, the lights in the hallway remained cold and dark. The storm must have brought down the power lines.

Her mind went back to her journey up here – the Rolling Stones song she'd heard on the radio about the traveller seeking shelter from the storm. It felt like an eternity ago. Like a scene from another life. Back then – before all this, although she didn't want to think about the idea of before – everything had been so much easier. Paul had been with her and she'd thought she was getting back on track.

And now all she had left was darkness.

But you aren't going to give up yet. You're going to find him. They're going to give Paul back to you.

Jasmin cast a glance into the living room. The French windows were open; the floorboards had swelled in the rain and the wind had blown leaves onto the rug, as if the room had become part of the forest over the last few hours. A layer of fine raindrops covered the sofa, clinging to the fabric like dew.

There was nobody in here.

Then she noticed the cellar door was ajar.

Of course, Jasmin thought. Things were coming to a head. And what better place than the cellar? 'We're going down there. Both of us.' She gestured with her gun for him to go down the stairs in front of her.

'Ms Hansen,' the stranger said again as he began to descend. 'Jasmin. You don't have to do this. You can still turn back.'

'What's that supposed to mean?'

'Put your gun away. We can talk about everything.'

He stopped halfway down the stairs and turned to look at her. His face was sad and disappointed, an expression that struck a chord in her subconscious which she couldn't quite place.

You know him. And not just because you saw his photo in Yrsen's notebook. There's more going on here.

Much more.

Once again, she saw lights flashing before her eyes, as though there was a storm raging outside that only she could see. Her hands shook. She thought she could smell petrol – could feel the cold fluid trickling over her fingers.

'Keep going,' she ordered him.

And then they were downstairs.

The gas heater made a humming noise but Jasmin didn't give it a second glance. The door at the other end of the cellar was wide open, and so was the gun cabinet. As if someone had recently taken a look inside – maybe to make sure there weren't any weapons inside it.

But they don't know about your little secret, she thought. *Nobody knows about it – not even Jørgen.*

And if he didn't know, the others wouldn't either. Not even Yrsen, who was working for him.

'Through the door at the back,' said Jasmin.

'That's enough,' said a quiet voice behind her. 'Good evening, Jasmin.'

She spun round. Behind her, as if they'd been watching her the whole time, she saw Henriksen and Yrsen – and behind them, on the staircase, were two men in white coats. Henriksen was wearing a suit she'd never seen him in before and Yrsen's face was clear of burn scars, just like earlier at her house. She was wearing a pair of rectangular glasses and her dark hair was tied back in a ponytail.

'This isn't a good evening,' she retorted. 'Not for you.'

'Put the gun down, Jasmin.'

'No.' From the corner of her eye, Jasmin saw the stranger moving a few steps to one side, as if he was trying to get round her so he could lunge for her gun and overpower her.

'Well? Where's the painting?' Jasmin smiled scornfully at Yrsen. 'Is it finished?'

'The painting is over there. And so is Paul.'

'He's . . . ?' Yrsen's words knocked her off balance. Jasmin hadn't been expecting such openness from her. 'Paul?' she called. 'Paul?'

There was no reply. 'What have you done with him? I swear to God, if you two—'

'Jasmin, what do you know? What have you found out?' Henriksen asked, lifting his arms in a gesture that was obviously intended to placate her, but only made her more furious.

'You've been fucking with me this whole time. That's what I've found out. And this woman' – Jasmin swung the revolver towards Yrsen – 'isn't who she claims to be.'

'Well deduced,' Yrsen replied. *No, not Yrsen*, Jasmin corrected herself. *The woman over there who's pretending to be someone she isn't.* 'And what else do you know?'

'I know you two are in contact with Jørgen. I overheard everything. And I know you're trying to frame me for Larsen's murder. I know what happened here and what you're all trying to cover up. The fire in the sanatorium. The massacre. The graveyard hidden in the forest.' Her hand trembled as she pointed the gun back at Henriksen. 'And I trusted you. You were there with me. You liar. Who are you? Are you even a policeman? What the hell is going on? You aren't going to catch me, I hope you realise that?'

Yrsen and Henriksen looked at each other. Then Henriksen spoke. 'Come here, Christian.'

The stranger gave him a long look before replying, 'I don't think that's a very good idea. She's growing unstable. We need to intervene.'

'You need to— What is this?' Jasmin fell back a step as the stranger tried to grab her gun. 'I'll do it!' she screamed, panicking, shaking with horror. 'I'll—'

'Stop it, Jasmin,' said Henriksen calmly. 'Stop all this nonsense. You aren't going to shoot anyone.'

'You won't catch me,' she retorted. 'I'll take Paul and we'll disappear, and none of you can stop me. And I'm going to tell the world about everything that's being covered up here. My colleague Sven Birkeland – his wife works for a major newspaper. What do you think will happen when the outside world hears about this? You're finished. Oh, I know very well why you lured me here. You're afraid. Your whole tower of lies is going to come tumbling down.'

'Jasmin, can I ask you a few questions?' Henriksen took a step forwards. 'Why don't we go upstairs? It's rather unpleasant down here.'

Jasmin looked over her shoulder at the door, which was wide open. For a moment, she was convinced she could hear the creaking of the rope with which the captain had hanged himself from one of the beams.

Because he'd lost his wife and son out at sea.

Because he couldn't bear to go on.

'I'm not leaving without Paul.'

She took a few steps backwards, without taking her eyes off the others. Cold air brushed against her neck – grasping at her like the stiff, clammy fingers of a corpse.

'Come on, Jasmin, that doesn't make sense.'

'I'm not leaving without him.' She turned around and for the first time in years – for the first time since her return – she peered into the back room of the cellar. It was empty. Cobwebs were draped over the rough stone walls and the wind whistled through narrow gaps in the rubblework. She saw the dark beams that spanned the room beneath the ceiling, and on one of them she could still clearly see the mark left on the wood by the noose.

Paul wasn't there. Instead, she saw a large, old-fashioned trunk lying on the floor in the middle of the room, of the kind people used to take with them on sea voyages. The lock was missing. Jasmin recognised it – it belonged to Jørgen.

She whirled around. 'Where is he?'

'Who?' asked Henriksen. He drew nearer, and Jasmin pointed her gun at him. 'We're here – you, me, Ms Yrsen and the others. There's nobody else.'

'Paul,' Jasmin repeated. 'Where is he?'

'He was never here.' Henriksen pointed abruptly at the trunk. 'That's all there is. Take a look inside. Don't you remember? That trunk contains your possessions, Ms Hansen. You and your husband packed them up before you checked yourself in with us for your course of therapy.'

'No. No, I won't look.' By now, the revolver was trembling so violently that she had to hold it with both hands to steady it. 'I want to see my son now.'

'Jasmin, please. That's enough. We've reached this point so often before and every time we do you start up with all this again. I'd been hoping you'd finally understand what really happened.'

Henriksen took another step towards her, his hand held out towards the gun – and Jasmin pulled the trigger. She didn't know what she was doing; it was barely more than an instinctive response to feeling threatened, cornered.

She pulled the trigger and the revolver launched its projectile with a deafening bang. Henriksen fell backwards, clutching his chest. The bullet had ripped through his charcoal-grey suit jacket and blood began pouring out of the hole. Yrsen rushed to his side, holding him upright as his legs threatened to give way.

Jasmin lunged forward, pointing her gun at the two men in white on the staircase. 'Out of my way!' she screamed. The men fell back, clearing a path, and Jasmin dashed up the stairs.

Outside, the storm was still raging. Through the front door, which was still open, she saw flashing blue lights.

Jasmin turned on her heel, sprinting through the living room and out onto the veranda. In the garden she saw Boeckermann in his long raincoat, his hood drawn down over his face.

How did he get here? Who set him free?

'There's no point coming this way,' he called through the rain. 'Stay in the house!'

Jasmin raised the revolver.

'Please, stop this,' said a voice behind her. On turning around, she saw Henriksen. He was walking towards her, his jacket completely intact. No blood – not even a drop.

'I – I just—'

'The gun is loaded with blanks, Jasmin. We couldn't let you put yourself or anyone else in danger.'

Jasmin opened the cylinder of the revolver. *You loaded the rounds yourself,* she thought – but when she took one out, she saw Henriksen was telling the truth. The ammunition wasn't live.

'You – you knew about the gun?'

'Of course. You told me about it yourself, Jasmin.'

'That's impossible – I didn't even know—'

'Not here. *Before* all this.'

'Before? But there is no before. We met for the first time when Paul disappeared.'

'That isn't true.' Henriksen shook his head. He gestured inside to the sofa. Only now did Jasmin notice he was carrying a folder in his hand. He was alone, and he looked sad and deeply concerned at the same time. Reluctantly, she came back into the house.

'Shall we sit down?'

'What's going on?'

'Nobody wants to hurt you. I promise.'

'But I heard you!' Jasmin exclaimed. 'You and Yrsen – I heard—'

'You heard what you heard, there's no doubt about it. But you misunderstood the meaning of our words.'

Jasmin felt him lay a hand on her arm. She sat down on the sofa but shuffled as far away from him as she could, still clutching the gun in her hand. The rounds had fallen out and lay glittering on the floorboards like pieces of silver.

Henriksen gave her a long, pensive look. 'I have to admit this whole thing didn't quite go to plan. I have to own up to my own mistakes. Maybe we went too far. Yes, I'm sure we did. You always were very good at finding things out and giving us the slip.'

'Where's Paul?' she asked again. The words seemed to echo through the room, as if she was inside a vast cathedral.

Then Henriksen spoke the words she would never forget. 'Jasmin, Paul is dead. He's been dead for so long now. It's been five years since he passed away.'

Chapter 18

It was raining.

Outside the house.

Inside her mind.

Henriksen's words forced their way effortfully through the downpour, through the white noise in her head. 'Jasmin, do you understand me?'

'Bullshit. He came here with me.' *Paul can't be dead. Henriksen is lying, he must be lying, there's no other explanation.*

But when he shook his head, it was like he was tearing strips from her heart with his bare hands. Breaking off pieces of her soul. 'No, Jasmin. That was all in your head. You were alone when you got here in your hire car. It was just you and your dog Bonnie.'

Jasmin felt as though his words were incinerating something inside her – burning and freezing it at the same time, until there was nothing left of her heart.

'You're lying. He was here at the house. And later on too – there are people in the village who saw him. There are people who talked to him. There's proof!'

'He's dead, Jasmin.'

'No!'

'He didn't talk to anyone, nor was he seen by anyone in the village. Think carefully. Didn't he always happen to be outside or in a different part of the shop or cafe while you were talking to the proprietor? And didn't he refuse to touch all the food and drinks you ordered for him?'

Jasmin swallowed. Her throat was parched and felt like it was filled with nails; her tongue was like sandpaper. 'I cooked for him. I read to him. He played with Bonnie.'

'The power of the human imagination is often impressive. It's unbridled, almost boundless in scope.'

'You're lying.'

Henriksen smiled sympathetically, but at that moment Jasmin wanted nothing more than to hit him and wipe the smile from his face. 'Think, Jasmin. What do you remember? From before you made your way here?'

'I . . .' Jasmin closed her eyes. Jørgen had been there; he'd given her a kiss on the lips, helped her load her bags into the car. Jørgen . . . He'd been talking to someone. A man who had come to their home. Or had it been different? Had she been the one who'd returned to the house accompanied by that other man?

Had that other man been Henriksen?

And did that mean . . . ?

Your memory is full of gaps. Your memory is different. You've – dear God, you've invented a story. Could it be true?

'I don't know,' she whispered.

'Do you remember the night of your accident?'

Jasmin cleared her throat and cast her eyes over the room, at the raindrops trickling down the windows overlooking the veranda. 'Could I have something to drink, please?'

'Of course.' Henriksen gave her a look that was equal parts caution and compassion. 'Do you promise to stay here and not try to attack anyone again?'

'Did I attack someone?' She recalled how she'd shot at Henriksen and felt certain she'd wounded him. All that blood . . . 'Apart from you?' she added, pointing at his jacket.

'Yes, Jasmin, you did. Even before you came here.' Henriksen got to his feet and left the room, but it wasn't long before he returned holding a cup in his hand that smelled of jasmine tea.

'There you go. Just how you like it.'

'Jasmine tea,' she said quietly.

'The best tea . . .'

'For the best Jasmin,' she said, finishing his sentence. That was something Jørgen used to say to her, back when they'd still been so in love. She wrapped her hands around the cup and took a sip.

'The night of your accident,' Henriksen began again. 'Do you remember it?'

'I – I was driving. In my car. Jørgen and I chose it together, back before Paul . . . We were so happy back then.' She took another sip, barely noticing that the tea was hot enough to scald the tip of her tongue. 'It was raining, as hard as today.' She glanced out of the window. 'Maybe even harder. I was coming back from the staff party, it was late. The rain had washed soil onto the road and I knew part of the route led through a forest, so I drove extra slowly there.'

'And then?'

'Then the Jeep appeared. It was hassling me. Tailgating my car.' Jasmin glanced at Henriksen, trying to gauge whether he was judging her, but right now he seemed to be concentrating solely on what she was saying. 'I got nervous. You hear all kinds of things, and see them too, when you work in a big hospital. Women getting attacked at night. Sven and I have operated on victims of violence before; you can't imagine what . . .' She paused. 'You really can't imagine, can you? You aren't a policeman, Hendrik. I think I've realised that now. You were so unsure of yourself when we met for the first time, acting like you didn't quite know what to do, like you were playing a role.'

Henriksen nodded. 'That's right. I'm not a policeman.'

'So what are you?'

'I'm a psychiatrist, Jasmin. *Your* psychiatrist. From the very beginning. That's the sole reason why I'm here. Why I've been watching over you.'

Jasmin felt her hands starting to shake again. Once more she saw those flashes of light, smelled the smoke in her nostrils, heard the crackling of a fire and felt the cold, slippery sensation of petrol running over her fingers.

The fox, she suddenly realised. *Paul found the fox in the wardrobe upstairs and he made one of his origami sculptures. And you put the sculpture in the grave Paul asked you to dig.*

So he isn't so alone.

The thought felt like warm sunlight after a cold night – like a lifebuoy floating towards her over the surface of a dark, ice-cold sea that she was on the verge of drowning in, and she clung to it.

You know where you buried it.

It'll prove you're telling the truth.

Jasmin leapt to her feet and stormed through the open doorway to the veranda as a new burst of energy and strength flooded through her body.

'Jasmin!' Henriksen called after her. 'Jasmin, come back!'

But she didn't listen to him. She refused to listen.

There had to be another way, another truth. The *only* truth: that Paul was still alive.

Boeckermann was still standing out in the rain, which trickled from his coat on to the ground, but this time she didn't let him stop her. Jasmin aimed her revolver at him as she dashed down the veranda steps. Her shoes slipped on the damp wood and she had to cling to the railing to prevent herself from falling.

'Let her through,' she heard Henriksen say behind her, and she hurried through the garden and sprinted down the narrow path to the woods, all the while feeling Boeckermann's piercing gaze on her back.

The rain rattled through the treetops, the wind swept twigs and stones into her face, and the gale roared with the noise and power of a jet during take-off – a raging, primeval force that had resolved to leave nothing but destruction in its wake. Jasmin shielded her face with her hand and drew her hood down. It was hard to breathe; she felt like the wind was sucking the air out of her lungs.

A branch the length of her arm crashed down at her feet. Jasmin leapt to one side and her shoulder collided with the trunk of a silver fir. The bark felt rough and swollen under her hands and reminded her of her first night on the island when she'd taken the fox outside. She'd buried it close to this tree.

There was the spot. She could see the pine twigs that she'd stuck into the soft black earth and the smooth, flat, grey stones surrounding the grave.

Jasmin fell to her knees and started digging with her bare hands.

Chapter 19

'Ms Hansen!' She heard Henriksen's anxious voice calling from among the trees. He was following her. *You have to show him*, she thought. *He has to see the fox, the origami sculpture Paul made. He has to believe you!*

I'm a psychiatrist, his voice echoed in her mind, sounding tinny, as if it was emanating from an old transistor radio. *Your psychiatrist.*

Jasmin's fingers soon started bleeding as she hurled the damp, heavy earth to one side. She heard herself whispering things she barely understood – felt the gale snatching at her with all its might, trying to grab hold of her and fling her to the ground, to hold her back.

'Jasmin, stop!'

She stared at a pair of men's shoes approaching over the dark forest floor, at the damp clods of earth clinging to the dark leather. It was Henriksen, who came to a halt ten feet or so away and looked at her in concern as the rain ran down his cheeks and plastered his hair to his head like a wet cloth. 'Stop, Jasmin. You're bleeding.'

'It's here,' she screamed at him over the gale. 'I'm not imagining it!'

'What's here?'

'The dead fox! The one Paul asked me to bury, along with a sculpture he made.'

'Jasmin—'

Suddenly, she felt her fingers brush against something new. Something other than damp earth and gravel. She felt hair, fur, paper.

'It's here! It really is . . .'

Jasmin brushed a few lumps of soil aside and glimpsed a small patch of red fur. 'It's here!' she cried again, her voice trembling with excitement. She dug on, her hands and fingers working on autopilot, and, ignoring the pain and the ice-cold rain running down her neck and under her coat, soaking her to the skin, she finally unearthed the fox, together with the origami sculpture that by now was so utterly sodden by the damp soil that there was barely anything left of it beyond a dirty lump of pulp.

She stared down at the grave.

'So he isn't so alone,' she whispered. 'That's what Paul said to me. This is the sculpture, and this is the fox, but – but how . . . ?'

'Come on, Jasmin,' she heard Henriksen say. He laid his hand heavily on her shoulder.

'I don't understand,' she whispered. 'I don't see how it's possible. I found it myself, it's been out here for days.'

'What you found back then is what you buried out here,' said Henriksen. 'A fox, yes – but . . .' He reached down into the grave and lifted the animal out.

Even in the darkness, Jasmin could see the metal stud sewn into the animal's ear. She could see its button eyes – artificial, like everything about the fox.

'It's just a toy,' she whispered. 'No – no, it can't be.'

'But it is, Jasmin. And this origami sculpture . . .' He shook his head. 'You made it yourself. Like all the others.'

270

Chapter 20

She felt the rain flowing down her cheeks, down her face, creeping under the collar of her coat. She felt it washing the soil from her hands as Henriksen gently led her back to the house. Her legs worked mechanically, as if they belonged to someone else. *The fox wasn't real. Those origami sculptures . . .*

Henriksen sat her down on the sofa in the living room. He closed the French windows, shutting out the bellowing gale and the driving rain, before picking up a blanket and placing it over her shoulders.

'I just wanted to—'

'Easy, now. I understand.' He took a seat beside her, the springs of the sofa squeaking quietly, and as he looked at her with a mixture of caution and sympathy, she felt like nothing had happened – as though her bleeding fingers and her little venture out into the rain had ceased to matter.

I'm your psychiatrist, he'd said. Maybe it was those words that had driven her out into the storm, because deep down she'd known he was telling the truth.

'What have I done? Something has happened, hasn't it? Is Jørgen here? Can I talk to him?'

'What else do you remember from the night of your accident?'

Jasmin tried to calm herself, to suppress the hysterical thoughts that were seeping through her mind like poison, but she couldn't quite do it. Henriksen – her psychiatrist? Was that why he'd seemed so familiar? Was he lying? What was going on here?

'The symbol on the back of your phone,' she said, her voice wavering. 'I knew I recognised it. The upside-down triangle.'

'We'll get to that in a moment, Jasmin, don't worry. Let's focus on the night of your accident for now.'

Jasmin tucked a strand of wet hair behind her ear. 'The Jeep. At some point he'd had enough and he overtook me. He drove off, far too quickly given the rain, and I was on my own again. Until . . .' She took a deep breath. 'Until he came back. He was coming straight at me. On my side of the road. I got scared – I swerved – and . . . There was a man at the edge of the road. A homeless man. I didn't have a chance to avoid him. My car hit him head-on. I can still remember the sound of his bones breaking.'

'When did all this happen? And what came next?'

'It was . . . Hmm. A few months ago. And afterwards . . .' Jasmin realised her memories of the immediate aftermath of the accident were shrouded in thick, grey fog. 'I don't know. I remember waking up in the hospital. Nobody believed me. It wasn't a man, they told me, it was only an animal. A deer.'

'But you never believed them. You never had any doubts that a human being lost their life that night.'

'No. Never.' Jasmin buried her face in her hands. She could smell the mud on her fingers: damp soil and decay. 'I thought I'd be able to find answers here. I could remember the upside-down triangle. The homeless man was wearing it on his coat. I knew I'd seen it before, here on the island. And as it turned out, I was right. It was the logo of the old sanatorium. And you have the same symbol on your phone. I just can't make sense of it all.'

'You experienced a terrible trauma that night – a terrible loss. In order to deal with an experience of this kind, to repress it, the human mind sometimes constructs an alternative version of events. An alternative reality.'

'But I didn't know the homeless man,' she said quietly. 'So how can that be what happened?'

'You didn't kill a homeless man that night. No, Jasmin.' Henriksen shook his head solemnly. 'That night, you lost your son Paul. He was the one who died in the accident.'

Jasmin stared at him. For a moment she couldn't breathe. 'But Paul wasn't with me in the car.'

'Yes, he was. It wasn't your original plan, but he was there with you.'

For a moment, she was back at the party on the evening of her accident. Through the windows, she could see the colourful lights decorating the lawn behind the consultant surgeon's house. She could hear the music thumping dully through the walls and could taste the alcohol in her cocktail – could feel it clouding her mind, making her drunk.

'That isn't a good idea,' she heard Sven Birkeland say behind her. He was pointing at her drink. She'd lost sight of him after she'd let him into the house, but he'd managed to track her down again and somehow they'd both ended up here.

'Oh no? But it's good to let your hair down once in a while. I'll call us a taxi afterwards.' Jasmin felt the chill from the ice cubes in her long-stemmed glass, and at that moment it felt good – felt right – to be here. 'That patient last night—'

'Shh,' said Sven. He looked pretty good this evening, Jasmin thought, in that suit of his. He wore it casually, with no tie. 'Let's not talk about work.'

'OK. Sure. Then let's . . .' She didn't finish her sentence.

'What about Paul?' he asked.

'Paul's outside with Sophie and the Brechts' two kids. Plus their au pair.' Jasmin noticed Sven drawing a little nearer and she looked up at him. 'He was meant to be at his grandparents' house tonight but something came up, so I brought him with me. That doesn't mean I can't leave him on his own for a little while though, does it? I mean . . .' Jasmin paused. Was she imagining it, or was there a twinkle in Sven's eye? They were alone in the kitchen. The party had moved outside, the guests gathered beneath the trees on the Brechts' extensive grounds. There was nobody around. That twinkle, his query about Paul . . . 'But what you're really asking is how long we're both going to be left here undisturbed, right?' She giggled.

'Undisturbed. That sounds good.'

Jasmin took a step towards him. Her legs felt like they were moving of their own accord. She noticed Sven's arm suddenly holding her somehow – his hand touching her in a way it shouldn't – and her thoughts briefly turned to the endless hours they'd spent together in theatre, under constant strain, always striving to save lives, always so close to each other. Too close to each other. And she also thought of all those evenings with Jørgen, their gruelling rows, the frustration that had crept into their everyday lives.

When Sven kissed her, Jasmin responded. He pushed her back gently but firmly until she felt the wall behind her and he kissed her again – this time much longer and more intimately. Jasmin could feel his excitement under her wandering hand.

'Don't,' she sighed. 'We shouldn't . . .' But when he lifted his lips from hers, it was she who leaned forward insistently, kissing him again. 'There's a guest room up in the attic,' she whispered, breathing heavily.

'Lead the way.'

Jasmin smiled, then pushed him towards the door and onward to the stairs . . . and everything happened the way it had to happen.

Afterwards, Jasmin took Paul's hand and led him back to the car. She could hear Sven's voice somewhere behind her. *You have to forget about it. We shouldn't have done it*, she thought. *Jesus, what were you thinking? Are you out of your mind?*

The way she felt even scared her a little. There was shame, anger at herself and Sven, and at the same time a secret and profound satisfaction at having done something Jørgen didn't know about. As if she'd been waiting for the chance to pay him back for his little fling a few years ago. The realisation was unnerving.

'Mummy, why are you crying?'

'It's nothing, sweetheart.' She sat Paul down on his child seat and got into the car herself. Her hand shook as she reached for the gearstick. Then the car lurched down the drive and she was on the road.

It started to rain.

Jasmin wiped her cheeks.

Things had happened. Things that couldn't be taken back.

OK. Calm down.

She drove on and the night enveloped her. The woods drew closer to the sides of the road, and soon they were alone in their small car – she and Paul.

Pull yourself together.

Lights appeared in the rear-view mirror.

Was that Sven? Was he following her? Or was it someone else? She turned off the road, deliberately taking a detour, but whoever was behind her took the same route.

They were following her.

The Jeep's headlights were on full beam, blindingly bright in the rear-view mirror. Nervously, Jasmin fumbled for her phone as the Jeep accelerated and overtook her.

She didn't recognise it.

Jasmin opened the window a crack. Fresh, cool air blew into her face. It was invigorating, exactly what she needed just now.

You'll be home soon. As for Jørgen . . . Think, Jasmin. You need to think about how you're going to handle this.

Jasmin glanced down at her phone only to realise there were no bars left on the display. *No reception. We must be too deep in the forest.*

When she looked up again, the blinding headlights had returned. This time there could be no doubt about it: the driver had come back for her.

And all of a sudden, she saw a dark shadow on the road. A deer with shaggy fur: bulky, enormous.

With a shriek, Jasmin flung the steering wheel to one side.

Too late.

The car started to skid.

She heard a dull thud as her car smashed into the creature; she heard snapping, cracking, the scream of the shock absorbers, and then the bonnet was doused in blood and the windscreen shattered as an object shot out from the inside of the car.

The Jeep pulled up beside her, tyres screeching on the wet asphalt. Jasmin felt blood flowing down her forehead, dripping onto her lips.

'Jasmin!' she heard a voice scream. It sounded familiar somehow, but the shock had wiped all rational thoughts from her mind and she was unable to recognise the person who had got out of the Jeep. In that moment there was nothing but shock, making her heart race. 'Jasmin, what . . . ?'

Then silence. Even the footsteps died away.

'Oh God, no! Jasmin, what . . . What have you . . . ?'

Jasmin tried to turn her head towards the window, but a terrible pain shot through her body. *Please, don't let me die . . .* More and more blood flowed down her nose, her cheeks.

'Paul,' she heard the man's voice calling. 'Paul! Shit, come on!'

In the distance, sirens approached, flashing blue lights.

Then endless darkness enfolded her.

Chapter 21

Paul is dead. He's been dead for so long now.

That thought – the memory echoing through her mind . . .

'How do you know? How do you know he was in the car that night?' Jasmin felt as though the ground was breaking open beneath her feet and all that lay below her was a bottomless void that threatened to swallow her up.

'You told me so yourself.' Henriksen tapped the folder he'd put on the coffee table. 'We've been at this point so many times before, Jasmin. We keep going in circles, and that's a great, great shame.'

'What do you mean?'

'You'd been drinking that night. A lot. You'd had a fling with your colleague Sven Birkeland. You were driving much too fast, consumed as you were with fear and shame over what had happened. And in your emotional turmoil, you saw the Jeep driven by your husband Jørgen – who'd come looking for you because he was too worried about you to stay at home – and you mistook it for someone pursuing you, attacking you. Deep down in your guilt-stricken subconscious, you were scared of how he'd react. Your car skidded in the rain and collided with a deer that was crossing the road. And in the accident, Jasmin, you were badly injured and you lost your five-year-old son. Paul. The boy you'd nurtured and cherished more than anything in the world, ever since you lost your second child in a miscarriage.'

Jasmin shook her head. 'No, no, that's not what happened, it was different, it—'

'Jasmin, what year is it?'

'It's . . . it's 2013. Paul was born in 2007. He turns six this year. The accident was in the spring, a few months ago. Jørgen and I lost our second baby over two years ago.'

Henriksen shook his head once more. '*Seven, not two.* Do you remember that? I expect some part of your subconscious mind has already grasped the truth. You lost your second child back in 2011 – not two years ago, but *seven*. It's now 2018. After your accident you spent over three years in a coma, followed by many months in a secure institution because you simply couldn't accept the truth. Paul wouldn't be five now, he'd already be ten years old – but in reality, he never lived to see his sixth birthday. Your family and your husband have done all they could to try to get through to you, but it was always in vain. You see, in your condition, something keeps resetting your conscious mind back to the moment of the accident. You've created an imaginary world in which Paul is alive, in which he even came with you to Minsøy. You've done everything you can to immerse yourself in that world. The pictures he drew here – *you* drew them. You bought food for him, laid out his things in his room. Your husband still loves you, but you have to understand that it's getting harder and harder to keep you in touch with reality. It's placing a tremendous burden on the people around you. Especially Jørgen.'

Jasmin felt tears running down her cheeks. What Henriksen had told her had to be a lie, and yet in a hidden chamber at the back of her mind, she understood he was right. It was a space she'd carefully locked up and hurled the key far out to sea, but it was still there.

'But the sanatorium on the island, the fire. Yrsen's painting. All the things that happened back then, that they were trying to cover up. The symbol—'

'All those things happened. There really was a psychiatric institution here, but that doesn't alter the truth. The symbol is the logo of Nordic Health Invest, a company operating a chain of exclusive private clinics across Scandinavia. Gabriela Yrsen really did live out here until she died of old age two years ago, but the woman who introduced herself to you by that name was someone completely different. It was none other than Solveig Moen, the medical director of the hospital where you were a patient. We had to incorporate the real history of the island into our project, and I'd hoped that building certain distinctive aspects of Minsøy's past into our little scenario would help jog your memory. So I asked Solveig to help me. What took place here was an unprecedented field trial – a kind of shock therapy designed to confront you with the truth once and for all. A unique experiment that we embarked upon with the agreement of your husband and the financial support of your parents. An experiment that might one day have won us the recognition of our entire profession. Everything you experienced here was based on things you're familiar with from your own past. You've been following a trail of memory, and we'd hoped you would manage to decipher the truth all on your own. We'd hoped your psyche would finally be able to adjust to the facts if you were confronted with them in a radical way.'

Jasmin tried to fit together the pieces of the puzzle, one by one. 'So the body on the beach wasn't real? If nobody died on the night of my accident—'

'In some iterations of your repressed memories, you invented a victim of the accident – a passer-by on the side of the road – whose identity varied, but who over time bore an increasing resemblance to Sven Birkeland. It was a way for your subconscious mind to deal with your suppressed guilt over your affair and your alcohol consumption. The dead body we confronted you with here was a direct reference to that. You didn't recognise it for what it was – a prop, a doll. On many occasions during your treatment, you would picture a dead body or something similar that would throw your subconscious into an alarmed state, prompting it to conjure up a fantasy or a scenario like this one in which Paul gets kidnapped. We've been through this so often already, and I'd been hoping so fervently that this time would be different. I'd been hoping you'd understand, Jasmin.'

'But Yrsen's face! Larsen – his house burning down . . .'

'You spent many, many months undergoing therapy in a secure institution, Jasmin. There were times when you tried to escape, to run away – sometimes because you thought Paul had been kid-napped back then too. You developed certain violent tendencies, which we observed once again here on the island. You started a fire at the hospital. Forty-five other patients were injured in the blaze and some were disfigured. Fortunately nobody lost their life.'

Jasmin threw her hand up to her mouth and bit her knuckle. *Forty-five.* The forty-five graves in the cemetery.

'And the fire at Johann Larsen's house was also started by none other than you, Jasmin. Do you remember? Instead of sleeping that night, you left your house, took a jerrican of petrol out of your car, which you'd brought over with you on the ferry, and started the fire. We know because we were watching you. We recorded the whole thing.'

Jasmin remembered the scrap of cloth in her coat pocket. The shard of glass. But no, he must be lying. This couldn't be the truth she'd been searching for all this time.

'Why would I do that to Larsen?'

'You wanted to incinerate the truth. Or should I say, Hanna Jansen wanted to? Larsen confronted you with the logo of Nordic

Health Invest – the upside-down triangle. He confronted you with a reality you'd been repressing. During your time under our care, you kept making paper sculptures of that logo, among other things, and you projected your obsession with origami onto your son.'

'But why would I—?'

'Johann Larsen checked himself into the same Nordic Health Invest clinic and was there with you for a long time,' Henriksen went on. 'That was when you became acquainted with his particular inclinations. His political views. We hoped that if you came face to face with him here, part of your memory would come back to the surface. He volunteered to help us with our unusual experiment.'

'Is he . . . ?'

'Dead?' said Henriksen. 'No, of course not. Only his house burned down. All the same, I had to use all my influence and powers of persuasion that night to prevent the experiment from being called off immediately and to stop you from being taken straight back to the clinic.'

'What about the drifter?' Jasmin asked weakly. 'Was he—?'

'His name is Christian Sunderberg. He's a nurse at the hospital. The man who's been looking after you all these years. Your closest confidant. All he wanted was to protect you, to watch over you the whole time. The scar on his face is because of you. You gave it to him.'

'He – he was really looking after me?'

'Some of my colleagues thought this experiment was futile. Some of them think you should be permanently sedated and locked away. You're on the verge of insanity, Jasmin, and frequently violent. You encountered one of those dissenting voices on the beach recently. Mattila tried to stage an intervention.'

'He wanted to hurt me!'

'He knows what you are, Jasmin. You've created a third personality. Alongside the Jasmin Hansen who believes Paul is still alive

282

and the Jasmin Hansen who occasionally acknowledges the truth during rare moments of clarity, you also developed a personality you call Hanna Jansen – a woman whom you claim Jørgen had an affair with. But Hanna Jansen is *you*. She's a violent part of your subconscious that's starting to emerge more and more often. I couldn't accept it, though. Not me, and not your parents or your husband either. We've always believed there's something of you left, a part of you that's capable of recognising the truth and accepting it.'

Footsteps approached down the hall. Jasmin looked up.

'Jasmin, your husband is here. Do you want to see him?'

'Yes. I do.'

'You have to promise us that you're willing to acknowledge reality. Otherwise I see little hope of convincing the others that you're on the road to recovery.'

Jasmin took a deep breath. There seemed to be an immense burden resting on top of her, pushing her down like a coiled spring. The footsteps fell silent, and when she looked up, Jørgen was standing in the doorway.

Jørgen, tall and blond, just like she remembered him. The smile on his lips was sad and affectionate at the same time.

Fresh tears welled up in her eyes at the sight of him. 'You're – you're really here.'

He walked over to her, holding out his arms, but then paused as if afraid of her reaction. 'Everything Dr Henriksen said is true. Nobody wants to hurt you. It was an experiment, but maybe it was too extreme. It was the last chance to make you realise what happened, and I'm sorry. I never should have allowed it. Your parents and I have discussed your situation with Dr Henriksen and the whole team so many times, and although I was hoping it would work, I realise now that I should never have given my permission.' He shook his head and looked at Henriksen. 'And nor should you, doctor. Everything we tried to do here is illegal.' Then he turned back to Jasmin. 'Your father funded the whole thing secretly. Henriksen, Mattila and Moen were the only doctors willing to get involved with the experiment, together with Nordic Health Invest, and so we planned it all on this remote island. It was hard to keep it secret, almost impossible, but—'

'It might still work,' Henriksen objected placidly. 'This might be the breakthrough we've been waiting for all this time.'

Jasmin stared at him. 'So this was a shot in the dark? Just a good opportunity for you? You want professional recognition for this bullshit experiment? Is that all I am to you? A guinea pig? What about Karl Sandvik and his wife? Or Jan Berger at the lighthouse? Were they in on it too?'

Henriksen looked sheepish and said nothing, but Jørgen nodded. 'Of course they were. We wanted you to find your way back to the real world, and some part of your subconscious must have realised it too. You avoided visiting Sandvik about his back pain because if you'd gone, you might have realised that you haven't practised medicine in years. And as for getting Berger to teach you how to shoot – Hanna Jansen would never have let you learn how to use a gun. That's *her* part of your personality. But you can manage it, I know you can! Don't let her—'

'When did you get here?' Jasmin cut him off abruptly. 'Where's Bonnie?' And then, with horror, Jasmin wondered, *If this is all true, does that mean you were the one who hit Bonnie and staged the break-in? The blond hairs they found in the room – did they belong to you?*

'She's outside. She's absolutely fine.'

'Was that me? Did I hurt Bonnie and break the window? Because I needed to make the kidnapping a reality for myself?'

Henriksen nodded.

'And the threatening letter? "I know what you are." Who could have . . . ?' She fell silent when she saw the expression in Henriksen's eyes.

'It was Hanna Jansen who sent the letter. It was you, Jasmin.' He nodded at Jørgen, who passed him a laptop with an NHI logo on the back. Henriksen put it on the coffee table between them and opened a CCTV software package. 'Do you remember? You showed me a video of the drifter putting the letter through the door while I was lying injured on your sofa.'

Injured. A thought occurred to Jasmin – one last way out, a lifeline in the storm. 'That cut on your head,' she cried. 'It can't have been me!'

'Can't it?' Henriksen pointed at the camera footage. 'Look. The threatening letter.'

Jasmin leaned forwards as Henriksen pressed play on a video taken from a camera mounted in the entrance hall. She saw herself hurrying over to the front door, peering out, and then taking the letter from a drawer in the sideboard and dropping it on the floor, as if she'd already prepared it and hidden it away beforehand.

'This was taken several hours earlier.' Henriksen opened another video, this one taken in her bedroom. Jasmin watched herself grab the drawer of the bedside table and tip it out onto the floor. A small mirror shattered, sending shards of glass everywhere. 'You see? You cut yourself while scrambling to gather up the pieces,' Henriksen explained. They watched as Jasmin tucked the bloody shard into her coat pocket before removing the false bottom of the drawer and taking out the silver revolver.

'Of course we knew it was in there. We replaced it with a fake, but you took it with you all the same, Jasmin. And you fired it at me twice. The first time was when you found me injured out there on the road. You were carrying the gun in your coat pocket and you cut yourself again on the piece of glass when you pulled it out. That's how you got the wound on your hand that Dr Gundersen noticed. And the second time was just now, of course, down in the cellar. I know it isn't you who wants to hurt me. It's that other woman. Hanna Jansen takes control of you during these moments, but Hanna Jansen only exists because you let her. Because you're suppressing the truth. But the night of your accident – that night is the truth, Jasmin. You mustn't let Hanna win!'

Henriksen played another video. This time, Jasmin was sitting alone at the kitchen table and talking to a person on the other side of the room – someone just outside the camera's field of view. She talked, and Jasmin heard a voice replying to her words that seemed to come from nowhere. Then she saw herself arriving in her rental car, recorded by one of the countless surveillance cameras they'd installed throughout the house, and watched herself get out and open the door for Bonnie. But there was no Paul following her into the house.

Jasmin drained her cup. The last of the tea tasted bitter, mingling with salty tears on her tongue. The truth felt like a drill boring into her temples with no anaesthetic.

'And what about us?' she asked Jørgen. She felt sick, as if every fibre of her body was rebelling against this truth, this agony.

'Us?' A cloud passed over Jørgen's face. 'After all that's happened – the accident, that business with Sven Birkeland – do you know how much I despised you? How badly you hurt me? And do you have any idea how hard it was for me to stay by your side, in spite of everything? You're ill, but . . .' He sighed. 'I want to help you, Jasmin. That's all. To see you like this – dear God, it breaks my heart.'

She looked up at him, her eyes blurred with tears. Jørgen, just as she remembered him. Or was it? If what both of them were saying was true . . .

'Has it really been years since it happened?' she asked incredulously. 'And I refused to believe it? Paul is dead? He didn't come here with me? We've lost *two* children?'

'The shock was too much for you, Jasmin,' Henriksen explained.

Behind Jørgen, the woman whom she'd known as Gabriela Yrsen appeared, along with Arne Boeckermann. The two of them fixed her with a penetrating look. They were on the alert, ready to act at a moment's notice.

And what if they're all lying? Jasmin thought. *What if none of this is true? What if Paul is sitting terrified out there somewhere, waiting for you to come back? What if Jørgen staged this whole thing to get hold of your money, like you suspected?*

You heard Yrsen talking about him. Yrsen is Hanna Jansen. Jansen and Jørgen. They both . . .

It was a possibility.

'Ms Hansen,' said Yrsen – or Solveig Moen, as Henriksen had called her – in a loud voice. 'You have to tell us now why you're here. I need to hear you say it.'

Jasmin wiped her cheeks and rubbed her eyes. She glanced at Boeckermann, who regarded her coldly and dismissively, and then back at Moen with her cool, analytical expression. Jørgen smiled encouragingly and Henriksen nodded curtly beside her.

'What do you think, Jasmin?' he asked her. 'What happened to Paul? Can you tell us?'

Paul. The name sounded foreign now. It was like a bitter taste on her lips. The taste of pain. Jasmin saw Sven Birkeland standing in front of her – saw him leaning in to kiss her. Not like a colleague, but like a lover. She coughed. 'I drank too much that night. I had an accident and I lost my son. Paul – Paul is dead. I spent my whole time here looking for a way out, a way to avoid admitting the truth. I was looking for a false reality. But I understand now. I know who I am and what happened. I'm sorry for all the people I hurt. When I set fire to the clinic, when I tried to shoot you. My name is Jasmin Hansen and my son died five years ago.'

Epilogue

The storm had passed; the night was over and the breeze whipped through Jasmin's hair as she got into the car beside Jørgen and they drove to the ferry that would take them across to the mainland. She looked back over her shoulder; Minsøy lay behind them.

She was overcome with a sense of relief. It felt so good to be leaving this lump of rock behind.

You made it.

'I'm glad you came.' Once they were on board, Jasmin and Jørgen got out of their car and walked over to the railing together. 'What a day.'

Jørgen threw his arm over her shoulder and looked happier than she'd seen him in a long time.

'And now?' she asked him cautiously. 'What comes next?'

'You need to get to grips with everything again, honey. With your everyday life, with 2018, with everything you forgot. But we're all going to help you. I'm so glad you're finally *here* again. *Really* here, I mean.'

Jasmin nodded, leaned against him and looked out to sea as the ferry left the harbour. The waves churned; the spray was clear and glittered brightly in the sun.

She wasn't quite sure what he meant by *here*. Hadn't she always been here?

'You know,' she said, 'for a moment I had the feeling we were being watched. But that's obviously absurd.'

'Is it?'

'Of course! Who would be watching us?' She closed her eyes. The murmur of the waves was soothing, and Jasmin felt the strain of the last few days melt away. When she opened her eyes again, she looked over Jørgen's shoulder. 'When we get back,' she said quietly, 'we need to buy Paul a birthday present. He'll be turning six soon. I think I already know what he wants.'

Jørgen looked down at her. There was something in his eyes that she didn't quite understand. It looked like resignation and deep regret.

'What's the matter?' she asked him and smiled. Paul was leaning against the railing beside Jørgen and he returned her smile, beaming the way only he could. The wind tousled his corn-blond hair as he lifted his hand and waved at her. 'Everything is going to be OK, isn't it?'

Jørgen nodded. The wind buffeted against them: a cold north wind heralding the autumn. 'Yes,' he answered slowly, gazing out to sea. 'Everything is going to be OK.'

ABOUT THE AUTHOR

Martin Krüger studied the dark arts of the law in Frankfurt before becoming an author and musician. He now divides his time between southern Germany and Switzerland. Find out more at www.kruegerthriller.de or www.facebook.com/kruegerthriller.

ABOUT THE TRANSLATOR

Photo © 2014 Jozef van der Voort

Jozef van der Voort is a literary translator working from Dutch and German into English. He studied literature and languages in Durham and Sheffield and is an alumnus of the New Books in German Emerging Translators Programme. In 2014 he was named runner-up in the Harvill Secker Young Translators' Prize and in 2020 he won second prize in the Geisteswissenschaften International Non-Fiction Translation competition.